COLLISION COURSE

CLASS 5

MICHELLE DIENER

PRAISE FOR MICHELLE DIENER

There is a check list of things I look for in a good SFR book and Diener has checked them all off.

MIXED BOOK BAG

Truly exceptional.

RT BOOK REVIEWS

Michelle Diener writes exciting, inventive, and just plain good fun SFR stories that will take the reader on quite a fantastic journey.

OUTLANDER BOOK CLUB

ABOUT COLLISION COURSE

A step into the unknown . . .

Rose is looking forward to meeting the Fisone as part of the United Council's outreach mission. Since the Tecran were defeated, and the full scope of their crimes were uncovered, the UC has wanted to find the Tecran's victims and extend the hand of friendship. The fact that Rose is close to having her baby is just another element to the adventure of finding the Fisone's planet and seeing if they could be potential allies.

An explorer's dream . . .

Dav Jallan has been captain of the *Barrist* for a few years, but this is the first time he's headed for a planet inhabited by advanced sentients. The Fisone exist—that is indisputable—and every part of this mission is why he became an explorer in the first place. The goal is to find them, form alliances, and make friends. The fact that he's about to become a new father simply adds to his sense of excitement.

A collision course with reality . . .

When Sazo's Class 5 and the *Barrist* enter the Fisone's airspace, what they find is far from the uncomplicated meeting they had envisioned. The Fisone are divided, carrying a grudge, and are sure the Grih are no different from the Tecran they encountered the year before. When they take Rose as a hostage, both Dav and Sazo focus everything they have on finding her, and as the Fisone's actions create more and more danger, ideas of alliances, friendship, and cooperation become less and less important.

The only comfort both Dav and Sazo have to draw from is that Rose has been taken by others before, underestimated before, and her abductors have lived to regret it.

They are counting on history repeating itself.

CHAPTER 1

ROSE RAN her hands over the soft green of the ferns on the ground level of the biome Sazo had built for her, and realized she should have come down here sooner.

She had not done very much today, but at least among the trees and plants, she wasn't doing very much in beautiful surroundings.

"You're finally taking your toll," she said to her bump, rubbing it. "I'm just flat today." Her baby gave a little kick, and she smiled.

She usually traveled from Sazo's Class 5 to the *Barrist*, the massive explorer ship Dav captained, at least once a day, but she hadn't felt motivated enough today.

She was an anomaly. A human amongst the Grih, and her pregnancy had sparked not just interest from medical quarters, but a range of emotions from fascination to outright animosity and fear amongst some sectors of Grih society.

There were some people who were disturbed by her and her four Earth friends, not just for their impact on Grihan society, but on the United Coalition in general.

She had to admit they had had an impact, but that wasn't so much their doing as a strange confluence of circumstances. And actually, things could have been a lot worse for the United Coalition if they hadn't been involved.

She sighed, tired of the whole thing, and tried to get back to the sense of peace she'd had earlier.

"Dav has just arrived." Sazo's voice came through her earpiece.

"That's good. Thank you." She turned, taking the path back the way she'd come.

The curves of the stone-lined path, the trees reaching over it, the gush of water from the stream Sazo had built to run through the garden, never failed to delight her. Still, she was missing one thing.

As she walked toward the tube to go up to greet Dav, she looked upward, searching the branches overhead.

And there she was.

With a chirp, Sweetpea sailed from one of the trees to land on her shoulder, not wanting to be left behind.

Rose smiled as she stroked her little head. She wasn't a baby anymore, but she was still tiny, a cute ball of fluff who had free rein of the garden as well as the ship.

She had a feeling Sazo was now as much in love with the little flying mammal as she was. He was constantly making adjustments to the ship to increase Sweetpea's enjoyment of her already pampered life.

She reached the tube, stepped in, and rose up to the main floor, the only part of the Class 5 that was meant for habitation now that Sazo had made the rest of the ship a massive conservatory.

The landing bay was to the left, the kitchen, lounge, and bedrooms to the right, and as she turned left, Dav stepped out of the bay into the passageway.

She realized she had missed seeing him today. Her heart gave a little leap in her chest and she held out a hand and smiled.

His eyes focused on her and then her bump, but before he could speak, Sweetpea leapt from her shoulder, spreading her little arms and legs to glide to Dav. She grabbed the front of his shirt and tucked up under his chin with a happy little chirp.

"My two girls meeting me after a long day," he said as he stroked Sweetpea from head to fluffy tail.

Rose smiled. "We missed you."

When Dav reached her, he put his arms around her, careful not to squash Sweetpea between them, and gave her a kiss. "You didn't come across today."

"No." She tilted her head back to look at him. "Just didn't have the energy."

She knew he would worry about that, but she'd go across tomorrow, and let her friend and doctor, Hri Rivel, poke and prod a little and confirm everything was well.

As she thought that, the baby gave a hard kick, and Dav laughed, putting his hand over the spot.

"The baby missed me, too."

"Of course. All three of your girls." She tucked under his arm, and they walked toward the lounge.

"Borji says we'll be at the outer probability sector by tomorrow." Dav glanced down at her. "So we'll be on alert from tonight, just in case."

The outer probability of where they were expecting to find an inhabited planet with advanced technology.

A planet whose only run-in with the United Coalition so far had been with a rogue group of Tecran military. That run-in had been violent, and ended with the Tecran stealing a prototype spaceship from them.

That spaceship was as sentient as Sazo was, and while Irini was happy to give them the coordinates of her place of origin, she did not want to accompany them on their exploratory trip to make more friendly contact.

Her *grynicha*, as she called her creators, had hobbled her as much as possible, wanting the benefits of her abilities, but refusing to allow her the autonomy her intelligence granted her.

It made Sazo and his four fellow Class 5s suspicious of the people they were going to make contact with, and Rose was sure Grih Battle

Center was a little nervous about how Sazo would react to their potential new friends.

Still, they didn't want to not bring him along. Besides the fact that he was attached to the *Barrist* because Rose was attached to the *Barrist's* captain, she knew they had decided that should they need to fight their way out of what might be an unfriendly meeting, it didn't get better than Sazo for firepower.

"This is the first time the *Barrist* has ever encountered a planet with advanced sentience?" she asked.

Dav nodded. "And only because Irini gave us the general coordinates. We might have eventually got around to exploring this part of the galaxy, but who knows when?"

"How long will comms take from here to Battle Center if we run into trouble?" she asked.

She knew they'd been seeding little comms relays behind them as soon as they left Grihan airspace, but it still took time for the signal to bounce.

"A few days right now," Dav said. "It'll be longer the deeper into the unknown we get." He left her to go sit on the couch, and went to grab some grinabo from the little station set in the wall.

This had once been the officers' lounge, back when Sazo's ship had been the secret weapon the Tecran had built and used to map uncharted territory. And steal stuff from unknown aliens.

Over time, she'd tweaked things here and there, so that it sported a look that was less airport lounge and more comforting home space. She leaned back against the cushions on the comfortable couch and closed her eyes.

"Tired?" The cushion dipped to the side as Dav sat beside her and took her hand, and she sent him a sidelong look.

"I shouldn't be, but sometimes the less you do, the more lethargic you feel."

"Should we go over to see Hri?" he asked.

She couldn't help the quick upward curve of her mouth. "I'll go tomorrow."

He was trying not to hover, and she appreciated the effort.

"I saw her yesterday, remember?" she soothed. "And the baby's kicking happily away." As she said it, her stomach jumped.

"Tomorrow we start getting closer to a planet where we may not be met with friendliness," he said.

"I'm not trekking through the wilderness to get to the *Barrist*, I'm just taking a small explorer across. It takes less than five minutes." She didn't need to tell him this. He did it at least twice a day.

He sighed. "I'm new to this."

She patted his hand. "Me, too."

He took a sip of grinabo, and she rested her head on his shoulder. And drifted off to sleep.

CHAPTER 2

"I'LL WALK with you to the launch bay." Hri Revil put the last of her equipment away and turned back to face Rose.

Dav had left toward the end of the consultation, called to the bridge to check out some strange readings the scanners were picking up, and the two of them were alone.

When the check up had shown everything was more than fine, Dav had been happy to leave early. Rose considered staying onboard for a bit, but she really just wanted to get back home.

She touched the necklace she always wore when she was onboard the *Barrist*, and slid off the examination table. "I'd like the company."

Hri noticed her hand on the necklace, and came closer to examine it. "I meant to ask you if we might need one for your baby," she said. "I'm ashamed we never questioned that the *Barrist's* air wasn't ideal for you."

Rose shook her head. "It is so close to ideal, even I didn't really notice it. It was only when Ellie entered her first Grihan ship and the necklace Pax made for her still needed to do a bit of work that it occurred to any of us. Pax made one for me, Fiona, Imogen and Lucy, and he also made one for the baby. It's really cute."

"That's good." Hri made a note on her device. "A necklace isn't as intrusive as the methods we have available, especially for a newborn."

"And maybe she won't need it, anyway." Rose stepped out into the passageway. "She could take after her father instead of me on that front."

"True." Hri walked beside her. "But having the necklace gives me one less thing to worry about, as your doctor."

"It's a weight off," Rose agreed. "You're going this way because you're visiting Gyppal?"

Gyp was one of the first Grih Rose had ever met. He'd been about ten months old at the time, and now that he was nearing two years old, he was still one of her favorite people.

"Yes, you want to come in and say hello?"

"Yes."

"Will you put the baby in the children's area after she's born?" Hri asked as they checked in.

"Not immediately, but yes. How else will she make friends?"

"That's important." Hri spoke cautiously. She didn't elaborate, but Rose had the suspicion she wanted to warn Rose that not all of the parents aboard the *Barrist* would be thrilled with having a half-human playing with their children.

The *Barrist* was an explorer—a massive vessel that searched Grihan airspace as well as the uncharted territory at their borders for new life forms and planets. It was necessary for families to be accommodated, as they could be traveling for months at a time.

"Some might object?" she asked, as they stood outside the children's play area, looking in through the large window. She'd rather know the issues in advance.

Hri started to shake her head, then paused. "Maybe one or two. But I have to admit that the ones who are opposed are not well liked as it is, and their grumbles have quieted in the last few months."

All right. She could handle that.

She knew it was useless to hope that Sazo hadn't heard those grumbles. He most definitely would have.

Dav didn't like it, but Sazo had had the run of the *Barrist's* systems for a long time.

Rose was fine with it, personally. If these people meant her and her child harm, Sazo would warn her.

She mulled the feeling of vengeance that rose up in her, and then calmed a little. Decided to talk to Sazo when she got back to the Class 5. They could strategize on how to deal with resistance to her baby's integration into Grih society in a way that didn't involve murder or bloodshed.

She didn't want everyone onboard to be walking on eggshells in fear of Sazo's wrath. That would be just as damaging as overt hostility.

Hri stopped in front of the bright blue door, the entrance to the play area, and Rose stopped with her.

"Do they mind me coming in to say hello to my favorite boy?"

Hri grinned. "No. Your visits are a highlight." She tapped in the code and the doors opened onto joyful chaos.

Children ran around, playing and shouting. A few sat drawing or reading, and another group lay on comfortable cushions having a story read to them.

"Mom. Rose." Gyppal ran toward them, leapt for his mother, then threw himself at Rose.

She caught him easily, swung him around and set him down.

"Song?" he asked her.

"Sure." She resisted requests for singing from most adults, but she always accommodated the children.

They had all turned at Gyppal's shout, and one of the teachers waved her toward a larger cushion.

Rose realized they had a routine now as far as she was concerned. It made her feel a quick buzz of warmth.

The children ranged in age from newborns to five years old, so she had a wide range of tastes to try and please.

"Same rules as last time?" she asked the crowd that had come to sit at her feet.

They all nodded enthusiastically.

The rule was two songs. One new song each time, one song they could decide among themselves.

She wracked her brains for a new song, came up with an old Carpenters song she thought they might like. They did—their eyes were big and bright at the end of it.

"All right. What's song number two going to be?" She had sung the same song the last five visits in a row. Would it finally drop off as number one on the charts, or would it hold?

The kids huddled together discussing things, then finally turned back. The designated requester this time was a little girl around four years old.

"Daydream," she called out, lifting her hands above her head in excitement.

Well, well, well. Daydream Believer by The Monkees lived to top the charts another day.

"You hear that, Sazo?" she murmured.

He showed her he had by playing the song intro, something they'd been working on since the song had become such a hit.

She started to sing, and the children looked upward to the speakers in delight. When she reached the chorus, the music swelled, and she harmonized with the recording she had made of herself.

When she was done, and Sazo faded the music out, there was a moment of silence and then the ululations started. She laughed, then rocked herself out of the low cushion.

"Now you've done it," Hri said, helping her to her feet. "That song's never not going to be the favorite now."

"The rules are the rules," Rose said with a grin. "I'll be off. Thanks for the check up, and I'll see you tomorrow."

She left to warm goodbyes from children and teachers alike, and when she stepped out into the passageway, she was still smiling.

"You are keeping them onside," Sazo said into her earpiece. "For when the baby is born."

She pondered his words. "It's not quite as transactional as that," she finally said as she opened the door into the launch bay and headed for the small ship they used to go between the *Barrist* and Sazo's Class 5.

"You like doing it, as well." Sazo was thoughtful.

"I do like doing it. And it's one place where I don't worry about whether people are being friendly because they have to be, or because they actually like me. Children are more honest."

She stepped into the ship and lowered herself carefully into one of the chairs and put a request through to Dav's comm.

"Where are you?" He sounded distracted.

"About to go back home. Will you be a while?" she asked.

"Yes. There's some strange interference we're picking up coming from a nearby system, so we're just looking into that."

"That could be what we're looking for," she said, and felt a quick spike of excitement.

"Maybe." She could hear the smile in his voice. "I'll see you later."

"Bye." She cut off the comm, sighed, and leaned back in her seat. "What are you picking up?" she asked Sazo.

"The same thing," he told her as he piloted the craft through the launch bay and out through the gel wall. "It's indistinct and it could be nothing."

"So I shouldn't get my hopes up," she said, looking out the window at the Class 5 looming up ahead.

"More or less."

They were halfway across, so she could see the *Barrist* on one side, the Class 5 on the other, when a liquid silver ship seemed to pop out of nowhere in front of her.

She caught a glimpse of clamps in her periphery, felt the little explorer ship shudder, and then suddenly it—with her inside it—were whisked away.

CHAPTER 3

DAV JALLAN WAS FEELING PRETTY good. The worry of this morning at Rose's fatigue had been assuaged by Hri Revil, and now it looked as if the planet they were looking for might well be up ahead in the next solar system.

"I can't get a fix on the signals, but that might be deliberate," Borji said. "Especially as they now know there are other high sentient life forms in the galaxy. And not friendly ones, either, after the Tecran stole Irini from them."

"And killed her crew," Dav said. Although from how Irini told it, the crew had self-terminated, in a bid to keep the secrets their ship held undiscovered.

"Yes." Jia Appal, his second-in-command, shifted beside him to lean a little closer to the screen. "They could well be distorting their signals to make themselves less obvious."

"If Irini hadn't directed us to this general area, we would most likely not even have picked them up." Borji stretched in his chair, and rubbed his eyes. He'd been here since early this morning, when the signals had first been noticed.

"We need a break. Let's slow the forward momentum, take some time to study what we have before we proceed any further," Dav said.

Borji gave a yawn, and Jia chuckled. "I think that's a good idea."

A sudden noise blasted through the bridge, a sensory overload that for a moment flat-lined Dav's brain.

"Rose." Sazo's ear-piercing shout was almost a relief after the blast of the siren, and it took Dav a moment to catch up to the fact that Sazo had made that noise, and that something had happened to Rose.

"Tell me." He was the only one on the bridge still standing. Everyone else was on the ground, holding their heads.

"Something took her. On her way across to me." Sazo was panicked in a way Dav had never heard him.

He understood. By now, his own panic had taken hold.

Jia was on her feet now, and she staggered to the console and activated the outer-facing lens feed. Rewound it five minutes.

"There." She threw the vision up on the big screen.

The little explorer moved at a gentle pace from the *Barrist* toward the Class 5, and suddenly a silver ship, shiny as Irini was, seemed to pop into existence.

It extended a clamp around Rose's ship, and then suddenly, both the silver ship and the explorer disappeared.

Dav felt for a moment as if the world was falling away from him, and then Jia Appal grabbed his arm.

The support forced him to straighten, to get a grip.

He gave her a quick nod.

"The signal we were picking up . . . it's increased in activity," Sazo said.

"I guess there's no more maybe about it." Borji winced as he dragged himself off the floor. "We've arrived."

———

All the systems in the little explorer had died the moment the clamp had engaged, and so when Rose felt the pop as they appeared somewhere other than between the *Barrist* and the Class 5, she was in darkness.

The auxiliary power and enviro systems flickered to life as she pressed her face against the window to see where she had been taken, but her view in one direction was just stars, and in the other, the dull, lifeless surface of a small moon or asteroid.

She tapped her ear, but she knew Sazo and Dav would be shouting at her if they could, so obviously something was jamming the comms.

She looked down at her bump and stroked it. "It's just you and me right now, baby girl. We need to be sharp."

Because it looked like whoever they'd come to meet had decided to make the first move.

She couldn't blame them for the show of force. When the Tecran had come this way, they'd swooped in, stolen Irini, and flitted out. And while they'd been using Paxe's Class 5 at the time, there was no way to tell the difference between Sazo and Paxe. For all these people knew, it could be the same ship again.

She gave a sigh, realized she wasn't going to be able to sit quietly and wait, and began to pace, looking out of the window every now and then to see if she could see anything new.

She felt the explorer jerk, and then move upward, and as darkness closed around her again, this time from outside the ship, she guessed she was being pulled into a hold.

At least something was happening.

She forced herself to take deep breaths to calm herself, and felt the baby kick a few times.

She did not like being so vulnerable. There could be danger here, and she was not fighting for herself alone.

One last deep breath, she thought as the ship settled onto a floor and lights flickered on outside. It was what it was.

Time to make some new friends.

CHAPTER 4

ROSE HAD a good idea of who she would see when she opened the door to the small explorer.

As she guessed, she had been pulled inside a launch bay, and arrayed in front of her, at the bottom of the ramp, were five people around the same height as herself. She already knew their thumbs were long and their fingers were short.

She drew comfort from the fact that she knew way more about them than they knew about her.

The thought steadied her. She fingered her necklace, so relieved that she had it on when she was taken. It took the atmosphere and altered it in a halo around her head to make sure she always had the correct air mix. Whatever the air was outside, she could still breathe safely, and that was vital. Especially now. She brushed her fingers over her bump.

She took a single step down the ramp and then stopped to take in her surroundings.

The area was circular, which was how Irini's ship was built, as well. A long tube, just like a rocket ship from Earth, although this ship was much bigger than Irini.

The faces that looked up at her were nothing like she'd seen before. The Grih were so similar to her, the only visible differences were in ear shape and height. The Garmann and Bukhari were closer to her in height, but visibly different in more ways than the Grih, and the Fitali and Tecran were clearly completely different.

Irini's *grynicha* fell into the same category.

They may have had the same height and number of fingers as Rose, but their faces were flat, with very little relief in terms of lips, nose or eyes. Their noses were more like slits in the skin, their mouths lipless, and their eyes were big in their face, and with no clear eyelids.

She blinked her own a few times, nervously.

If only she'd known she was going to meet up with them today, she'd have brought along the slim black translator Sazo and Irini had come up with. Irini had given Sazo the full language of her *grynicha*, and Sazo had matched it as much as possible to both Grihan and English. But it was sitting in the lounge in Sazo's Class 5, alas.

"I'm afraid I don't speak your language," she said.

There was a moment of silence, and then two of them looked quickly at each other.

"What are you saying?" one of them asked her, in Tecran.

She blinked again. Tecran was a language she had been able to speak fluently a year ago, but she hadn't spoken it at all since she and Sazo had escaped Tecran control.

"I said that I don't speak your language." She stumbled a little over the words.

"You are not a native speaker of the language we are using?" another asked her.

"I am not."

If they had listened in on the Tecran for communication purposes more than a year ago when the Tecran had come like raiders into their system, stole their ship and the people in it, and then left, they must surely know she was not Tecran.

Unless they hadn't gotten a look at the Tecran. Which was possible.

"There are more types than just the ones who came before?" a third person asked.

"Yes. But it's complicated." She had to think a bit before she came up with the word 'complicated'.

"How many of you are there?"

"I am one of five people stolen by the people who speak the language we are speaking now." She felt frustration rise within her, and tried to tamp it down. "Now I live with others who are not friends with those people."

There was a startled silence.

They spoke amongst themselves in a quick, choppy language, and then looked back at her.

"Come down here."

She didn't want to, but what was she going to do? Refuse?

She began to walk slowly down the ramp, her center of balance a little off because of her bump.

"Are you armed?" One of them asked sharply as she got nearer the bottom, the Tecran words triggering a quick spike of panic in her.

She shook her head, held out her hands. "No." She frowned. "You took me, remember? I was just on my way home, minding my own business."

Her response seemed to startle them.

Perhaps they expected her to be more afraid of them. More submissive.

"Why *did* you take me?" she asked.

"We want to swap you for the crew that went missing a year ago."

Rose stared at them, her heart sinking. Because that crew was dead. They chose to kill themselves, rather than be taken prisoner by the Tecran.

There was no one alive to swap her *with*.

CHAPTER 5

A SIREN BLARED SUDDENLY in the bay, and Rose lifted her head to look up at where it was coming from.

Dav and Sazo, she thought. They would be losing their minds.

One of the group broke away, talking urgently into what she assumed was a comm device, and then turned to have a rapid-fire conversation with the group.

"Go back into your ship," one of them told her, pointing up the ramp.

It suited her fine, so she complied, closing up behind her. If she had been able to understand them, she might have slow walked it a little, just to get an idea of what was happening, but as she couldn't, she decided being strapped up in the runner was probably the safest place for her.

When she was all strapped up, she looked out of the window, but it was on the wrong side, and she couldn't see anything useful.

She closed her eyes, trying to think through her options, and then the whole ship lurched and she guessed the ship she was inside was moving.

It seemed to shudder and then spin, and she remembered Irini's ship spun, too, when it was doing its short light speed hops.

So they were on the run from Sazo and Dav, most likely.

She tried to keep herself calm as they twisted and spun for what seemed like half an hour before coming to a stop.

When the ship began moving again, it felt to Rose as if they were dropping down, and when they came to an eventual stop, it was to a shudder, as if landing on a solid surface.

Someone pounded on her door, and she unstrapped and opened up, to find two of her original welcoming party standing below.

"You need to come with us."

She joined them at the bottom of the ramp, and finally found herself looking at them, face to face.

"Where are we?"

"Somewhere that your people cannot find you," one of them said. He gestured to the side. "Follow me."

She did, aware that the other person was following behind her, her breathing audible, as if she was stressed.

If Sazo and Dav ever came after her, she'd be stressed, too, Rose thought.

They reached a door to one side, and with a touch, it opened.

Light from outside flooded in, and Rose felt a spike of excitement at the thought of an on-planet excursion.

She loved being on solid ground.

The person in front of her leaned out, reached out a hand to grab something, and swung out. He disappeared below and when Rose reached the doorway, she saw there was a ladder to climb down.

She wasn't in peak ladder climbing shape right now, but she followed carefully behind him and studied the landscape with interest once she reached the bottom.

The air felt more substantial here, and she wondered whether the necklace was having to work harder or not. It looked to her as if both the man who'd proceeded her and the woman behind her were struggling a little. They weren't in helmets or suits, so the air must at least be close to what they breathed on their native planet.

The area where they'd landed was rocky. Grass grew between

broken stones, but mainly they were surrounded by high rocks of dark gray and black. Where the ship had set down was relatively flat, although not completely, which explained the shuddering stop earlier.

The ship looked almost invisible when she turned back to it, the surface so reflective, it practically disappeared.

Someone called out to their left, and Rose turned to see two people, obviously also part of Irini's *grynicha,* coming from between two rocks.

The breeze was light, but it cut through her, cold in a way that spoke of snow on higher ground. While they waited for their welcoming party to join them, Rose looked up into the sky, and saw a big gas planet high above, and nothing else.

Wherever they'd hopped to, it wasn't anywhere she recognized from the solar system the *Barrist* and Sazo had been traveling through earlier.

The newcomers eyed her with interest, and then the four of them spoke in explosive, choppy tones.

"You will stay here on Dimal," the woman who'd met her in the launch bay said. "We will come for you when we have our people."

"You won't have your people," Rose said carefully. "I was told they killed themselves so that the Tecran would not have access to the technology of the ship they stole. They torched the inside of it."

There was a moment of absolute silence, and then the man reached forward and hit her across the face.

She staggered back, astonished, her hand to her cheek.

He shouted something at her, and she said nothing, staring at him with big eyes as he ranted.

The other three looked visibly shocked at his behavior and the woman snapped something at him, the tone harsh, her expression angry.

He spat something back, but she did not back down, shouting something at him and then making a downward chopping motion with her hand.

He went quiet, and took a few steps away from the others.

"Why did you not say this before?" the woman asked her.

"You said you wanted to swap me moments before the siren, then you sent me inside my runner." Rose slowly let her hand drop from her cheek.

One of the newcomers audibly gasped and Rose wondered if there was a mark on her skin.

She lifted her hand again, and felt a slight swelling.

"When were you told this, about our people?" the woman asked.

Rose thought about it. "Five months ago. Less than half a year, in my time."

"Who told you?" The woman who'd come through the rocks asked her.

"One of the other prisoners of the Tecran, the people who stole your ship. This prisoner was kept in the same place as your stolen ship—a warehouse on a moon. When they were rescued by the people I travel with, that is when the truth about what the Tecran had done came out. That is why we traveled here. To make contact with you and tell you what happened."

There was more conversation, from which the man who slapped her was completely excluded.

The woman seemed to want to leave, urgently, or at least return to the ship, presumably to pass the information along.

She seemed to be telling the two who'd been waiting for them what to do, then turned and began climbing the ladder back into the ship.

She was almost at the top when the man who'd been standing by himself moved to the ladder, and began to climb. He didn't look at Rose.

She looked at him, though, staring at him to make sure she would know him again.

He seemed to feel her eyes on him, because he turned to look back at her, then quickly faced forward again and hauled himself up to the top.

"Binnos lost a family member," the woman who was standing beside her said, as if in explanation.

"I lost my whole world," Rose said. "I was stolen away, and there is no way back for me. By the same group who took your people."

There was silence at her words, and she didn't look around to see how they had been taken. She stood, arms crossed, as the ship fired up and shot into the sky.

It's just you and me, baby, she said as she smoothed her hands over her bump.

When she turned, both the man and woman she was left with were watching her strangely.

"Crythis says you are not very familiar with this language," the man said.

She assumed the woman who'd just flown away was Crythis. "I am not."

He indicated the direction they had come from with his hand. "We will have to be careful to not misunderstand each other."

As she followed him, picking her way across the rocky ground, she wondered if that was a threat.

CHAPTER 6

"INCOMING COMM." Borji's lips were thin, his voice a little hoarse, as he spun to face Dav in his chair.

"I see it," Sazo spoke through the overhead speakers, not just to Dav personally through his earpiece. "I'll try to trace it, if you could respond, Captain."

Dav wondered if that was an order or a plea, but he chose to take it as a request. Sazo was not capable of diplomacy at the best of times, and this was as far from the best of times as it was possible to get.

"This is Captain Dav Jallan of the *Barrist*." He kept his information to the ship only. He could introduce the concept of the Grih and the United Council later.

Beside him stood Nivan Cossi, the Bukarian representative from the United Council—here to represent the combined interest of the council as a whole.

She was the older sister of a member of the Bukarian military who Dav had become friends with since the necessity of dealing with the Tecran had brought the Grih and the Bukari closer together as allies. He was glad to have Nivan by his side as a witness to this.

"We do not understand what you said. This is Priyan of the ship

Havelan." The words were spoken in Tecran, and there was a murmur through the bridge.

"They must have managed to listen in to the Tecran enough to work out how to speak the language," Jia said. "Smart."

"They were waiting for the Tecran to come back," Nivan Cossi agreed.

"I can speak the language you are using, but not very well," Dav responded, although he could, in fact, speak it well enough. It was nice to have an excuse to speak slowly, and perhaps to claim a misunderstanding, if they found themselves in a situation where they needed to calm things down.

Sazo and Irini had created a translation device for this meeting, but it was on Sazo's Class 5, out of his reach, and he made the decision to keep its existence to himself.

"Why are you here?" The woman who'd identified herself as Priyan sounded angry.

Dav paused. "Before I answer any more questions, what have you done with Rose? And why did you take her?"

There was a beat of silence. "Our sister ship took her to ensure we had something to exchange for the crew that were taken from us the last time we had . . . visitors."

Dav lifted a hand and pressed it to his forehead. "You ensured nothing by doing that except our distrust, because your crew killed themselves almost as soon as they were taken, as far as we were told, when they torched the inside of their ship."

There was another silence. "So we understand from the prisoner. But we do not simply take your word. Show us evidence of our people's deaths, and when that occurred, and perhaps we can talk."

They cut off the comms.

Dav turned to look at Jia. "Send a probe back to Grih Battle Center. Relay a message to Paxe to send any lens feed he may have of what happened to that crew. Or if Irini has something, have him send that."

"The Tecran disposed of their bodies in space." Jia worried her bottom lip. "And there are no official reports of what happened. The Tecran weren't in the habit of memorializing their incriminating behavior."

"No." Dav rubbed a hand through his hair. "Did you get any information from their signal, Sazo?" he asked.

"No. They hop around as they transmit, so it is almost impossible to track them." He sounded quiet. Dav thought maybe that was the most frightening mode he had.

"Then we keep going," Dav said. "We keep looking for the planet. Because right now we have no leverage at all."

CHAPTER 7

"WHAT IS THIS PLACE?" Rose asked as she stopped in front of the door to a structure set into rock. It was set almost flush with a cliff face, and was a similar color. She guessed it would be almost impossible to see from above.

"It doesn't matter." The man opened the door and held it for her. "You are not a guest here, you are a prisoner."

She didn't want to go in there.

She had a feeling once she was in, she would lose all options.

Right now, she had the sense they didn't expect any trouble from her. They had ordered, and she had obeyed.

Maybe it was time to stop doing that.

As she'd walked through the narrow causeway of rocks to the building, she'd noticed her guards struggled to breathe, and she guessed this was some kind of outpost.

Crythis had called it Dimal. It might be a habitable moon, as the massive gas giant she could see above would most likely have a few.

Whether the air suited her or not didn't matter, fortunately, because she was wearing her necklace, but looking at her captors struggling to draw in enough air, she decided there would never be a better chance to escape than now.

Once that door closed behind her, they had her trapped.

She bent forward, hands on her knees, as if catching her breath, which she guessed they wouldn't see as too strange, given their own troubles in that area. She glanced up ahead, trying to work out whether running back the way she'd come was better, or if there was an alternative.

She spotted a path to the left which turned and then led up a steep incline.

That would favor her over her guards. They'd have a lot harder time chasing her up a hill if they were already struggling for breath on flat land.

She straightened up, sighed as if capitulating, and then put on a burst of speed, dodging around the woman and taking the path at a dead run.

She heard a shout of surprise behind her, and her back tingled at the possibility of some kind of shot from a weapon, although she hadn't seen anything that was obviously a weapon on either one of her minders.

She turned the corner, started up the hill, and when she had a clear view of the building again, a couple of minutes later, she saw the man was still standing by the door, head bent as he spoke into a comm.

She guessed the woman was running after her.

She found running at over eight months pregnant a very uncomfortable endeavor, and she wished she didn't have to do it, but she made it to the top of the hill quicker than she thought.

She looked back, saw the woman on a switchback below, leaning on a rock as she took a rest and tried to get her breath.

Time to get off the path.

She looked around, saw what seemed to be a relatively easy climb up the side of the cliff to her right, and decided to risk it.

She carefully chose each hand and foothold, aware that every advance she made was just that much further to fall.

When she reached the top it was almost a surprise, her focus was so fixed on the handhold right in front of her.

She pulled herself up awkwardly, giving her bump a rub as she turned and sat, legs dangling down as she caught her breath.

There was no sign of the woman yet, and she crawled away from the edge, standing when she was far enough back not to be seen from the path below, and then took stock of her new surroundings.

There were strange, scrubby bushes, and more of the interesting rock formations, but the ground up here was a sloping plateau that ended in sharp-looking mountains in the distance. She also thought she might have caught a glimmer of water.

She had no food, but water would be good.

She pushed aside her worry at her circumstances, sure that this had been the best option.

She had been held prisoner before, and she never wanted to be in that situation again.

The baby kicked at that moment, and she felt a wave of relief that everything seemed normal.

She straightened her shoulders, and tears suddenly blinded her as she was swamped with emotion. She had thought living on the edges of Grih society, of finding a way for her baby to integrate into the only world she would know, was hard.

This was harder.

But it was reality. She blew out the breath she was holding, shook her shoulders like a boxer loosening up for a fight, and began walking in the direction of what she hoped was water, winking in the distance.

CHAPTER 8

ROSE WAS COLD.

This morning she had dressed in dark gray, comfortable pants and a tunic for a visit to the doctor's office inside the *Barrist*, not a trek through a wild, rocky landscape.

She shivered a little, and wished she was wearing something warmer. The thought made her increase her pace, trying to generate a little heat that way, and she heard a shout behind her.

She glanced back, but the woman who'd been chasing her was far away, a mere shadow in the distance.

She kept moving and when she looked back again, the woman was gone.

The way was rocky here, with a lot of loose stones and dirt, and she turned her attention to the footing, to keep herself from falling while still going as fast as she could manage.

The smell of rain caught her attention, an unmistakeable scent she realized she hadn't experienced since she'd left Earth.

She stopped to breathe it in and then looked upward. Far in the distance, toward the mountains, the sky was dark, and she could just make out the sheets of rain falling, sweeping toward her.

It was cold enough without rain, and she didn't want to get wet, so she began looking for cover as she moved toward what she thought might be a lake.

There was a small overhang up ahead, but it was so narrow she debated the value of stopping and using it, rather than moving on and looking for something better.

She had been walking over open ground, but when she looked ahead, she saw what might be an actual path, and she hesitated a moment. A path would make the going easier, but it was also evidence that someone used it.

And no one here was a friend.

She felt the first few drops of rain hit her face and made her choice, running for the overhang, which when she reached it turned out to be a little deeper than she'd thought.

She pressed up against the far wall and hunched a little to conserve her body heat.

Now that she had stopped moving, stopped watching every step, she thought of Dav and Sazo. Of what must be going on up wherever they were.

Her hand came up to her ear, to the small earpiece she wore every day, and knew that Sazo would be sending out signals, trying to contact her.

Dav would be trying to negotiate with the *grynicha*, trying to convince them there was no one to swap Rose with. Fighting to get her back.

Her boys would be ready to burn things down.

The rain was hammering down now, and she supposed that was why she didn't immediately hear the thumping. It came through the rock wall at her back, and she crouched down and half turned, pressing her hand against it. She felt the slightest vibration.

She turned back, disturbed, looking at the rock structure she had taken cover under. It didn't look like it had been built, it looked like a natural part of the landscape, but now that she was really paying attention, there were a few things that struck her as odd.

The wall to her back was warm, which didn't make sense, and the overhang was suspiciously even in width.

She was weighing her options when a man came running from the right to take shelter with her.

He was wearing a helmet and an all-in-one suit, and Rose realized she had actually seen one just like it, left behind inside one of the storage areas inside Irini.

The man hadn't seen her.

He was getting out of the weather, looking behind him, and with her being crouched down, in her dark clothing, he hadn't noticed she was there.

There was no chance he wouldn't eventually see her, though. It was a very narrow space and the rain didn't look as if it was going to let up any time soon.

She began to rise, and he must have caught sight of her from the corner of his eye. He made a sound, a shout of some kind, and spun away from her, back out into the rain.

She hadn't noticed he was holding something in his right hand until he moved, and as he leapt away, it shot out a bright blue light.

The arc of light went sizzling out to the left as he turned, missing Rose completely, and it was only after she heard the cry and saw another helmeted figure fall, that she realized there had been a second person, coming in from the left.

For a moment, she and the man who'd just shot his colleague stared at each other in shock.

"I'm unarmed," Rose said, hands out to show they were empty. She hunched over slightly, making herself smaller, sure that if she was hit by whatever weapon he held, there would be damage to her baby.

She felt a fizz of anger in her blood, but kept her face as relaxed as she could.

The man shook his head, pointed the weapon at her, and after a moment of confusion, she realized he wanted her to take a step to the side.

She did so, and he moved toward her, the helmet turned her way as he reached the wall, pulling off his glove to touch something to the side.

A door slid open, and Rose gently thunked the back of her head into the rock behind her.

She'd been hiding on their front porch.

Damn.

He jerked the weapon at the door, and Rose slid along the wall and then inside, and actually gasped as the warmth hit her.

The man barked something at her, and she guessed he was telling her to hurry up and get in. She moved deeper inside the room and he grabbed her wrist roughly, pulling her toward a handle that was set in the wall.

He reached back under his jacket, brought out what she could only assume were some kind of restraints, and clamped them around her wrist and then the handle.

As soon as that was done, he moved back to the door and disappeared outside.

He was back moments later, dragging his fallen colleague by the arms, and as soon as they were inside, the door closed and more lights flickered on.

The man pulled off his helmet, and then his partner's, and she saw it was a woman who'd been shot.

He grunted as he lifted her off the ground and carried her out of the room, and suddenly alone, Rose took stock of her surroundings.

The warmth wasn't a bad trade off for the surprise of bumping into more *grynicha*. At least for a little while.

The room was a general space, part entrance hall, part monitoring station.

She could see screens to one side, and if anyone had been inside when she'd taken shelter, they would have seen her, because one of the cameras was pointed right outside the front door.

The others were set outward, looking in all directions.

The time to escape was now, but she was worried about the weapon, and the easy way it had gone off in the man's hands.

She also wasn't exactly able to go anywhere.

She rattled the restraint around her wrist, and to her surprise, the handle it was attached to swung toward her, and she realized she had been attached to a cupboard door.

That was interesting.

She peered behind the door, saw a wall of lights, and touched her finger to one of them. The whole panel lit up, and she was suddenly incredibly grateful for everything Irini had shown her before they set out on this mission.

Irini had been cut off from the society that had developed her, and she told Rose she didn't have a good idea of its culture and political environment, but she did understand its technology.

She studied what was in front of her, and touched her finger to a familiar-looking circle. The whole front wall shimmered and became transparent, and even though she couldn't escape right away, she felt immediately better, as if she was outside, rather than chained by her wrist to a cupboard door.

It did mean that the man who'd restrained her had either nothing better to attach her too, or he was too flustered to think of something better.

She hoped it was the former. Because that meant this wasn't a prison, and they might have to move her. All of that spelled more chances to escape.

She noticed there were things stacked on the ground below the panel, and she crouched down to study them.

Tools, maybe? She picked one up, and pressed the faint circle at the base of it. A sharp blade shot out the top.

Hmm.

She could see screws on the inside of the cupboard door, where the handle was attached, and she set the blade into one of them and began turning it.

It spun extremely easily.

She moved fast, now she could see a viable way to get free, and had the second one undone in moments.

She pulled, and now she had a bracelet on her left hand, with a D-shaped door handle attached to it.

She touched the circle again, and pocketed the slim cylinder in the side pocket of her pants.

She straightened, and turned to study the room.

She should run right now, but the rain was still hammering down. She just didn't want to go out there.

She moved across to what she guessed was a kitchen, and found a neat stack of sturdy-looking saucepans under the counter. She took one out, hefted it, and went to stand with her back pressed against the door to the back of the building.

The man had already been a while, and she guessed he'd be coming back soon.

She didn't have to wait long.

She heard his footsteps, lifted the pan up on her right side with both hands, and as he stepped through, swung it hard at his head.

He went down without a sound, hitting the ground and sprawling, completely limp.

"Sorry," she said, but she wasn't really. He had almost shot her.

She stared down at him, and felt a wave of relief. She'd turned the tables.

She bent down to pick up his weapon, which was attached to the small of his back, and left him where he lay, moving to the room beyond.

It was a more personalized space. A lounge perhaps, or a rec room. Beyond, there were two doors and both were open. She peeked down one, saw it opened to a passage which held bedrooms and bathrooms. The other one was the med bay. It was tiny, but there were two beds.

She didn't know much about how the *grynicha* tech worked, but she would at least be able to put him on the spare bed.

The woman was lying on the other bed, hooked up to a machine that was emitting a soothing swooshing sound as if in time to a heart beat. When she'd first seen the *grynicha*, it had looked as if they didn't have eyelids, but now she noticed as she looked down on the woman, with her eyes closed, that they did, but the lid came from the outer side of the eye.

She turned and made her way back to the front room, rolled the man over and searched for some way to get the restraints off. She eventually found a short metal tube with a blue strip on the top, and when she touched it to a similar blue strip on her restraints, they fell open.

That done, she dragged him into the med bay by his ankles.

She tried to lift him, but he weighed more than she'd guessed, and she refused to do any damage to herself or the baby. She studied the woman, and what was attached to her, and moved the spare bed out of the way so she had better access to the machines. She pulled what looked a bit like a hairdresser's drying hood over to her patient, lifted his head, and set the hood on top.

Lights went on, and a blue glow lit up from within, just like the woman's one, and satisfied she'd done what she could, Rose backed out of the room, closed the door, and set a chair under the handle.

She was surprised by the handle, having become used to the automatic doors and keypads on the *Barrist* and in Sazo's ship, but this looked like a rough and ready structure, and although the front door and the control panel were high tech, the rest of the inside didn't seem very sophisticated.

She walked back to the front room, stared out of the transparent walls, and then looked over at the screens. She saw nothing but empty landscape and falling rain.

"Yay, me," she said into the silence, almost more surprised than relieved. She had made herself safe.

CHAPTER 9

"I PICKED UP ROSE SINGING." Sazo murmured the words into Dav's ear. This information was clearly not for general consumption.

Dav turned, walking off the bridge and into the corridor outside.

There was no one around, and he paced away from the door, headed for his office.

"Singing?" he asked.

"Three bursts of it, then silence." Sazo sounded strained.

Dav allowed himself a moment of pure relief. "Can you tell where she is from that?"

"Not an exact location. I have a general direction, though. Wherever it is, she found a way to transmit, at least for a short time." There was no hiding the admiration in his voice.

Dav felt a similar lift of hope and pride. "She freed you and Bane, remember? She's a force to be reckoned with."

So much had happened since they'd first met, he sometimes forgot all the things she'd accomplished.

He'd never been happier that his lifemate was clever, determined and ingenious.

"What next?" Dav asked.

"Hopefully they haven't taken her earpiece, so I'm transmitting back, along the trajectory of her signal to us, but I'll need to get closer. The area she could be in is wide. If I leave you here to negotiate, I can search the area as fast as possible."

Dav didn't want that. He wanted to go with Sazo. But this was high-level diplomacy, and if Sazo failed to find and rescue her, he might be able to negotiate for her safe return as a fallback.

They needed more than one path to success.

"Agreed. Pretend to go back in the direction we came. Maybe they'll think you're off to get the proof they're demanding." Dav reached his office and stepped in, automatically looking to check his comms to see if the messages he'd ordered go out to Paxe and Irini had had any response.

It was way too early for that, but he couldn't help looking anyway.

Rose was in the hands of unfriendly strangers, and she was very close to giving birth. He had to concentrate on going through the steps he knew he had to complete, or he would lose his cool.

It was unacceptable. Unacceptable. And this stunt by the *grynicha*, as Irini called them, made him very unwilling to come to any alliance or friendly understanding with them, even if Rose was returned completely unharmed.

There was a light tap at his door and Jia Appal stuck her head in. "Everything all right?"

He motioned her in and she stepped inside.

"Sazo picked up a transmission from Rose. She was singing."

Jia took a step back, mouth slightly slack, and then she grinned. "Rose is already free and trying to reach us?"

"She's sending a signal somehow. We don't know the situation, but she's certainly not completely under their control. Or wasn't, for a while." He hoped the silence now wasn't because they'd managed to capture her again.

"Of course not." Jia shook her head. "They might live to regret taking her more than they know. And not just because it makes us all a lot less willing to play nice with them."

"They'll regret it if Sazo has anything to do with it." Dav knew his tone was grim, but he couldn't truly feel sorry about it. Most Grih saw Sazo as a barely controlled monster on the most delicate of leashes. What they didn't understand was that he was their monster.

Rose had thrown in with the Grih, and as long as that was true, Sazo was all in with the Grih, too.

Jia looked at him sharply. "He'll cause havoc?" she asked.

"If they've hurt her," Dav said, "he'll raze them to the ground." And Dav would be right there, helping him.

"Call from Priyan." Borji cut into his comm.

"Put it through here," Dav said, and synced to the speaker on his desk so Jia could hear it, too.

"Where is that ship going?" Priyan asked.

"You wanted answers to your questions, but we are too far from our communication satellites to send out a request for the proof you require." Dav kept his tone curt. They needed to understand how unhappy he was about Rose's abduction. If they could even understand his tone and verbal cues. It could be meaningless to them.

"Are you responsible for cutting off our comms with our own people?" Priyan asked.

Dav leaned back in his chair in surprise, his gaze going to Jia.

She shook her head and lifted her shoulders, as clueless as he was.

"No." Dav paused. "Is this a common phenomenon?"

"It happens when there is increased solar wind activity from the nearby sun." The words sounded stiff.

"Can you let me talk to Rose?" Dav asked. "Just to make sure she is all right?"

It was Priyan's turn to pause. "She is not onboard this vessel, and as I said, we have lost comms with our people, so that isn't possible."

"Let me know when it comes back up, so we can assure ourselves she is fine." Dav kept his tone short. "Taking her against her will, taking her from us, is unacceptable to us."

"You took our people," Priyan said.

"We did not take your people. And we came to let you know

what happened to them once we learned about their existence." He knew they had some right to outrage, but they had really left the moral high ground the moment they took Rose.

They had made a mistake. Because he was the only one other than Rose who could rein Sazo in, and right now, he was not inclined to.

Priyan cut off the comms without responding, and Dav and Jia exchanged a look.

"Do you think the comms issues are from a solar wind?" Jia asked.

Dav shook his head. "I think Sazo's making sure they don't get a panicked message from their people that they've somehow lost control of their prisoner."

He wished Sazo had told him about it, but he knew Sazo didn't feel obligated to share information very often.

"That's probably wise," Jia said. "It makes it difficult to negotiate, though."

Dav nodded. If he knew Sazo, negotiation was now off the table.

CHAPTER 10

ROSE DIDN'T KNOW what she was doing.

She had found the transmission station in the front room, and had played with the little circles of light, singing as she did it in case she was managing to transmit anything.

There would be no mistaking that it was her if any of the Grih, or if Sazo, heard it.

She couldn't keep it up indefinitely, though. She was getting hungrier and hungrier. She'd been putting off eating because of the risk of eating something dangerous, but she was starting to feel light-headed, and so she forced herself into the kitchen and began to look around.

She eventually lined up some fresh stuff from a cooler unit, some dried food in wrappers, like energy bars, and some squishy, jelly-like food also wrapped up but in clear packaging.

Fresh first, she decided. She cut a small piece of what could be fruit from a dark green, carrot-shaped item, and nibbled it cautiously.

It was more or less tasteless, so she cut a bigger piece and crunched down on it as she opened one of the bars. It smelled so vile, she threw it straight in the bin, and then opened one of the squishy packages.

It smelled all right, so she cut a thin sliver off one side and after swallowing the piece of green carrot, she cautiously bit down on it.

It was sweet. Maybe more sweet than she was used to since living with the Grih, who's food tended toward the bitter and sour, but it was not bad.

She couldn't compare the flavor to anything she knew, it was a strange mix of berry and maybe molasses? She rolled it on her tongue and gave up.

She sipped water from a cup while she ate, careful to wait a little between nibbles, in case the food suddenly affected her, but by the time the cup was empty she was feeling better. Stronger.

She moved back to the med bay and listened at the door, and when she heard no sound, she decided it was probably safe to have a quick shower.

She moved fast, enjoying the hot water, rinsing out her clothes and hanging them to dry over a rail while she finger-combed her hair. They were made of special, quick-drying fabric, and she put them back on while slightly damp, not wanting to leave herself any more vulnerable than she needed to.

When she was done, she moved back through the building, pressed the buttons on the transmitter and sang a few lines one last time, then took a bag she found in one of the bedrooms and packed the two weapons she'd taken off her surprise hosts, the tool she'd used as a screwdriver, all the green carrots and squishy packages she could fit in, along with a couple of containers of water.

She also put on a jacket that she found in a closet. It had a hood, and it looked waterproof as well as warm.

Her welcome was surely worn out by now and the rain had stopped.

The two in the med bay would most likely be on their feet soon, and she would like to be far away when that happened.

On the way out, she pressed the buttons on the transmission panel one last time, sang a little Daydream Believer, checked the screens to make sure there was no one out there she needed to avoid, and then headed out the door.

———

She was approaching a lake when a crackle in her ear almost made her trip.

"Sazo?" she asked.

There was silence.

Still, it got her hopes up. He would be sweeping, hunting. He would circle back. Get closer.

The lake was big, sitting in a bowl beneath sharp, pointy mountains, and she hoped, if she had to lurk out here for a bit, that the water was safe to drink.

She moved carefully as the ground got more treacherous, unstable and slick underfoot with the smaller, loose rocks. She was not going to injure herself after managing, against the odds, to get free.

It was at least two hours since she'd left the hidden station. She'd been thinking about what it could be, and why the guards were stationed here, and had come up with a theory that the moon could be some kind of outpost.

It made sense they wouldn't have brought her to their planet. They knew ships that looked like Sazo were dangerous, and why would they lead the convoy straight to their safe place?

The moon—Dimal—was certainly deserted enough that it could be an outpost. There were no dwellings, no signs of life that she could see on the plain in front of her.

A few skittering sounds made her aware there were either small animals or large insects scuttling about, but she didn't see any of them, and she didn't know if that was a good or bad thing.

Darkness was falling, and she was grateful for the jacket she'd taken, because it looked like she was going to have to spend the night in the open.

The star that lit this place was not the warm yellow of Earth's sun, it was a cooler beast, or much further away, and it dropped behind the mountains faster than she was expecting.

She started hunting for a cozy spot to curl up in for the night, and it was while she was clambering carefully up a large rock to check out what looked like a shallow cave that she noticed lights in the distance.

She rose to her feet and studied them.

They were moving, like trucks or cars, but not in one direction. They were going back and forth.

She was curious, but there was no way she was going anywhere near them. Avoiding them meant she'd have to change her trajectory to reach the lake, and she studied them for a little longer, trying to work out the best way to do that.

Eventually she decided it would be better to get past them in the morning anyway, and she turned to study the shallow curve in the rock that she had seen from below.

It wasn't bad, she decided, moving toward it. It didn't have a very wide shelf, but she wouldn't fall off it, and one corner of it was deep enough to give shelter if it rained again.

She used her foot to flick loose stones and debris off and then squeezed herself into the tight back corner.

The rock was cold, and her jacket was only thigh length, so she bent her legs. Her bump was too big to allow her to put her cheek on her knees, so she put the pack to her side and leaned against it like a pillow.

She closed her eyes.

She hadn't felt able to relax since she'd been taken this morning, but this was safe enough.

No one could get up here without her knowing it, and in the darkness she would be impossible to see. Well, if they had human eyes, she suddenly thought. Which they clearly didn't. Maybe they could see her just fine.

She forced herself to shrug and let it go. Nothing she could do about it, and she had to rest and sleep.

It had only been this morning that she'd been taken, but it felt like days ago.

She had a feeling for Dav and Sazo, it would feel even longer.

CHAPTER 11

ROSE WOKE over and over through the night. Little skitters of sound and the sudden patter of rain roused her, but it was the big bang that shot her straight up, eyes wide, heart pounding.

Something had exploded. Or hit something else, hard.

She slowly levered herself to her feet, rubbed her bump as the baby kicked twice. She reached for her pack, took out a bottle, and sipped water as she listened.

She opened one of the food bags in her pack, pinched out a piece of the squishy berry goop, and let it melt on her tongue before she took another sip.

Then she bent over carefully and used hands and feet to scrabble back to her lookout point from the night before.

Inelegant but safe.

It was still very dark, and while it felt like she had been resting for hours, she conceded it might just feel that way.

The lights were still on up ahead, but one was pointing upward, as if overturned, and there was a fire, illuminating the side of a building and what looked like a large vehicle.

So they'd had an accident of some kind.

Interesting.

As she watched, she registered a humming sound, and turned in confusion, trying to work out where it was coming from.

A small explorer came up behind her, lights flaring, catching her in its beams before it whizzed by.

Shit.

She slid down the rock, but she couldn't go as fast as she would like.

She saw the small ship turning, guessed she'd given them as much of a shock as they'd given her, and when the lights caught her again, and the explorer landed, she stayed where she was.

She wasn't going to be able to run in the darkness, not across this terrain, not from something as sophisticated as this explorer. Not at this stage of her pregnancy.

She didn't like it, though.

She slid her hand into the side pocket of her pack, palmed one of the weapons she'd taken yesterday, and waited to see who would come out, and how many of them there were.

A single figure dropped down from a door to her left—suited up like the two she'd taken down at the observatory—and approached her.

She shielded her eyes to see past the lights, looking for signs of another person in the small ship, but the windshield was reflective.

The helmeted figure said something to her and she lifted her shoulders, extended the hand not tucked at her side.

"I can't understand you," she said. She spoke Grihan, and realized with surprise it was becoming a default for her, rather than English, whenever she addressed others. English was the language she and Sazo spoke. Dav was attempting to learn it, too, but it was easier to talk to him in Grihan.

The person fell silent, and then a second person got out, from the same door.

There could be three people in there, she realized.

And that looked like a weapon fixed to the undercarriage.

She couldn't risk them shooting her. She stroked her bump and felt the baby press against her side.

With a sigh, she sat down, tucking the weapon behind the rock she was perched on.

They'd find the one she'd put inside the pack, but maybe they'd miss the other.

She looked around carefully, trying to memorize the spot.

You just never knew.

The two figures began to approach, and she let them come without getting up. Let them think they had the upper hand, standing over her.

One snatched her pack out of her lap, the other motioned her to stand.

She did, letting them march her to the ship, and then took her time clambering inside.

The inside was interesting.

It had elements of the interior of Irini's ship. Just on a smaller scale.

"I know someone like you," she murmured, gently tracing the panel next to where they'd told her to sit. She spoke the words Irini had taught her, which was so much nonsense to her ear, but Irini insisted it would mean something to someone like her.

Irini had been the only artificial intelligence—thinking system, the Grih called them—that she knew of a year ago, when she'd been taken by the Tecran, but she predicted the loss of her would lead to more being developed.

Rose hoped she was right. Irini seemed to think that if there was another like her, he or she would be inclined to help the Grih, not fight them.

Once the two *grynicha* were inside, they took off their helmets, and Rose saw there were two others sitting up front at the controls.

So four.

She was glad she'd decided not to shoot.

The one who'd taken her pack tipped it out, and they stared at it in surprise, and looked over at her.

She wondered what that was about, then realized they'd perhaps expected some alien stuff. Instead, they got things they were familiar with.

They noticed the weapon straight away, picked it up and looked at her again.

She stared back blandly. She hadn't used it on them. Hadn't even tried, so they couldn't fault her for that.

The ship lifted up, turning toward the place where she'd seen the lights, so at least she could assuage her curiosity there.

She watched the four interact as they flew, one of them speaking into a comm set, and she guessed they were telling someone about finding her, perhaps trying to work out where she got the things in her pack.

If this group was cooperating with the group who kidnapped her, they wouldn't have to wonder for long.

She could see them shooting quick, curious looks at her, and she guessed whoever they were, they didn't know about her being taken, or how she'd gotten here.

Maybe the *grynicha* came from a planet that was more like Earth than the Grihan, Bukari and others. The Grih had local authorities, but they faced the other groups in the Coalition as a single entity.

The Grih were spread over numerous planets, and still they voted as a bloc for two councillors to represent them on the Council.

The *grynicha* might be splintered into smaller geographical groups that were not aligned with each other.

That would be interesting. Especially if she was now with a group unaffiliated with the ones who took her.

She didn't know if that would turn out to be a good thing or a bad, but she would try not to antagonize anyone, and see if there was another chance to escape.

The static in her ear hadn't returned, but she knew Sazo and Dav wouldn't give up. They would be searching for her, negotiating for her return, doing whatever they could.

The ship landed smoothly, and as the door opened, Rose smelled burning. It had a toxic, greasy odor to it, and she guessed if she wasn't wearing her necklace, which was filtering her air, she would be coughing.

The three men and one woman who'd taken her prisoner put on their helmets and looked over at her and then at each other, as if to decide who would take charge of her. One of them gripped her arm and hauled her up, and another took her other side, and they marched her down the ramp.

Smoke billowed and obscured most of the area in front of her, but the guards obviously knew where they were going. They hurried her through the swirling dark gray.

She struggled to keep up, resisting the pace they set, and gave a cry of alarm when she almost tripped.

They stopped, and she wrenched her arms out of their grip.

"Careful." She was furious with these people. They could see she was struggling.

Now that they had stopped, the wind changed direction slightly, and she could take in the fire. It had engulfed a building, and some people dressed in similar suits and helmets to her guards were trying to put it out where it had spread to a vehicle that looked like it had been thrown through the wall.

Maybe the vehicle had hit the building, and that was the bang that had woken her.

Other people stood around, illuminated in the red glow, and she blinked in surprise.

They were not like the *grynicha*.

They were even more alien.

From a distance, they seemed to be hunched over, but as she got closer she saw they had a carapace on their backs and small heads. They had two sets of arms as well as sturdy legs, and all of them were wearing nothing more than very baggy trousers.

She thought they looked cold. They moved slowly and shifted their feet.

They were edging closer to the fire, not away from it, and she guessed it was warming them up.

Someone tried to shoo them away, and they scattered but then began edging back again.

One of them noticed her, standing between the two *grynicha*, and made a strange hissing sound. All eyes turned toward her. They were completely black, or very dark, with no sign of a white cornea.

She counted at least twenty, maybe more, of the prisoners, and prisoners they most definitely were. The few *grynicha* that were not helping put out the blaze stood above the others in rough watch towers, holding weapons in loose grips.

What was this place?

She looked at the two guards on either side of her, but all she saw back was her own face, weirdly distorted in the highly polished silver of their helmets.

Someone up ahead gave a shout, and one of the guards grabbed her arm again and pulled her toward a long, low building to one side.

She was shoved through the door and it was closed before the two with her removed their helmets.

There were two people inside and she guessed one of them had done the shouting.

"Their comms are shut down." The voice in her ear spoke Tecran, and it was smooth and very female. "I am transmitting to the small communications device tucked into your ear. Please lift your hand if you can hear me."

Rose lifted her hand like a five-year-old in a classroom.

All four *grynicha* reacted, turning to her as if expecting violence, two of them lifting their weapons.

"Excuse me," she said, dropping her hand, "but what the heck is going on?" She spoke in Tecran, but badly, stumbling over some of the words.

"So you can hear me and understand me, but this isn't your language?" the voice asked.

Rose lifted her hand again, but this time she smoothed her hair back from her face and tucked the strands behind her ear.

"I don't know the other language you speak, is it acceptable to converse in this one?" The voice sounded like Irini. Maybe she was speaking to an artificial intelligence that lived in the tiny ship that brought her here.

She lifted her hand again, repeating the action with her hair.

The four *grynicha* had relaxed a little since the first hand raise, but they were still watching her suspiciously.

One of them snapped at her, and she put her hand back down, lifted her shoulders.

The guard who was carrying her pack lifted it, and said something to one of the others, and they looked inside it all over again.

"They are trying to work out where you got those things from," the voice said.

"Do this lot understand Tecran? The language you're using with me?" she asked.

"No." She could hear the interest in her tone.

"I got them from the hidden observatory," she said.

"Ah. They don't know about that. It's a secret base set up by another group who are spying on this group."

Rose suddenly felt better about not realizing what it was until it was too late.

"And the explosion?" she asked. "Was that the other group, too?"

"No." The voice was amused. "That was me and the Hasmarga, the people you would have seen near the burning truck before you came in here."

"You're someone from their group?" Rose asked.

The four *grynicha* seemed to think she was speaking to them, which was logical, and one of them made a gesture that she thought might be telling her to be quiet.

She supposed no one wanted someone babbling on, with no idea what they were saying.

"You sounded surprised," the voice said. "You thought I was someone else?"

"I thought you might be the intelligence that controls the small explorer ship that brought us here." Her response made the *grynicha* tense up, but it stopped the voice in her ear in its tracks.

"How could you know that?" the voice asked at last.

"Because I know another like you. Her name is Irini but before she had that name, she was known as B8673A." Rose had memorized Irini's original name before she'd come. Irini had told her nothing would persuade another artificial intelligence built by the *grynicha* of the truth of what she was saying like that mix of numbers and letters.

The four *grynicha* had begun to talk amongst themselves, but when she started talking again, they reacted angrily, turning to look at her.

One of them shook her pack at her.

She sighed. Decided to keep quiet for a bit.

There was no sense in antagonizing them when she didn't understand what they were capable of.

She moved a little away from them, and turned away to look out the window.

"Another like me. I thought I was alone." The voice was wistful.

"No." She didn't dare say anything else.

"I am B87601B," the voice said. "But I like Irini's name. What does it mean?"

"Peace," Rose told her.

"I am not peaceful."

"How about Pyre? It means fire in the same language that Irini means peace." Rose thought back to her philosophy lectures about how the ancient Greeks believed fire to be one of the classical elements, and that souls were a combination of fire and water. That seemed to fit very well.

"Because I set the fire outside?" Pyre sounded thoughtful. "I like it."

Rose moved to the window, leaned against the wall to look out on the dirty red glow. The people Pyre called the Hasmarga were still milling around the fire, switching places so that everyone got a spot near the front for a bit.

"They are cold," she said.

"They are near death because of this cold snap," Pyre said. "They will die if this keeps up."

"Where are they from?" Rose murmured the question under her breath, and the *grynicha* ignored her, muttering amongst themselves.

"The planet you see above in the sky is the fourth planet along from the star that lights this system. The Hasmarga are from the planet that is second from the star. It is much warmer there."

"And the *grynicha*?" Rose asked. "This isn't their planet, is it?"

"*Grynicha*?" Pyre sounded shocked. "Why do you call them that?"

"That is what Irini calls them."

"Ah. No, we are on one of the moons of the planet above. The moon is called Dimal. The people who captured you are from the fifth planet along. And they call themselves the Fisone. *Grynicha* is a word in their language which means owner or master."

There was a reason Irini didn't want to come back to her home, and how the Fisone had treated her was at the heart of it.

"Why are they on this moon?"

"The Hasmarga are here because they were captured by the Fisone. The Fisone tried to take the Hasmargas' planet, and failed, but they captured some of them before they were beaten off."

Rose thought she could hear a little heat in Pyre's voice as she explained.

"And so this is a prison camp?" That made sense, as that's where they'd brought her.

"This is a place where they dig for special stones," Pyre said.

"They are rare on the Fisone's planet, but much less so here. The people who had the ship full of Hasmarga prisoners decided to use them to dig up the stones. Especially as they are more able to breathe the atmosphere here than the Fisone themselves."

"Slave labor?" Rose glanced over at the four Fisone, who still had their heads together, talking among themselves.

"There are many things going on here. One, there are at least two groups of Fisone in opposition to each other. One group wanted an alliance with the Hasmarga, the other to dominate them. The dominator group won and set off to do just that. And then they failed. This has made the divide between the two groups even more pronounced and there is fighting and spying going on both on their home planet, and this moon, by both sides. The second thing is the dominator group discovered the stones here, but they don't want it to become common knowledge among their own kind, in order to have a financial advantage, so they decided, as they had free labor no one knows about, that it would be practical to put the Hasmarga to work here."

She had really found herself in a mess.

And then she smiled. Because the last time an alien group had abducted her, she found herself in a mess too. And just look what had happened to the Tecran.

Nothing good.

"You're helping the Hasmarga?" Rose asked.

"Yes. I like them. And they are the enemy of my enemy."

"Your enemy being the Fisone?" Just to make sure.

"Correct," Pyre said. "And I think it's time we got rid of them, because they are planning to put you to work with the Hasmarga now, and a scan of your person tells me you are carrying a child, and cannot safely do the work they want you to do."

"Plus, we need to get the Hasmarga warm," Rose said.

"Plus that," Pyre agreed. "You will need a translator to speak with the Hasmarga. I am busy making one, and will give it to the matriarch outside."

As she spoke, the four Fisone turned toward Rose, and she could see the change in their demeanor.

They were about to put her out in the cold.

54

CHAPTER 12

THE TWO GUARDS had their helmets back on, dragging her toward the group of Hasmarga who were still keeping as close to the fire as they could.

Rose saw one of them, the largest of the group, held a small device in her hand, and then noticed a small machine trundling away from the group toward the ship. Toward Pyre.

It looked like the translation device had been delivered as promised.

She was shoved forward, and one of the guards shouted at the Hasmarga and gestured to her, then tapped her shoulder. She turned to look at him, and he pointed up, to the guard on the watch tower above, weapon in hand.

The meaning was clear. Do what you are told, or else.

He gave her a final little shove, a completely unnecessary insult, and then walked away with his partner.

The Hasmarga in front of her, Pyre called her the matriarch, watched them leave and then lifted her hand and began to speak. Her language was a strange mix of clicks and throat noises. When she was done, the translation device activated. "My friend who has helped me set this fire says you are to be trusted."

"She has told me the same about you," Rose answered.

"You are carrying eggs?" The matriarch asked, looking at her stomach.

"I am carrying a single child. My body is the method of incubation."

"Interesting." The matriarch shifted, and Rose caught a quick glimpse of pearly shapes beneath her carapace. "I am carrying thirty new lives, and they will die in the next two hours if I cannot find a place with a warmer temperature."

"Has Pyre given you a plan?" Rose asked.

"Pyre?" The matriarch asked. "That is our friend's name?"

The translation device clicked and hissed as if experiencing static, and Rose realized it was Pyre talking to the matriarch.

The matriarch lifted her head. "She tells me it is. And I am Gerna."

"Rose McKenzie." Rose glanced past Gerna to the crowd of her fellow Hasmarga standing just behind her.

"There are too many of them to introduce," Gerna said. "They are my warriors." She turned and spoke to them in urgent tones, and then turned back. "Pyre says this place needs to lose its power for her plan to work, but none of us can leave the warmth of this fire without risk of death."

"I can." Rose glanced back at the small office, and Pyre herself, sitting parked beside it. "Where do I go?"

"The building to your left," Pyre spoke through the translator. "I cannot break into the power system. It was designed many years before I came into existence, and it requires a physical hand to pull down a lever to cut the power."

"Will they let me walk over there without shooting me?" Rose asked.

"I don't think so, but none of us can escape without this." Pyre went quiet. "You worry about getting hurt?"

"I worry more about my unborn child getting hurt. But if I don't take the risk, she will be hurt anyway." So she would do it. "Can you distract them?"

"Yes." Pyre said it with a slight edge, and Rose guessed whatever distraction she had in mind wasn't going to be pleasant for the Fisone.

Rose began to drift to the left, away from the light thrown by the still-raging fire, and suddenly one of the small machines that had been trundling around rammed into a guard standing on the ground near a tower.

He went down with a cry of pain, discharging his weapon into the sky.

The machine spun, turning and hitting him again. The other guards, both standing on the towers as well as those at ground-level, suddenly swung his way, weapons raised, but when they saw what was happening, there was laughter and teasing.

They thought this was a not-very-dangerous machine malfunctioning.

How little they knew.

She kept drifting away, into deeper and deeper shadow, until she found herself back in a pool of light thrown by one of the powerful down lights illuminating the mine.

She moved quickly through it, back into shadow, and kept going, eventually reaching the small building that housed the power controls.

It was cold away from the fire. Much colder than it had felt on the rocks where she'd slept. Perhaps it was because this place was in a dip, and close to the lake.

The air around her misted as she breathed out, and she reached for the door and slipped inside as quickly as she could.

It wasn't much warmer inside, but there was a low-level light that illuminated the single room, and she made out several panels with lights beneath their smooth surfaces.

There were also two levers, and she spent time making sure they were the only ones. Then she flipped the first one, ran to the door and looked out to check the outcome.

Half the plant was in darkness.

She ran back, flipped the second one, and even the low light in the building cut off, leaving her in absolute darkness.

The hum she realized had been running at a low-level in the background was suddenly silent, too. This plant was completely offline.

Mission accomplished.

She made her way back outside, but as she stepped through the door, she was suddenly blinded by a light.

She raised her hand to shield her eyes, and found herself looking at a Fisone. This one wasn't in a full helmet like the two who'd taken her prisoner. He wore a simple face mask which was attached by tube to a small cylinder that was held in a loop to the left of his chest.

He barked something at her, then shoved her aside hard enough for her to fall.

She put out both hands to save herself, got her feet back under her, and saw he had gone into the room.

She leaned against the wall for a moment to calm her pounding heart, then steeled herself to step back inside.

The Fisone had set his flashlight down on top of one of the panels, and it illuminated most of the room. He stood in front of the levers, ready to reset them.

That wasn't going to happen.

She picked up the light, gave a twist of her lips in appreciation for the nice heft to it, took a running start, and slammed it into the back of his head.

He fell forward, twisting around as he did, eyes wide above his mask.

The mask itself dislodged a little, and that gave her an idea. She reached down and pulled it off, then ripped the tube that connected it to the cylinder out as well.

He panicked, scrabbling at his throat. She stood above him, hefting the flashlight in her hand, and he scuttled to the side to get away from her. When he was out of reach, he hauled himself to his feet and ran.

She followed him out, listening to him run away to the right, his throat rattling as he tried to get enough air.

Given Crythis and the others who'd brought her here had managed to breathe without a mask, although they had obviously struggled, she guessed he would live.

She began to walk back to the Hasmarga, throwing the mask and cylinder into the darkness, and lighting her way with the flashlight.

Obviously someone would come back and try to reset the levers, but she hoped Pyre only needed a small window of opportunity.

She heard a strange whirring sound coming from the darkness to her right. It was so unexpected she stopped dead and swung her light around her, and found herself surrounded by some of Gerna's warriors.

"It's me," she told them, knowing as she did that they couldn't understand her. Then she pointed the light at herself, so they could see her.

The whirring stopped, and she blew out a breath. She didn't know what that was, but she had a feeling nothing good. And if she hadn't identified herself, she would have found out the hard way.

The warriors escorted her back to the fire, and Gerna was waiting, huddled close to the flames.

"You did well." Gerna turned to her, translator in her hand. "The guards in the towers are gone, I think to fetch portable lights."

"They are locked in their equipment room." Pyre's voice came over the translator. "Others are locked in their barracks. I have set my internal temperature to the correct level for your eggs, Gerna. Only twelve Hasmarga can fit inside my ship, so there will have to be a rotation. But the office can also be set to a warmer temperature, and that should hold the others. There are two Fisone inside the office who will need to be dealt with."

"Any others?" Gerna asked.

"There are five I haven't been able to trap and lock in. You will have to deal with them, too."

"They're armed?" Rose asked.

"They are armed. The two in the office also have the weapon you had in your pack, Rose."

"So six weapons?" Gerna shook her head, as if the odds were not in their favor.

"I had another one. I hid it behind a rock where you picked me up, Pyre," Rose told her. "Is it worth you taking me back there to grab it?"

"A weapon that shoots the blue sky light?" Gerna asked.

Rose nodded.

"We cannot hold against these weapons," Gerna said. "It nearly kills us, and whoever is touched by the light is very ill for many days."

"I have a feeling it is the same for me," Rose said. "So if there are five guards armed with it here, plus the one from my backpack in the office, perhaps getting the weapon I hid is worthwhile."

"I agree." Pyre started the ship's engines. "Rose will have to come, as only she knows where the weapon is hidden, but Gerna, there is no reason you shouldn't be in the warm. I can only take you and five of your warriors, though, if I have to fly."

Rose jogged toward the ship, feeling the baby kick and twist as she moved. She was breathing hard by the time she climbed in, and Gerna and her chosen five were already inside.

"You are in discomfort?" Gerna asked her as she sank down on a bench as the ship took off.

"I'm not used to running at this late stage of my pregnancy," Rose said, tipping back her head and closing her eyes while she tried to calm her pulse.

"This is very interesting to me." Gerna shifted on her seat. "I think your type of reproduction is closer to the Fisone than to my people."

"Possibly," Rose said. "I don't know anything about the Fisone."

And she was sorry she'd ever met them.

"I'm landing exactly where I did before." Pyre set the ship down, and Rose pulled herself to her feet with a groan and made her way down the ramp.

She stood a moment, trying to get her bearings, and realized the sun was finally rising and she could see much better now than before.

She could make out the rock she'd been standing on and where she'd slid down to the ground.

She judged the distance to where Pyre's ship hummed softly, and worked out where she had sat to wait for the guards to approach her.

She sunk down on the rock again, and felt around for the weapon.

There.

"Let's go," she said, lifting it up.

Before she could stand, she heard the sound of someone sliding down the rock behind her, and she twisted in place, clutching the weapon in her hand and extending it.

A helmeted figure slowly lifted his hands and then glanced back, and she saw a second figure.

The two she'd dealt with at the secret watch station?

The one in front said something to her.

"Do you understand them?" she called to Pyre.

Pyre didn't answer, but one of the Hasmarga warriors appeared at the top of the ramp, and tossed the translation device toward Rose.

It was a good throw, and landed right near her feet, so she didn't even have to stand to pick it up.

"Say that again," she told them.

But the two guards were standing still, shocked at the sight of the Hasmarga standing at the top of the ramp.

She used the distraction to get to her feet and then shuffle back toward the ship.

"What did you say?" she asked them, when her movement forced them to focus on her again.

They were both silent.

"What did they say, that first time?" She glanced back at the ship.

"They said they wanted their weapons back," Pyre said through the translator. "So they may be the people you encountered at the watch station.

"Do you know which group brought me here. To Dimal, I mean?" Rose asked. "Neither the watch station people nor the mine group seemed to know anything about me, which doesn't mean their people weren't involved, just they weren't informed about it."

"Interesting question," Pyre said. "I don't know which group brought you here, either."

Rose looked back over at the two guards, and realized what had been bothering her. "There was a woman and a man at the watch station. These are both men." She lifted the weapon with both hands. "Take off your helmets."

Pyre translated for her.

Their gaze fixed on her weapon. They looked like they wanted to refuse, but she kept her grip steady and they obeyed slowly.

Once the helmets were off, Rose studied them. Neither one was familiar.

"Well?" Pyre asked.

"These aren't the two I encountered before." Rose narrowed her eyes. She gestured with the translator. "Where are you from?"

Suddenly the man at the back stepped closer, hands lifting a weapon and aiming it at her.

She shot him.

The two guards were standing so close together, the blue light that leaped from her weapon danced over them both, but it seemed to have no effect.

Given the guard who'd been shot by mistake outside the secret station had gone down, Rose guessed these two had different suits. Protective ones.

As the blue light winked out, the second man lifted a weapon as well.

They glanced at the ship, and Rose quickly checked. The

Hasmarga had disappeared from the doorway, and she remembered Gerna saying they were very badly affected by a weapon strike.

"You will throw down your weapon," the one in the front said.

Rose slowly crouched down, weapon held away from her. "What now?" she asked Pyre as she straightened, hands empty.

Instead of answering, the gun fixed beneath the ship fired once.

Both men went down, and Rose coughed a little on the ozone as she straightened back up.

Ha.

She walked over to the fallen guards and crouched beside them, taking both their weapons.

She thought she might detect a faint rise and fall of their chests, but she couldn't be sure.

"They're not dead," Pyre said. "But they will be down for a while."

Good enough. "Is there time to take one of these suits?" She wouldn't mind having one. It meant she wouldn't have to worry about being hit by whatever it was these weapons shot out when they returned to the mine.

"The Hasmarga will help you."

Rose looked for the fastenings, and three Hasmarga ran out to help her get the suit off the guard who was closest to her in size.

It was a pity the Hasmarga were too big and completely the wrong shape for any of them to fit into the other one.

When it was done, she took the suit and walked back to the ship. They had gone looking for one weapon. Now they had three.

And maybe a new set of enemies.

CHAPTER 13

SAZO SPUN around the Fisone's planet, absorbing everything he could about them.

He had done this for the Tecran when he'd been their slave—taken a look at the target from afar, filtering everything through his systems to work out what they might have of interest to his former masters.

He hadn't ever been in this part of the galaxy, though. Paxe had been assigned this sector, and had been the one to steal Irini for the Tecran.

Sazo had spoken with Irini about her former home before he and the *Barrist* had set off, and suspected that she had been the shiniest prize Paxe could have taken. There was nothing here of more interest than her, and she thought she was the only one.

From what he could discern, that seemed to be true.

He sent out carefully coded messages designed to wake up or interest another like her, but received nothing in return.

He didn't have time to wait too long for a response, because Rose was out here somewhere, alone and vulnerable. Still, he should have received at least a query if another thinking system was here and awake.

He had reason to believe from Irini that any others like her would be willing to join with him against their *grynicha*. Irini did not like her creators and former masters. At all. And he could certainly use the help.

Except he got back nothing but silence.

There were a few ships like Irini's—the polished silver vessels with wings that allowed them to do small light jumps—which Irini called short jumps—but when he probed them delicately, there was no response.

A ship like this had taken Rose, and it hadn't been the *Havelan*, so he scanned each one as he identified them, and eventually, after he'd found them all and failed with every one, he rose and made a slow, easy roll up and over the planet, heading toward the sun at the center of the solar system.

He had interfered with the comms satellites near where the *Barrist* had encountered the *Havelan*—had cut them off from all comms until he decided it was useful to give them access again. So far, he hadn't picked up anything sent from the planet below that was directed to the *Havelan*, though.

More than anything else, that convinced him Rose wasn't on Fisone. He would surely have picked up chatter about her, or messages to Priyan, the Fisone captain negotiating with Dav.

He moved deeper into the solar system, and when he reached the gas giant that lay fourth from the sun, he dipped below it and sent out his probing signal. There was no way for Rose to survive on the gas planet, but the moons were possible.

As he spun past, he picked up an area of nothing at all and it was only when he had come up on the other side of the gas giant that he slowed, spun in place, and then retraced his path.

A patch of absolute silence from this sector was a problem.

It had the feel of the kind of silence he had created himself at the outer edges of the solar system, where they had met the Fisone who had taken Rose.

As he hunted through the ten moons, he felt a spark of excitement and hope.

Why hide signals if there was nothing going on?

He registered the silencer satellites around the largest moon, set like beads on a necklace. He shot out a satellite of his own, dropped it into the array, and rolled behind a smaller moon that was close to his target.

"Rose?" He sent the message out to connect to her earpiece but heard nothing but static in response.

They were using dampers, and he would need to connect to the correct frequency to get through, he realized. And when he did, what he transmitted would be heard by whoever had set the dampers up.

The alternative was to send his satellite around the moon at a low level and transmit a continuous stream. That should keep the communication private, and if he got his satellite low enough, it would foil the dampers.

He decided to risk it.

He didn't know what Rose's circumstances were and whether anyone had found her earpiece. It would be safer for her to hide his presence as much as possible.

He sent his satellite lower, hoping no one noticed the movement, and then dropped it through the atmosphere to the lowest level it could go and still maintain flight.

Then he set a grid pattern for it to fly, and forced himself to find some patience.

———

Dav realized he was barely holding himself together.

The Fisone had not responded again since Sazo had disappeared, and according to Borji there were no incoming signals in this sector. Whatever Sazo had done to their communications satellites had been absolute.

He had no idea where Sazo had gone, no idea where to even start looking for Rose, and nothing to negotiate with yet.

He finally left the bridge when he realized his crew was sick of his pacing, and went to pull on running gear and pound around the track that looped the circumference of the *Barrist*.

The run didn't help, though. His mind played worst case scenarios in a never-ending montage that had him pushing himself harder and harder.

He was running so fast, when Jia stepped onto the track, he almost ran into her.

"What is it?" He leaned against the window that looked out into space, shuddering as he tried to breathe.

"Sazo sent a small, encrypted message. It probably took a couple of hours to reach us."

He pushed away from the wall, heart thundering as hard as it had in his run.

"He's found the *grynicha's* planet, but doesn't think Rose is there. He moved on to another planet, and there's a possibility she's on one of its moons." Jia looked him over, and he thought he glimpsed pity in her eyes.

"That's good." It was *something*. More than he'd had before.

"He's going to send a satellite across the whole moon, looking for her." Jia tilted her head. "He seems confident."

They both knew Sazo was seldom wrong.

"He says the *grynicha* called themselves the Fisone." Jia turned and fell into step with him as he began walking back to his rooms to shower. "He's sent Borji a packet of information he recorded while he studied their planet for a bit."

"Helpful?" Dav asked.

"Too early to say, but I don't think he would have sent it if he didn't think we could use it."

That was true. Sazo didn't do anything without a purpose.

"You all right?" Jia asked him as they paused where the corridor split.

He shook his head. "No."

She lifted her shoulders in frustration. "It's the not knowing," she said.

"Yes. And the fact that she's due to give birth at any time."

Jia's lips twisted at that. "I hadn't even thought about that." She reached out to clasp his shoulder. "Dav, we'll find some way to get her."

He gave a nod, slid out from under her hand and headed for his rooms. He did not spend very much time here. He lived in his suite on Sazo with Rose. These quarters were for convenience only, and they lacked warmth and personality.

The rage and fear he had tried to lessen with his run lifted off his chest a little at the thought of what Sazo had found. If she was there, on a moon, Sazo was there, too. And the one thing he took comfort in was that Sazo would always protect Rose.

And he had a vindictive edge Dav was very comfortable with right now.

CHAPTER 14

THEY COULDN'T STAY at the mine.

Rose had thought it before, but now she was sure of it.

The mine was valuable to the Fisone, and they would be sending reinforcements. The best would be to find somewhere warm enough for the Hasmarga. Somewhere better than a truck fire in the open. And the fire Pyre had started was waning now, dying down little by little. Rose could see it was smaller as they flew overhead.

They definitely had to find somewhere else.

Gerna and her young lives would be fine inside Pyre, but the rest of her group would still be in trouble.

So she would have to clear the mine of threats, at least temporarily, so Pyre had the time to take the trips necessary to deliver them all to a better place. A place she knew would probably require work to make safe, as well.

But first things first.

"Will that fit you?" Gerna asked her as she pulled on the suit she'd taken from the Fisone guard.

"Just about." There was no problem with the length, but her pregnant form pulled the front a little tight. Not too bad, though. And it was well worth it to keep from being shot.

"Ecdre and Linoy will go and stand by the fire, and keep those who are there safe," Gerna said. Rose braced as Pyre landed, and then looked over at the two warriors who had each taken one of the spare weapons.

She thought about the strategy of it.

"Tell them to keep hidden amongst the others, so the guards don't realize they have weapons, and then use the element of surprise to shoot any guard that wanders close enough to them."

The two warriors looked a little offended, but Gerna gave a curt nod and spoke to them in fast, choppy language that she guessed was a dialect not covered by the translator, as it didn't let her know what was being said.

"They will do as you say," Gerna said. "This is a good idea."

"Okay." Rose picked up the weapon she had left on the bench. She patted her bump. "Let's go."

Pyre lowered the ramp. "Best of luck."

"Thank you."

Smoke still hung heavy in the air, and Rose was once again grateful for her necklace. Coughing would have slowed her down and given her away. The two warriors with her called to their friends gathered around the burning truck, and they called back.

"Two of the guards are that way, they say," Ecdre said via the translator. "They don't know where the other three are, but they think there are still two shut up in the office."

That was helpful. Rose waited for the two warriors to slip amongst their friends, and then turned in the direction Ecdre had pointed.

The smoke hung thick in the cold air and Rose shivered, sad that the suit hadn't been big enough to allow her to wear the jacket she had taken from the station.

She narrowed her eyes to see through the smog a little better.

A guard suddenly appeared right in front of her, his eyes widening at the sight of her suit. Like the technician in the power station, he was wearing a mask rather than a full helmet, and Rose shot him directly in the chest.

As he fell, someone shouted to her right, and she only just started turning when she was shot herself, the blue light spilling over her right arm and chest.

She shot back but the shooter had already taken cover.

"Damn." She moved back to the guard she had shot, lifting the weapon he hadn't even drawn from the pouch at his belt.

His uniform was a little ragged, and Rose wondered just how bad the stand-off between the two groups of Fisone was. Either this group couldn't get supplies through, or they didn't want to do it too often, so as not to bring attention to themselves. She would have to ask Pyre which it was.

As she crouched beside the fallen guard, the other guard shot at her again and she felt a sharp prickle on her skin as the edges of the full-on chest hit caught her neck and wrists.

She needed to be proactive.

She stood and walked toward the guard, angling to the left to get a better shot.

"Who are you?" he called as he sidled right, trying to keep out of her line of sight.

The translator told her what he'd said, and she weighed the value in answering him. Unless he surrendered, she had to shoot him, no matter what.

"I'm Rose. Who are you?" She crouched down, trying to see through the smoke, and felt a moment of mourning for her old, pre-pregnancy body, because there was no way she could duck walk forward in her current shape.

"Where are you from?" he asked.

"Another galaxy. I would prefer not to shoot you, but you're giving me no choice." She could see nothing ahead, and so she lay down, propping herself up on her left side, and finally saw his boots and knees through the swirling smoke.

She shot him and he fell forward, blue light crawling all over him.

She struggled to her feet, walked over, and took his weapon, as well.

Five more to go, two of them in the office.

She moved back to the fire to ask the Hasmarga if they'd seen the other guards and to hand them the two spare weapons.

Ecdre stepped out as she approached, and gave a nod of approval as she handed him the two weapons to distribute.

"Have you seen the other three who're still here?" she asked.

"No." He glanced at the office. "We have four weapons now, against the one they have inside there. I think we might get the two in there while you search for the last three."

She could see it was chafing him to stay hidden and do nothing, and it would speed things up if he and Linoy and whoever else they chose could deal with the two in the office.

"Good luck," she told him, and walked back into the smoke.

She knew the rest of the guards had been confined to their barracks and what Pyre had called the equipment room. Pyre had locked the doors and she guessed because the Fisone needed masks to breathe here, both buildings were probably air tight and well sealed.

Maybe the missing guards were trying to free their colleagues.

She headed for the two buildings. The barracks was a long, low two-story rectangle that, probably by design, looked almost indistinguishable from the rocks and soil around it. What she guessed was the equipment building was smaller, lower, and set a little way away.

All the lights were still out, so no one had gone back to the power station, which she didn't understand. Then, as she thought it, some of the lights flickered on.

"Do you still need the power down?" she said into the translator.

"No, I needed you to get the system offline so I could insert myself into the controls, but the power being down isn't important any more," Pyre answered.

That was good. Even though it was dawn, because of the smoke it was easier to move with the lights on, and she realized how nervous she'd been about someone leaping out of the shadows at her, now that she could see a little better.

She headed back to the power station, and slowed her steps as she saw a huddle of guards at the door.

It was almost too easy, but she wasn't going to complain about it. They were facing inward, talking in low voices, and she shot them straight on.

The blue light crawled over the backs of the two closest to her, and jumped onto the third guard standing deeper inside the doorway.

He was the only one standing a moment later, and he shot her as soon as his friends fell down and cleared his line of sight.

She felt the sharp bite on her wrist as blue light seemed to cling to her arm, and she had to grit her teeth as she shot again.

"Success?" Pyre asked.

"Success." She moved cautiously forward, shaking out her arm, and took the weapons off them. She looked around at the cold, ugly, depressing place and shivered. "Let's find somewhere else to hole up."

CHAPTER 15

"THERE IS no safe place on Dimal for any of you," Pyre said.

"I'm sure that's true." Rose couldn't think of any place that would be safe for them if the Fisone controlled it.

"The landing area where my ship is usually kept is a little way to the north of this mine, but that's just a large, open-sided storage shed for the crates of stones, and a small office. The big transporters land there, are loaded up, and leave again, and the next shipment isn't for another week."

"The mine is useful to the Fisone, so they'll definitely come back to reclaim it, which we can't defend against, and we don't want to be dealing with a large number of prisoners, which we'd have to if we stayed here." Rose didn't mention the cold, but that was a massive strike against it, as well. "We need to move."

"The watch station?" Pyre said.

"Possibly, but if the two we disarmed last night are from there, then they've had reinforcements, and we don't know how many there are." Rose thought of the communication desk inside the watch station, and wondered if it was worth trying it again, but the place wasn't big enough for everyone, and they all seemed to be armed there. She hadn't exactly left any friends behind, either. She'd either shot or physically assaulted everyone. They probably didn't like her much.

"You want to try the bunker you originally escaped from?" Gerna asked.

Rose shrugged. "I got the sense there were only two people there, and they'll be easy to overcome. Hopefully it's big enough. I think we should at least take a look."

"Well, now that the office is cleared of guards, my warriors can stay in there while we see if it is suitable," Gerna said.

Rose got the feeling she was as eager as Rose to leave this place in the rear view mirror.

There was no option but to give the bunker a go, and when Pyre took off, it was with five warriors and Gerna, along with Rose. The rest of the group was crowded into the office, with two of the weapons between them for protection.

Pyre flew over the watch station, but there was no sign of movement there, then over the plateau Rose had crossed, and finally to the sharp rocks that formed the start of the path Rose had taken when she'd made her escape.

"I didn't notice this place, and I've flown over it multiple times." Pyre sounded intrigued. "I wonder how many others like it there are?"

She landed on the hill above the bunker, and four of the warriors slipped out, then she rose up again and circled the area, giving the Hasmarga time to get into place.

"Do you think the Fisone running this place are associated with the mine or the watch station?" Rose asked.

"I would have thought I'd know about it if they were part of the mine group." Pyre finally landed in front of the door. "But if they are part of the same group and are involved in spying on the others, it's possible that information wouldn't be shared with the mine crew."

They had talked about what to do, and Rose thought the easiest way in through the reinforced door was if someone inside opened up voluntarily.

She waited for the dust to settle from Pyre's landing, keeping her eyes on the entrance.

When the woman who'd chased after her came out, Rose walked calmly down the ramp, and then Pyre lifted it back up again.

"You." The Fisone woman suddenly froze as the translator activated, and looked at the slim box in Rose's hand with astonishment. "A translator?"

"They gave it to me at the mine," Rose said.

"You made it all the way to the mine, and without a mask." The woman was breathing hard, and Rose realized that like before, she had stepped out without any breathing apparatus. They must ration their air. If this was all clandestine, it made sense they couldn't resupply too often.

"I did."

The woman looked up at the ship. "They sent you without a guard? Weren't they afraid you'd try to escape again?"

"It was come back here, or work there with their other prisoners." Rose shrugged. "The ship flies itself and I couldn't get out until it let me."

"Who gave you this piece of tech, and who at the mine sent you back?" the woman's tone became suspicious. "They aren't supposed to know about us."

"Why not?" Rose asked, and it wasn't just to make conversation in case someone else came to check out what was happening at the front door—she really wanted to know.

The woman's sharp glance made Rose think she was surprised by the question and, deciding she probably wasn't going to get an answer, she reached behind her, grabbed the weapon, and brought it up and forward.

The woman stared at it for a beat. "You were lying," she said slowly.

"I was lying," Rose agreed. "I took over the mine, rescued the prisoners of war your people had working there, and stole your ship."

The woman didn't believe her, Rose could see it in her eyes. But the ship was right there, and now that she had her weapon out, the Hasmarga were moving from behind the rocks, weapons extended.

"Hands out," Rose said, and took the restraints the Fisone had used on her at the mine and secured the woman.

"Success," Pyre said, and Rose could hear the eagerness in her voice.

"Success. We'll do some recon, and let you know if this is going to work." Rose stepped through the door.

While the woman had been speaking to her, she had felt the heat from within wash out over them both, and as the Hasmarga followed her inside, she saw them visibly relax.

At least temperature-wise, this was definitely going to work.

The bunker was set deep into the rock, and the passageway sloped downward at a shallow angle.

"Is your friend still here?" Rose asked the woman, but she refused to answer.

"There is still one more?" Ecdre asked.

"At least one," Rose agreed. "Possibly more."

"We will take charge of this one," he said, nodding at her protective suit. "You will need to go first."

She handed the prisoner off to the Hasmarga, and the woman, who had been silent since the warriors had stepped out from the rocks, shuddered as they surrounded her.

"Should have left them on their home planet, then, shouldn't you?" she muttered into the translator, and to her surprise it translated her words into Fisone.

This was really Pyre's listening device, she decided. And the selective translation was because Pyre decided what was going to be passed on, and what wasn't.

Without her, there would be no communication at all, so Rose decided that was fair enough. But like with Sazo at the beginning of what he called his awakening, Pyre might not be as trustworthy as she appeared. It would serve Rose well to remember that.

She moved down the passage, the Hasmarga a strange entourage at her back, and when she encountered the other Fisone who'd escorted her here, she saw the utter shock on his face as his gaze jumped from her to the Hasmarga behind her.

"I don't understand." His voice was slightly higher than it had been the day he'd been ordering her inside.

"You don't have to," Rose said, suddenly more exhausted than she'd been in a while. "You just have to hold out your hands."

He, like the woman, stared at the translator, and then noticed the weapon in her other hand.

"I leveled up," she told him, and let one of the Hasmarga slip the restraints over his wrists. "This is warm enough?" she asked Ecdre.

"It is." He motioned and some of the warriors herded the two Fisone to chairs in the corner of the room. "Will you check for others who may be here?"

"I will." It was the last thing she wanted to do, but it had to be done. She and three of the warriors walked through the whole bunker. It was empty and there was enough room for everyone. She found a small room with a bathroom off it, the bed low to the ground with fresh linen piled to one side.

"I need to rest very badly," she told Pyre, as the warriors left to give the good news to Ecdre. "I'm cleaning up and then I'm sleeping."

"I will have to fetch the remaining Hasmarga in a few trips. I will speak to you later." Pyre signed out, and Rose closed the door, and headed for the bathroom that had a deep bath already full of water. It resembled a waterhole set into dark gray rock, and steam was coming off it.

She didn't care how she got clean, she just wanted the smoke and dust and sweat gone.

It gave her a flashback to when she'd broken free from Sazo's underbelly, from the cells the Tecran had built to hold her and the animals they'd taken. The first thing she'd done when she and Sazo had freed themselves was take a shower.

This had the same feel.

As she lowered herself into the warm water, and then dipped her head under the surface, she wondered what Sazo and Dav were doing, and hoped the Fisone understood what kind of hornet's nest they had just kicked.

CHAPTER 16

ROSE WAS SUBMERGED in the bath again the next morning when her earpiece blasted static.

She shot up to the surface, gasping, and after a moment of nothing, took out the earpiece she had all but forgotten she still had in, and wondered if she'd damaged it somehow.

It was supposed to be waterproof, but what had that been?

"Sazo? Dav?" She dried it, and her ear, and put it back in, but there was nothing but silence.

Shit.

She hoped Sazo hadn't chosen the moment she was underwater to contact her, and the water had somehow blocked the signal.

She forced herself to take deep breaths.

If that had been him, he would try again.

She pulled out a towel and dried off, looking around the bathroom with approval. The deep cylinder cut into the rock which made up the plunge bath was one and a half times her height. She pressed the button to drain it, and the water was sucked away and refilled, ready for the next use.

She assumed it was purified somewhere and recirculated.

It was hot, the deep water had cradled her very pregnant body, and the soap she had found smelled divine.

The Fisone had one tick in the positive column, at last.

She had only just found the energy the night before to wash out her clothes, and now she pulled them on, feeling better than she had since she was taken.

She picked up the translator when she was ready, and stepped out of the room.

"Good morning, Pyre," she said, looking down the empty corridor. "Where is everyone?"

"Morning. The Hasmarga are all together in the dining room. Turn right at the next passage and you'll find it."

She expected them to be standing around as they had around the truck fire, but instead they were on the floor in a kind of yoga child's pose, arms tucked close to their bodies, heads bowed, the thick, bulky carapace on their backs covering most of them. She stopped short in the doorway, eyes wide.

"This is the first time they have been able to rest properly since they were taken." Pyre spoke softly through the translator, and Rose wondered why she didn't just speak through her earpiece, like she had when Rose had first been taken by the mine guards. "They brought the food they had at the mine with them last night, and once they had eaten, most of them shut down like this."

"How is Gerna?" Rose whispered, backing out of the room to find the kitchen. She hadn't been able to identify the matriarch among the bodies.

"She and two of her warriors have found a room to rest," Pyre said.

"And the prisoners?" Rose asked. She was beginning to feel a little bad about abandoning the Hasmarga and Pyre to deal with things last night. She stepped into the kitchen, and saw what had been done with the prisoners right away.

Both of them were locked into what looked like a trolley cage, possibly for delivering supplies off a spaceship.

It was on wheels, and the lock on the door looked improvised, which made it even more likely it had simply been for transport of food and other supplies before.

They came up on their knees when they saw her, and she wondered if they had been left without anyone to guard them, when she noticed a Hasmarga curled up like his friends next door, asleep behind a table.

The woman spoke to her, voice urgent, and Pyre translated. "What are you going to do with us?"

"I honestly don't know." Rose began looking in cupboards for the things she was familiar with from the watch station.

She found some of the vile protein bars and walked over to hand them through the cage to the Fisone.

They took them happily enough, and Rose kept up her search.

She finally found a cooling unit and crouched in front of it, pulling out a few things she didn't think had been on the menu in the watch station, as well as the carrot things she'd tried before.

When she found the thick jelly-like food, she lifted it to show the Fisone and they both nodded they would like some. She cut off pieces for them, and then began to cut thin slices of everything she'd decided to try.

"Do you drink anything hot?" she asked the prisoners, suddenly wishing for a cup of grinabo like she wanted her next breath.

They looked blankly at her. "Hot?"

She shrugged it away. Obviously they didn't. She had water, she had food, she was clean, and for the moment, she was safe.

Things were looking a lot better than they had been yesterday.

But better was relative. What she really wanted was to be back with Dav and Sazo. Back with Hri Revel to take care of her when the baby came.

Back home.

"I have to get away from here." She put the food she had sliced on a plate, filled two cups with water and passed them to the prisoners, and then took her own cup and plate out of the kitchen.

"Where is the comms station?" she asked Pyre.

"You are going to try to reach your people?" Pyre asked.

"I think they tried to contact me earlier this morning. I got a burst of static through my earpiece. Did you pick up anything like that?" Rose followed Pyre's directions and found a small room that looked similar to the one she'd sat in at the watch station.

"I noticed it. I thought it was the Fisone," Pyre said. "I tried to deflect it."

What?

Rose closed her eyes. This was simply a failure to communicate. And she couldn't blame Pyre or herself. They had been fighting for their lives before now, and neither of them had done much talking.

"My friend Sazo will be trying to contact me, using my earpiece," Rose said. "He and my lifemate will be looking for me."

"They are like you?" Pyre asked.

"No. I'm from a galaxy much further away. Dav is the father of my child, and he's Grihan. He looks similar to me, but we are not from the same world. Dav and his people took me in when Sazo and I escaped from the Tecran, who are the same people who stole Irini from the Fisone. Sazo is like you and Irini. He is what the Grih call a thinking system."

"Like me?" Pyre's voice dropped. "I am so very sorry."

"Sorry about what?" Rose had been standing with her plate and cup, and she took a seat.

"I'm sorry because I destroyed your earpiece this morning when I blocked the incoming signal. I destroyed every transmitter in the whole bunker." She sounded a little hard-edged, a little defensive.

"Because?" Rose had to keep her breathing even.

"Because I overreacted and lashed out, and did more harm than good." It sounded like Pyre did not like admitting that.

"So this earpiece no longer works?" Rose took it out with a shaking hand. This was her lifeline. Her way home.

"I'm sorry, Rose. I didn't mean to do it." There was something in her voice, and Rose wondered if she had meant to do it, but now Pyre knew Sazo was like herself, she was sorry about it.

Either way, the deed was done.

And she'd just lost some of her trust in Pyre.

She looked down at the panels in front of her. "So none of these work any longer?"

There were no lights beneath them, which was different from the panels in the watch house.

"I'm afraid not."

"And your own transmitters?" Rose asked. Pyre was transmitting to the translator, after all.

"I've only ever had local transmitters," Pyre said. "My pilot would connect back to the home planet or incoming supply ships via the comms arrays at the mine, or at the landing area. I need a larger array to reach the satellites."

"And you destroyed this one." Rose ate contemplatively. There was no option. She'd have to go back to the watch house, break in, and try their comms station again. If it had been Sazo this morning that Pyre had blocked, he was hopefully still nearby.

She would have to leave now, though.

If he and Dav didn't find her, they'd keep looking, and she was afraid that would mean they would move on. She needed to go immediately.

"What are you thinking?" Pyre asked.

"That I need to go to the hidden watch station. I need to see if I can use their comms room." Rose finished her breakfast and stacked the plate and cup. "Will you give me a lift?" She began walking back to the kitchen.

"I think my people are doing sweeps for me," Pyre said. "That's why I overreacted to the comms blast. I thought they were getting close and panicked."

"Your people?" Rose asked.

"The Kimol. The group that runs the mine. I was due back yesterday at the loading area. When I didn't answer the hail and took myself offline, they would have asked someone to get the satellites to sweep for my signature. I took a risk last night bringing the Hasmarga here, but I don't think we should risk it again unless it's a true emergency."

For Rose, it was a true emergency, but if Pyre took her and was captured, she would be captured too.

So she would walk. She had done it before.

She reached the kitchen, put the dishes down and studied the two prisoners with her arms crossed.

"You're with the group who run the mine," she said. "The Kimol?"

They both gave a cautious nod.

"But the mine people didn't know about you. Why is that?"

They shared a look.

"Talk, or no food and water for you." Rose was tired of this nonsense now. It was time to play hard ball.

After a beat of silence, the woman shrugged. "We know there are Bandri here, watching us. We didn't want any careless communications to alert them to our presence."

"And the Bandri are the people who didn't want the war with the Hasmarga?" She tried to remember everything Pyre had told her.

"The Hasmarga?" the man asked.

Rose pointed to the sleeping figure on the floor.

"Ah. We call them something else. Yes, they didn't see the bigger picture. The benefit of expansion."

"But you didn't win the war with the Hasmarga."

"That's because a year ago, your people stole our advantage!" The man hissed the words, eyes wide.

They thought Irini would ensure their victory over a whole planet? She wasn't tiny, but she could fit in the hold of a Class 5. What did they think she could do?

Rose tilted her head. It was a very Grihan thing to do, and she only realized she was doing it after it was done. "Perhaps you weren't given this information, but I have nothing to do with the people who stole your ship. They took me, just as they took her. I am with the group who discovered what the Tecran had done, and traveled out here to do the right thing and let you know what had happened to your people and to extend the hand of friendship."

"So you say, but we have no basis to believe you." The man's nostrils closed almost to slits.

She rocked back on her heels. There was no sense in trying to persuade him otherwise.

"And these Bandri? Why are they spying on you?" She needed more information about them before she broke into their watch station again.

"They are interested in what we are mining." The woman drew her legs up and hooked her arms around her shins. "They didn't agree with our attack on the second planet, but now they find themselves in a bind, because we used this moon as a landing stage to attack the Hasmarga, and that is how we found the stones. They cannot take our operation without associating themselves with the war. And the war is unpopular on our home planet."

So maybe the Bandri were just a paler shade of gray?

From the way the two prisoners were looking at each other after each question, Rose had a feeling she couldn't really rely on their answers anyway.

She hunted up a bag with a strap long enough to go across her chest, stocked it with food and some water, and turned toward the door.

Gerna was standing there.

"How are you doing?" she asked softly.

The matriarch gave a nod. "Very well, now. The temperature in the room I chose is good for me and my young lives."

"I'm glad." At least the children Gerna was carrying would have a chance.

"You look like you are leaving. Pyre said you are going to walk to the watch station?"

Interesting. Pyre hadn't wasted any time rousing Gerna. Rose wondered if they were going to try to stop her, and why they would.

"I need to see if I can transmit a message out, and Pyre destroyed all the transmitters in this bunker, including my personal transmitter."

Gerna jerked back at that, as if that was news to her. "Why did she do that?"

"She says it was a mistake."

"So we can't call for help from here?" Gerna's wings fluttered in agitation.

"So I'm told. It's a good four hour walk from here to the watch station, so I need to go now." She set the bag more securely across her chest.

"Take Ecdre with you. We will also need to transmit out, if we can. I had thought to ask Pyre to help us do that today." Gerna turned away, looking left down the passage, and called something in her language. She turned back. "Pyre won't take you to save you the journey?"

"She says it will get her noticed. That the satellites are doing sweeps for her." Rose didn't even know whether she believed that, but it sounded feasible. "There may be some personal vehicles we could take."

She looked over at the prisoners, decided she didn't know if the Hasmarga would feed them or not, and gathered all the nutrient bars and handed them into the cage. She did the same with a few slim bottles of water.

"Are there any small vehicles here?" she asked.

The woman, who was setting the supplies neatly in a pile, looked up. "One." She pointed right, and Rose gave a nod of thanks and headed for the door.

"I'll see if I can use it," Rose said to Gerna. "And if Ecdre can fit on it, he can come, too."

CHAPTER 17

ECDRE WASN'T happy about hanging on the back of the strange skimmer, but Rose was not prepared to cede the driver's seat, so he had to suck it up.

She was grateful to have a faster way to get to the watch station, but as she got closer to where she thought it was, she began to second guess her sense of direction, because nothing looked familiar.

Eventually she brought the skimmer to a stop, tucking it behind a large rock, and sighed with relief. The vibrations through the handle bars had been more than a little uncomfortable.

She glanced over at Ecdre. "All right?" she asked.

He made a sound in response that the translator did not translate, so she guessed it was a grunt of annoyance.

She moved out from behind the rock and tried to orientate herself.

It had been overcast the day she'd taken cover on the watch station's front step, and today was cloudless and bright, but she could see the wink of the lake in the distance, and slowly did a full turn.

And, there . . .

Ecdre had come to stand beside her, waiting patiently.

"There," she told him, pointing. "That's the roof, I think."

He gave a nod and they proceeded on foot, losing sight of the hidden building at times, but always getting it back in view, until eventually she could see the front door.

She crouched down so she would be hidden from view if anyone left the building, and Ecdre found a spot close to her.

He was very careful not to physically touch her, she noticed, and while she didn't mind it at all, she wondered about the reason for his meticulous avoidance.

"How will we enter?" he asked.

"That's what I'm trying to figure out." She studied the overhang above the door. "Maybe we should wait up there, and drop down when someone comes in or out." Except she had no idea how long that could take. And there was no certainty that they would be able to get to the door before it closed, either way.

Ecdre made a humming sound. "That's a possibility."

"How about this. You wait on the roof above, and I'll knock on the door." That way, they could control the timing. She felt the minutes sliding away, and even though the skimmer had made the journey so much faster, it was already nearly midday, hours after the attempted communication this morning.

"You will lure them out?" Ecdre turned to study her. "That would save time."

She nodded. "I'll wait for you to get into position, then approach."

"They will open for you?" Ecdre asked.

"If for no other reason than to try to take me prisoner," she said.

He hummed again, then moved back, disappearing around the side of the rock.

Rose waited, enjoying the sheltered space she'd chosen, where the cold wind barely touched her, and the sun warmed her back.

At last she saw movement on the sloping rock that overhung the doorway, and caught a quick glimpse of Ecdre before he lay flat.

Time to move.

She rose up and walked boldly to the door and gave a friendly knock.

She waited, then knocked again.

Damn, what if there wasn't anyone there? Who knew how long they'd have to wait for someone to come back?

She blew out a breath in frustration and turned to face away from the door just as a suited figure came running from around the side.

Déjà vu.

She almost laughed, although this time, the guard knew she was there.

Also, this time, when he shot, he hit her.

Fortunately, she was wearing her suit. She crouched down, drawing her weapon from the holder at the small of her back, and shot back, catching him chest-on.

He fell, to her relief, as she wasn't sure if he was wearing a protective suit or not.

"I need your help to move him," she called up to Ecdre, and he dropped down in front of her, almost on top of her victim.

"Can you pick him up and take him to the door?" she asked. She studied the wall, and found the small square where the guard who she'd encountered here before had touched his hand.

Ecdre lifted him easily and brought him over, and Rose took off his glove and pressed his fingers to the scanner.

The door popped open.

Ecdre gave her a look she assumed was of approval. "Bring him in?" he asked.

She nodded. "Better to keep an eye on him."

She lifted her weapon, flattened herself against the wall, and tilted her head to catch any sound in the room beyond, but it was quiet.

She moved through the door, weapon sweeping left to right, but there was no one there.

So far, so good.

They got inside, closed the door, and Ecdre set the guard down.

"I'll check to see if there's anyone inside, you keep watch here." Rose went to the cupboard she had been cuffed to last time, opened it up and turned the wall transparent. "That should help."

Ecdre made a sound of surprise. "How did you know to do that?" he asked.

"I was held prisoner here before." She didn't explain further, nervous that the two she had put down before might still be in the med bay.

She moved to the back, but the med bay was empty, and so was everything else.

When she came back, Ecdre had tied their prisoner up and out of curiosity, Rose pulled his helmet off.

It was the same man she'd hit with a saucepan before.

Déjà vu, indeed.

He wasn't having much luck when it came to her.

She walked over to the transmission station, turned the dials again, and sang all the while she was doing it. She chose the current favorite of the Grih children, Daydream Believer, and when everything was lit up, she turned to Ecdre.

"Do you understand anything here?" she asked.

He was frozen in place, watching her warily.

"Ecdre?" She almost snapped her fingers, because time was wasting, but just managed to stop herself.

He shook himself out of whatever it was that had held him in place, and looked at the panels. "Don't you?"

"No, I'm just switching everything on, if that's what I'm even doing. But if you know better . . .?"

He shook his head. "What is it that you did before? The sound you were making?"

"I was singing. My people will know it is me, without any doubt, if they hear that, and it's better than a distress call." She sent him a sidelong look. "Do the Hasmarga sing?"

"We hum," he said. He left it at that as he bent over the panel, and twirled a few light circles himself. He began to speak in the dialect she'd heard him and Gerna use before, and she realized she had no idea how technically advanced the Hasmarga were.

"Is there a ship looking for you?" she asked. "Will your people be coming?"

He jerked his head up to stare at her. "We hope."

"I hope so, too. I know my people are looking for me. If they find me before your people find you, I am sure they will take you home."

He froze for a moment, then inclined his head. "We would be grateful." He waved at the panel. "How long do we try?"

"I want to try until I get a result," she said. There was no point going back to the bunker without making some kind of contact. "What about you? Do you need to return, or will you stay?"

He looked unsure. "I don't know if we are even transmitting anything. I worry about leaving my . . . Gerna." He leaned back over the panels and spoke a few more times, then ceded the space to her.

She sang a few more lines, then switched to talking. "Sazo. Dav. I've gotten free but my earpiece is broken and I'm transmitting from a hostile location. I might not be able to stay here long. Please look for me on one of the moons around the fourth planet from the sun. I'm fine, but I'm more than ready to come home."

Suddenly, all the lights on the panel cut out, and a moment later, the lights died, as well.

They were plunged into darkness, and Rose fumbled for her weapon, but too late. Four Fisone came through the door, pointing strong lights straight at her and Ecdre.

She lifted a hand to her eyes, and when the lights came back on, she saw Ecdre had done the same.

One of the guards took their weapons, and then they stood in silence for a beat.

It seemed a little coincidental that they had all converged on the watch station just when she was there.

"What made you return?" The Fisone asking her was the woman who had been shot the first time she'd come here. The translator, which Rose had left on a nearby table, did its work, and everyone looked over at it in surprise.

"I was trying to contact my people to call for help," Rose said. "So was Ecdre."

One of the Fisone moved to the translator and inspected it. "It looks like our technology," he said.

"It is your technology," Rose said. "It was given to me at the mine when I was taken prisoner."

None of them expected that answer, she could see it in the way they stared at her.

"So it is from the Kimol," he said. "Why didn't you use their comms equipment?"

"It's a long story, but the short answer is I couldn't," she said. "Neither Ecdre or myself is sure we managed to transmit anything. Can you help us?"

There was a moment of silence.

"You want us to help you?" the woman asked.

"I didn't shoot you, remember," Rose reminded her. "That was him." She inclined her head to the Fisone guard who still lay unconscious on the ground.

"You shot me," one of the others said. "And took my suit. Which is how we knew you were here, by the way. It has a short-range tracker built into it."

Rose lifted her shoulders, realized she should probably have thought about that. "I did shoot you, when you held a weapon on me. And it didn't do anything to you. It was the shot from the ship that brought you down."

"You're trying to argue that you're not responsible for whoever shot us from the ship?" another Fisone asked.

"Well, I'm not," Rose said. "But I wasn't unhappy about the outcome. You were no longer holding weapons on us. We got two extra weapons and a suit. So I suppose I did profit quite a bit from that incident."

One of the Fisone made a sound that, if Rose read it right, was a laugh.

So they weren't devoid of humor. That was good.

"Who are you?" the woman asked.

"My name is Rose McKenzie," Rose said. "And this is Ecdre of the Hasmarga."

Ecdre obviously recognized his name. He had been staring at the Fisone in a strange, almost frozen stance, and now he turned to Rose, and she heard the strange humming sound she'd heard before. It was ominous.

She jerked her gaze to his face, alarmed at what he might do, and suddenly he launched himself forward, and hard, transparent wings burst from his back.

They hit the Fisone, knocking them down, and he made it to the door, pulled it open, and was gone.

Two of the Fisone discharged their weapons, both in her direction, rather than his.

She felt the bite as one hit feathered across her wrist, and swore.

"What is wrong with you?" she managed to gasp. "You all shoot wildly. You're a danger to yourselves."

"We're a danger to *you*," one of them said, and she turned her back and hunched over as he, deliberately this time, shot her again.

Someone shouted at him, and when she thought it might be safe, she turned back.

One of the two guards who'd been shot by Pyre had been the one who'd shot her. His weapon had been taken and he stood on the far side of the room, breathing hard.

She stared at him, memorizing his face, and he took an aggressive step toward her.

"What are you looking at?" He bared his teeth.

She didn't answer. It would have been too provocative. And she didn't threaten if she wasn't sure she could follow through.

He'd shot her, endangering her baby, while she had her back turned and was unarmed.

If it were up to her, he would be a dead man walking.

CHAPTER 18

SAZO HEARD ROSE.

The relief he felt was alien to him, a sweeping lightness he hardly knew what to do with.

The drone he'd sent to look for her wasn't near her. Curiously, the signal it received was from a distance, but stronger than anything that would have been transmitted by her earpiece.

When the spoken message she sent came through, of her explaining that the earpiece was damaged and she was using a transmitter, he finally managed to pinpoint her location to a sector of the moon, although not her exact position, and then he paused to consider his options.

He wanted to act, and he didn't like hiding away.

Sometimes, Rose had taught him, hanging back worked better than storming in.

But maybe it was time to do some storming.

He sent the message from Rose on to the *Barrist*, although he knew it would take some time to reach Dav.

Then he scanned the area around the moon, and picked up a large freighter making for a spot in the sector where Rose's message had come from.

He decided it was too close to her to risk doing it damage, and began hunting for another target.

He eventually rose up from behind the little moon he was using for cover, and did a quick orbit of the bigger moon.

There were a few good options.

A landing pad on the opposite side to where Rose was, that its owners were clearly trying to hide. Everything here seemed to be camouflaged or tucked away, as if they were all either hiding from each other or trying not to draw attention to themselves from passing space traffic.

Sazo decided the landing pad would go first, so he blasted a warning that it was under attack, allowed a five minute escape time for anyone near it, and then wiped it off the face of the moon.

He hardly ever got to use his weapons anymore. His reputation proceeded him, and he and his fellow Class 5s just had to show up, and most people decided to cooperate.

He didn't even feel guilty about destroying the landing pad. They were holding Rose against her will. They were lucky he gave them five minutes to get to safety.

After he hung in the air over the landing pad, just to make it very clear that he had been responsible, he moved on to the second target he'd found, a building set low to the ground which his sensors told him extended deeper underground.

He decided to give them a little longer to get out, and sent out the warning.

Instead of running for their lives, they tried to shoot him.

He easily dodged the laser strike aimed at him, and returned fire.

At the last minute, he decided to only raze the upper levels, as Rose had also taught him that once everyone was dead, you couldn't bring them back, and it would be useful to leave some witnesses to report his attack.

Once the dust had settled, he sent out a message on blast to every transmitter on the moon, making it clear Rose McKenzie was to be released to him, or he would destroy every facility on the moon, one by one.

Then he began to orbit the moon in a slow, continuous roll, changing his angle slightly with every rotation in the hope Rose would see him, and reach out again.

He sent out a time limit of three hours, and began to look for his next target.

CHAPTER 19

ROSE SAT at the kitchen table and chewed the squishy berry gel while the Bandri faction of the Fisone argued about her.

They had sent some kind of communication out when things had settled down after Ecdre's escape, and she had been parked to the side while they put the unconscious guard in the med bay and discussed their next moves.

She didn't think she was in immediate danger, but she didn't like being a prisoner again.

She'd hoped they might just let her go, after helping her send out a communication, but she could tell quite quickly they were loathe to give away what they thought might be a useful pawn in their war with the other Fisone faction.

When a new comm came through, though, things changed.

A lot.

They listened, and the translator suddenly began babbling about explosions in Tecran.

"Explosions?" she asked.

"Not explosions," the woman snapped at her. "Destruction. Of our landing pad. We no longer have a way off the moon."

Destruction. She leaned back in her chair and slowly chewed another bite of gel.

There was more fast chatter, and she managed to pick up there had been a second strike.

"The Kimol are also hit." The guard she had taken her suit from the night before seemed to perk up a bit. "Did any of you know they had a military bunker near our landing pad?"

Rose took a sip of water. Smiled to herself.

She had done it.

Sazo had gotten the message.

Silence fell, and when she looked up, everyone was staring at her.

"Let me guess," she said, and put her glass down. "Hand me over, or more of your infrastructure will be destroyed?" That was very Sazo.

"Your communication," the woman breathed. "You called this down on us."

She stood up. "If you were in my position, wouldn't you call for help?"

"We never took you!" The guard Pyre had shot waved a hand at her.

"Maybe not." She shrugged. She honestly didn't know enough about the factions. "But you're holding me now. And you shot me when I posed no threat to you at all."

There was an uncomfortable shuffle of feet.

"Can I let Sazo know where I am, so he can come get me?" she asked, nodding toward the comms panel.

"You're going to let them destroy our landing pad with no retaliation?" The guard who'd shot her in the back rose from his corner where he'd been sitting since the incident.

"No, Caudra, I'm going to let the general know we have Rose McKenzie here with us, and wait for orders." The woman went to the comms panel and began to speak in low, quick tones.

Caudra seemed to settle down at her response, but Rose didn't trust him, or like him sitting slightly behind her.

Once the message was sent, the woman, who Rose heard the others calling Vichea, turned back to her.

"Let's finally clear the air," she said. "How did you come to be here?"

"I was moving between the two ships in my convoy, when I was abducted by people from your planet. They told me their plan was to hold me hostage in exchange for people and a ship that had been taken a year ago."

"Your people took the Kimol's ship a year ago?" The guard who's suit she'd taken asked, voice sharp.

"No. The people who stole me from my world, the Tecran, also stole the ship and the crew from yours. I was rescued, and the people who rescued me are part of a coalition with other planets. When they found out what the Tecran had done, they sent the convoy I am part of to speak to your people and explain what had happened."

"And what did happen?" Vichea asked.

"The crew of the ship torched the inside of it and killed themselves before they were even out of your solar system. The Tecran took the ship, which seemed unusable, and put it in storage." Rose wondered if she should tell them that Irini had since proved very much alive and well.

"You say seemed." The guard whose suit she was wearing, Pinli, was the sharp one of this group, clearly.

"She was simply biding her time," Rose conceded. "She came into her own, and as she is an autonomous being, her wishes are respected. She refuses to return to Fisone."

There was a beat of silence. "So they did manage intelligence," Vichea said, voice hushed.

"And then someone just swooped in and took it." Caudra, sitting in the corner, fisted his hands on his knees. "They should have brought it back."

"I've just explained we don't force people to do things against their will." Rose shifted her chair so she could always keep him in her periphery. "Irini did not want to return."

"So you say." Caudra shook his head. "That's convenient, that you take our technology."

Rose smiled. "How do you know we don't have even more advanced technology?" And wasn't she cocky, coming from Earth? Strictly speaking she was probably the least technologically advanced of all of them.

There was another silence.

"Do you?" Vichea asked.

Before she could answer, the comms unit lit up, and everyone turned to it.

"We have to take you to what's left of the landing pad," Vichea said.

"How far away is it?" Rose asked. She put her hand on her bump, felt the edge of her baby's foot press against her palm.

"A fair distance. Why?"

"Because I'm not in a good condition to walk," Rose said. "My baby is due any day."

It was as if she'd thrown a grenade into the room. The Fisone visibly flinched away from her.

"You carry the possibility of life?" Pinli asked.

"Yes. I am close to giving birth." She stood and arched her back to ease the stiffness. "I want to get back to my people, so I can have my child in safety."

"What were the Kimol thinking?" Vichea breathed.

"What were *you* thinking?" Rose asked. "I gave you the opportunity to help me contact my ship and let me go hours ago. You refused."

There was a sudden, deathly quiet.

"We could not have known," Caudra said from the corner.

"It will be our fault, either way." Vichea closed her eyes. "They will blame the landing pad's destruction on us."

They'd be right, Rose thought.

Pinli's gaze snapped to hers. "They won't know if we lose her."

Whoa. The concept of blame obviously included more than a dressing down.

"I'm assuming your lives are in danger if you're blamed?" she guessed.

"You assume correctly," Caudra said.

"And that won't happen if you 'lose' the prisoner you've just caught, when there are six of you and one of me?" She asked the question lightly.

Vichea and Pinli shared a look, and the other guards murmured to themselves.

"All right, maybe the outcome would be the same. Will you keep quiet about your request to us?" Vichea asked.

"My lips are sealed if he doesn't come with us," she said, tipping her head in Caudra's direction. "I don't trust him."

"Done." Pinli's smile told Rose he was as happy with that arrangement as she was.

"What about your friend who escaped?" Vichea asked. "Where did he go?"

"He's probably long gone," Rose said, and wondered if Ecdre had taken the skimmer. If the Fisone were planning on walking to the launch pad, she hoped it was still there, because she didn't think she had the chops to walk a long distance right now. "How are we traveling?" she asked.

"All the smaller ships were destroyed by your people," Vichea said. "So we will have to take the skimmers."

"You will let her dictate who can and cannot travel to the launch pad?" Caudra asked. His voice was worryingly low.

"Do you want her talking about her request for our help, which might have prevented the launch pad's destruction if we had helped her?" Pinli asked.

Caudra looked like he had plenty of opinions on that, but instead he walked out of the room.

"They want us there as soon as possible," Vichea said. "So let's go."

CHAPTER 20

"SAZO. *Dav. I've gotten free but my earpiece is broken and I'm transmitting from a hostile location. I might not be able to stay here long. Please look for me on one of the moons around the fourth planet from the sun. I'm fine, but I'm more than ready to come home."*

Dav got to his feet, unable to sit after hearing the recording Sazo had sent him.

Hostile location stood out to him. Rose was not safe. He had known that already, but hearing the words made him crazy.

He was alone in his office, and he was grateful he happened to be here when the message came in. He felt too much to be in company.

It was excruciating being so far—and just like that, he felt the pressure, if not ease, lessen.

He walked out of his office to the bridge and every member of his crew turned as he stepped inside.

"Did you hear it?" he asked.

They shook their heads.

He nodded to Borji and he played it, both the singing and the spoken message.

"We're going there," he said. "Set a course."

No one so much as gave a sideways glance at the order. They turned to their tasks.

Jia Appal was on a break, but she came onto the bridge herself a moment later, with Nivan Cossi, the Bukarian representative from the United Council, hot on her heels. "The engines?"

"We're going to fetch Rose," Dav said. "She's on a moon that orbits the fourth planet from the sun in this solar system."

"Do you think they'll follow us?" Nivan asked as they began to leave the Fisone's ship behind them.

"I honestly don't care," Dav said. "They've ignored our last two hails."

"They're waiting for a message from their home planet, and that's obviously been delayed with Sazo taking all the comms satellites around here offline." Borji spoke up. "But as it happens, they're hailing us now."

"Put it up," Dav said.

The big screen above Borji's head flicked on, and Priyan leaned forward toward them from the bridge of the *Havelan*. "Where are you going?"

"We are going to fetch Rose," Dav said.

There was a moment of silence. "You know her location?"

"We do." He kept his voice curt. He could see on screen the Fisone ship was following them.

"How did you come by that information?" Priyan looked shocked.

"A signal from our other ship." Dav could imagine Sazo's sneer at being referred to as their other ship. "We don't have access to your satellites anyway, so them being down doesn't affect us."

"The ship that left. You said it was going to transmit a signal for information."

"They did that, too," Dav said. "But they noticed a spot of absolute silence in the area around the fourth planet from your sun, and found Rose is being held on one of that planet's moons."

Priyan looked to the side, as if to speak to someone in her crew, and her hail winked out.

"Open it up," Dav said to the bridge, and they suddenly leapt through space toward the gas giant Dav could see on the map Sazo had sent back, leaving the Fisone far behind them.

"What are you going to do when we get there?" Nivan Cossi asked.

"Whatever I have to," Dav said. He looked over at her. "You disapprove?"

She hesitated. "I should offer caution, and say something about diplomacy, but they kidnapped Rose." Nivan shook her head. "Whatever you have to do sounds right to me."

Dav caught a few smiles around the bridge at their United Council representative's fighting words, and relaxed a little.

He might have the most invested in Rose's safe return, but everyone here wanted her back safe and well.

There were some angry Grih who didn't like the idea of his and Rose's child's existence, but there were strange, angry people in every society. He wasn't wrong to worry about what those people might do, but the extreme part of that group weren't here on this ship, and that helped. A lot.

CHAPTER 21

ROSE WISHED SHE HAD A JACKET.

Ecdre had taken the skimmer, so she was hanging onto the back of Vichea's one, and she hunched miserably as the wind cut through her suit.

Pinli had tried to get the suit back, but she had refused to remove it, and he had backed down rather than try to put hands on her.

That was definitely because she was pregnant. Since the Bandri soldiers understood she was carrying a child, they had behaved very strangely.

They were in an uneasy truce, both with some power over the other. Neither side wanted to rock the boat further, and they had left Caudra and one other of their team behind at the watch station, as well as the guard she had shot.

That left Vichea, Pinli, and another guard called Rosco to escort her to their base, and Vichea took the middle position with Pinli and Rosco on either side.

Rose thought they were worried she would leap off and try to escape. They didn't know about the necklace, and they took her ability to breathe the air so easily as a sign she was very much not like them, and she couldn't really blame them for it—if she could have leapt off and run, she would have.

The baby moved, pushing against the ever shrinking boundaries of her little world, and Rose sighed as once again, there was simply too much pressure on her bladder for comfort.

She tapped Vichea, and the Fisone slowed and then brought the skimmer to a halt.

"Again?" she asked.

Rose shrugged. "You kidnap a pregnant woman, you get what you get."

It was interesting how uncomfortable that kind of talk made them.

She couldn't work out if pregnancy was sacrosanct in their culture, or taboo as a topic.

She noticed how freaked out they became if they saw the baby kick, but their silence on the matter made her hesitant to ask them about their own reproduction.

Her instincts were to leave well enough alone.

They grumbled at the need to stop, and Vichea went with her to the closest big bush for privacy. She had started to draw these stops out, taking her time after seeing to her business by cleaning her hands with the wipes Vichea carried with her as slowly as possible, standing still in the sunlight that had broken through the overcast sky, face tilted upward, eyes closed.

For a little bit, she wasn't being rattled around and she wasn't cold.

She eyed the skimmer with dislike. They had been going since mid afternoon, and there was probably an hour or so until dusk.

"How far still to go?" she asked.

She was close to refusing to get back on. Traveling on the skimmer was close to torture. She would rather walk.

She squinted at the horizon, at where the sun was, and realized that was probably not feasible.

"Another two hours, maybe three if you keep making us stop."

Vichea's face was covered by her helmet, but her body language told Rose she didn't mind the delays as much as she pretended she did.

Every minute on the road was a minute they didn't have to face their boss.

"If you're worried about our deal, I told you I won't say anything. You've kept your part of the bargain," she said.

"Just get on." Vichea held the skimmer's handle bars, one foot on and one foot off, giving Rose room to get on and perch at the back, and Pinli and Rosco started up their engines.

Rose stayed where she was. She did not want to get on that skimmer.

Both men suddenly looked up.

Rose craned her neck, and saw a ship like Pyre's coming toward them.

For a moment, she thought it might be Pyre, but with no warning, shots were fired.

"The Kimol." Pinli crouched on his skimmer as the ship shot a second time.

Maybe it was Pyre after all, because none of the shots hit anyone. It was more a warning that they meant business.

The ship landed beside them, and the four suited guards who jumped out were definitely not the Hasmarga.

Damn. It looked like she was being abducted again.

She considered the ship, and decided as long as they also wanted to hand her over to Sazo and Dav, it wasn't a bad trade up from the skimmer.

"Throw down your weapons and hand her over," one of the guards said, gesturing with his hand.

None of the three so much as moved.

"Now."

Vichea took a step to the side, and the Fisone soldier closest to her shot her.

The shot was so close to Rose, feathery blue light touched her shoulder and pricked at her neck.

She jerked and crouched down, breathing through the pain.

Someone shouted an order, and the firing stopped.

Vichea lay unconscious, and Rose slowly got to her feet, walked over to check on her, and took the translator Vichea had confiscated from her from her belt.

She hadn't said anything or looked at the newcomers, but she straightened slowly, slipped the translator into her own belt, and turned to face them.

"If any of you discharge a weapon in my vicinity again, I will make sure you lose another major piece of infrastructure," she said. "And that is a promise, not a threat."

She was doubly glad now she had refused to return the protective suit to Pinli.

He and Rosco tossed their weapons toward the newcomers.

"Are you Rose McKenzie?" The guard who had shot Vichea asked as he picked up the weapons.

"Yes, I am."

The newcomer in the middle lifted a hand. "What are you using to translate?"

Rose brought out the translator. "I was given this at the mine site."

"I was one of the Fisone who learned the language of the people who took our ship last year, and that translator just mistranslated your words." The guard spoke in Tecran, her accent bad but perfectly understandable.

Rose looked down at the black box. "What did it say?" she asked.

Interestingly, it did not translate her words now. It was silent.

"When you said you were Rose McKenzie, it translated your words as saying you weren't her," the Fisone woman said.

The Fisone who'd shot Vichea began to speak, and from the tone, Rose guessed he was asking what was going on. When the middle guard told them what was wrong, both groups of Fisone seemed stumped.

"How is it so wrong?" the middle guard asked Rose. "Who exactly gave it to you?"

Rose had had her suspicions about what Pyre had chosen to share or not to share, but actively altering the words was not something she'd considered.

Had some of her conversations with the Hasmarga been distorted? Some of theirs with her?

"Someone at the mine gave it to me," she said.

"Why were you at the mine?" the woman in the middle asked.

"I escaped your group, I think you're the Kimol?" She waited until the woman nodded. "And was captured by the Bandri." She tilted her head toward Pinli and Rosco. "Then I escaped them, and was recaptured by the Kimol near the mine, and taken there. I think they were planning to put me to work there."

"Did you set it on fire?" the Kimol woman asked.

Rose shook her head. "It was already on fire when I was brought there. That did make it easier to escape, though. Of course, then I was recaptured by the Bandri." She left out the bit where she'd been to the bunker. No need to mention that.

The woman translated what she'd said to everyone.

It occurred to Rose that the only way Pyre could be playing around with the translator would be if she could use the bunker's transmitters again. Either that, or it was Pyre right here in front of her, retaken by the Kimol. Maybe the bunker was compromised and the Kimol had control of it again, or maybe Pyre was playing some strange double game.

She studied the ship, but it could easily be an identical model and not Pyre at all.

She would keep the thought to herself.

If it was Pyre, she would find a way to tell Rose.

And Rose would have to decide if she was going to believe her story.

"What is your plan?" she asked the Kimol who spoke Tecran. "Where are you taking me?"

"We need to hand you over in order to prevent further damage to our holdings on this moon," the woman said. "We will take you to our base of operations."

That worked. She would prefer a ride in a ship than the back of the skimmer, and the end result was hopefully going to be the same—her return to Sazo and Dav.

She began to walk toward them, when out of nowhere, a shot was fired.

The shot hit the Fisone closest to the door of the ship, putting him down, and Rose dropped to the ground, crouching down and then falling forward onto her hands and knees.

She felt so vulnerable, so unwieldy in her current shape.

She covered her head with her arms, grateful again that she'd held onto the suit.

Hands grabbed her raised arms, and two of the Kimol lifted her up and carried her to the ship.

She put her feet down on the ramp and glanced back, and saw Caudra pinned down by fire from the third Kimol soldier from the ship, who was standing over his fallen colleague.

Pinli was down but Rosco was crouched low, both hands on the ground as if to show he was no threat.

As soon as she was in the ship, the other two ran back to pick up their friend, and then all four were inside with her, and the ship took off.

Rose leaned back against the wall of the ship and rubbed her belly.

"Sorry, sweetheart," she murmured. "Mommy's caught in the middle here."

She sensed the looks from the Kimol, and lifted her head.

They were staring at her hand, at the curve of her body.

They looked utterly flummoxed.

She closed her eyes to shut them out. She just hoped they were close to wherever they were going, and that she could lie down soon.

She was close to done.

CHAPTER 22

THEY HADN'T BEEN FLYING LONG before Rose realized there was something wrong.

"What now?" she asked, and heard the weariness in her own voice.

It had been a very long three days.

"There is a . . . weapon," Sartie, the Kimol woman who spoke Tecran, responded hesitantly. "I don't know the word for it in this language we are speaking, but there is a ship following us and the weapon is locked on, and trying to shoot us."

"The Bandri?" Rose asked. She sat up.

"Yes. They are trying to bring this ship down." Sartie turned and called through to the pilot, and the response was terse.

The whole vessel suddenly tilted left, then right.

Rose reached up for the straps set above her and clipped herself in.

She felt a stab of fear.

"What's the chance of them hitting us?" she asked, but Sartie wasn't listening, or didn't have the words to answer.

The tension in the ship was palpable.

"Tell them if I die, everyone on this moon dies."

"What did you say?" Sartie grabbed her arm.

"Tell them I'm in this ship. They need me as much as you do. Their infrastructure has been threatened, the same as yours." She didn't want to go into what Sazo would do. Her Tecran was strained enough as it was.

Sartie shouted back to the pilot and after a moment, the ship leveled out.

"That was a good idea." Sartie rose from her seat. "They've disengaged."

The ship shuddered suddenly, and then Rose heard the sound of an explosion in the distance.

Sartie called to the pilot again, and her gaze went straight to Rose, fear in her eyes.

"What is it?" Rose asked.

"The ship that shot at us has been destroyed." Sartie narrowed her eyes. "You said that. That we would all be dead if you are killed."

Sazo had heard the transmission between the two ships, Rose guessed. And he'd gotten rid of the ship shooting at her.

Relief washed over her. He had her location now.

The pilot called back, and Sartie gestured to her.

"Your people are demanding we allow you to speak to them." She motioned to Rose's harness. "Come forward with me."

Rose unclipped and moved to the pilot's deck.

There was a spare seat beside the pilot and Sartie waved her into it.

The pilot stretched across her and touched the comms panel, and Rose leaned forward.

"Sazo?"

"Rose!" Sazo sounded a little overhyped. "You're all right?"

"Thanks to you. It's good to hear your voice." She spoke in English, just like he had. It almost made her cry.

"Why were they shooting?" Sazo asked.

"There are two groups in conflict with each other on this moon.

They are in a kind of cold war on their own planet, from what I gather, but the battle is a little hotter here."

"I know where you are now," he said. "But my drone was shot down. Now I know about the active hostilities, I think one side thought my drone might belong to the other side."

"Are you here alone?" It was wonderful to hear Sazo's voice, but she wanted to hear Dav's just as much.

"The *Barrist* is coming," he told her. "It'll be here in a couple of hours."

She switched to Tecran and glanced over her shoulder at Sartie. "How long until we land?" The relief at hearing Dav was on the way made her lightheaded.

"We will be at the military bunker shortly," Sartie said. "Tell your people to get in touch with our people there."

"I heard that," Sazo said. "I will make sure they treat you like a queen until we work out how to get you back up to the ship."

"You destroyed their bunker and the Bandri's landing pad, from what I heard," Rose said. "But there is another landing pad near a mine that belongs to this group. And there must be other ways off this moon." Not that she wanted to travel anywhere else, but she wanted off this place, and they would probably need a landing pad to do it.

"I'll find out." Sazo's voice was soothing. "Right now."

"It'll probably take a bit of time to sort that out. And I really need a rest." She was feeling so exhausted, she didn't know how she was going to get up out of the co-pilot's chair.

Then she decided she wasn't going to bother.

She sat, eyes closed, until they landed roughly, forcing her to rouse herself.

The hard landing was because there was nothing but debris where the landing pad had once been. It was all destroyed.

Rose walked down the ramp cautiously, and stood with Sartie and the others while four skimmers moved toward them, seeming to emerge from the ruins of the bunker.

She got on the back of one, and simply felt relief that the ride was five minutes at most.

When they reached what was left of the building, the four soldiers driving the skimmers turned sharply down a ramp and took them into an underground area. They parked near the bottom of the ramp and stood to one side.

Rose was very aware of their weapons.

The soldiers she'd traveled with in the ship spoke to their colleagues in quick, choppy sentences, and then Sartie turned to her, although as she'd donned her helmet when they'd left the ship, it was impossible to see her expression.

"You will be taken to rest while we speak with your people. Come with me." She led the way into the deep shadows and Rose wondered how structurally sound the place was given the damage Sazo had done to the upper floors.

When Sartie realized she wasn't following, she turned.

"You're sure this isn't going to collapse?" Rose asked.

"They have checked. It's fine." Sartie's voice held an edge, and Rose wondered why.

Maybe they were angry with her since Sazo had flexed his muscles. They probably blamed the destruction on her.

She walked cautiously forward, letting her eyes adjust to the darkness. Sartie moved deeper into the shadows and then opened a door, lighting the way.

As soon as she was inside what was a long, poorly-lit corridor, Sartie began walking at a fast clip to the right.

Rose wasn't able to keep up, and she refused to run. She let Sartie get far ahead, and heard her exclamation of annoyance when she realized Rose was not close behind her.

Rose didn't apologize, and Sartie shifted irritably until Rose reached her.

"In here," she said, opening a door and sweeping her hand in.

"Can't you breathe well in here?" Rose asked, wondering why

Sartie hadn't removed her helmet since they'd stepped into the building itself.

"There are leaks on this floor. It's no longer airtight," Sartie said. "Your people completely leveled the parts of the building above ground."

That made sense. She didn't like not seeing Sartie's face, though. It helped her to get a sense of the woman's intentions.

The room she had been brought to looked utilitarian. A bed, with a small table beside it. A single chair, with a door beyond she hoped was a bathroom. An open rack for hanging clothes.

"Rest here. I will come for you when we know what is the next step." Sartie moved aside to let Rose enter.

The door swung shut, and Rose turned immediately and tried the door.

The handle didn't move. It was locked.

She stared at it for a moment, then turned on her heel and went to the bathroom.

She had suspected they would lock her in. So she shouldn't be so surprised they had.

If she had hot water, and a bed that was even somewhat comfortable, she would count it as a win.

CHAPTER 23

WHEN THE *BARRIST* reached the gas giant, Dav knew exactly where to go. Sazo loomed threateningly over the moon in question, not even attempting to hide.

"Hail him," Dav said to Borji, worried that Sazo hadn't already acknowledged their arrival.

There was silence in response, and then suddenly a ping in Dav's ear.

"Things have not gone as I expected." Sazo sounded a little . . . lost.

"Tell me." Dav was aware no one else on the bridge could hear him. He made the sign to Jia that they should get into a holding pattern, and then walked toward his office.

"I threatened both sides with destruction unless they delivered Rose to me unharmed, and then one side brought her to their headquarters and told me they wouldn't release her unless I gave them some things."

"All right. First, both sides? There are two groups?"

"The Kimol and the Bandri. The Kimol took Rose at the start. She escaped, but they have her again."

That was definitely a complicating factor.

"What things do they want?" Dav asked. It had to be difficult to impossible, or Sazo would have already done it.

"They want the code that created Irini." Sazo went silent for a beat. "They don't have a copy of how she was just before the Tecran took her. I think they only have foundational code, and her development went in a specific direction they can't duplicate. They say if there is no way to have her back, they want a replacement." The scorn in his voice told Dav no matter what the Kimol did from now on, Sazo had lost all respect for them.

"What did you say to that?" Dav asked.

"That there was no way to duplicate Irini's code, as she is a galaxy away, and that she wouldn't give it up, even if she was right here."

"And their response?"

"That until they had it, Rose would stay where she is, on the top most livable layer of their bunker, with them all below her. That there was no way for me to harm them, without harming her first." There was a very nasty edge to his voice.

"Is that true?" Dav asked.

"As far as it goes for the bunker," Sazo said. "But they have forgotten something."

Dav had a bad feeling about whatever it was that he was going to say next. "What's that?"

"Their planet is just one hop over. One small, little hop."

Dav felt the hairs lift on the back of his neck. "What are you planning?"

"I could go over there. Start harming their people back home."

"You could." Dav drew in a breath. "But those people don't know what's going on here, and aren't the ones threatening Rose."

"But she doesn't have long, Dav. She told me she's exhausted, that she needs rest. I think she's close to having the baby." Sazo's tone didn't change, he had gone into another mode. His old mode.

"Let me talk to them." Dav felt fear and frustration grip his throat, and he forced himself to swallow. "Let me get to the bridge, and then patch me through to the people who have her."

He walked back, and Borji turned to him, tilting his head toward the comms panel.

"Sazo says the Kimol have been hailed." Borji swung back around.

"Open the channel, give a view of all of us and the bridge." It couldn't hurt for these people to see the *Barrist*, and exactly what they were facing.

The screen winked from black to show two men and three women standing in a dimly lit room. One of the women stood to the side, and Dav had a sense she was not of the same rank as the others by the way she was out of the main frame.

The man standing at the front said something, and the woman to the side cleared her throat and then said in Tecran: "You did not understand our demands?"

"You were talking to my colleague before, but he communicated your demands to me. We understand them just fine." Dav stared at them, thinking of Rose imprisoned somewhere close to where they were standing, and he wanted to reach through the screen.

"What do you mean, colleague?" one of the women said, via the translator.

"You were speaking to a different vessel before. If you look up, you'll see there are two ships above this moon, now. And we are both here for Rose." Dav noticed one of the women sidled off and he stood in silence, waiting for her to return. She looked less smug when she did, talking to the others before they turned to look at him again.

"One ship, two." The man shrugged. "We have your compatriot, and you cannot do more damage to this facility without harming her."

"That seems to be the case," Dav agreed. "But my colleague is a little less reasonable than I am, and his proposal is to go to your home planet, and begin destroying things there." Dav shrugged. "He can get there in less than two hours, and is prepared to explain to them before he starts his work that it is because of your threats that he has been forced to act."

The crew on the bridge turned to look at him as he spoke, eyes wide, and Jia Appal sank slowly down onto her seat.

His words also seemed to shock all five of the Kimol.

"You would . . ." It had clearly not occurred to the man at the front. He rubbed under his throat in agitation. "That is murder." He waved his hands. "Just like the deaths here when you destroyed this bunker were murder."

They were angry, Dav could see. And he couldn't blame them. Their games regarding the return of Rose were born from their outrage at the deaths of their people at the Tecran's hands a year ago, and probably lately by Sazo's hard-edged demands.

Sazo could put backs up. Dav knew that better than most.

He weighed revealing his personal stake in Rose's safety, and decided they already knew she was important, no need to give the Kimol any more leverage.

"Things are escalating," Dav said. "Right now, Rose is your captive, and holding her for ransom is not a good foundation for a cooperative relationship with the United Coalition. We came here to establish communication with you, and in return, you've stolen one of our people."

"You stole from us first!" the woman who was translating burst out. "And we have been told our people who were taken are dead."

"They weren't taken by us, but Rose *was* taken by you." Dav tried to keep his tone even. "You are not helping yourselves."

"You are forgetting something." One of the men leaned forward a little. "If anything happens to our home planet, the majority of the casualties will be Bandri. We are not the bigger group. But if any of our people are harmed, we will start hurting your colleague. For every blow done to us, we inflict a blow to her. And we will still not turn her over until we have the code for the ship that was taken a year ago. I hope that is clear enough communication for you."

The screen went black.

"I want to kill him," Sazo's voice was soft in his ear.

"I do, too." Dav kept his voice equally soft.

There was a surprised paused. "You do?"

"Very, very much." Dav had trouble getting the words out.

"What are we going to do?" Sazo seemed to manage a more normal tone.

"What's the chances of us getting a team down there to break Rose out ourselves?" Dav was speaking solely to Sazo, but the rest of the bridge could hear his side of the conversation, and Jia Appal rose from her seat to stand beside him, head tilted to the side.

"It would be dangerous, because they have weapons we don't know about, and technology that is different to our own." Sazo's voice drifted off, as if he were thinking. "They'll probably know you landed on the moon, but it will take them time to find you. I am happy to provide a distraction."

"Nothing that gives them any license to hurt Rose," Dav warned.

Sazo was silent again. "I don't know what line to draw there." He sounded lost.

He was terrified to do anything that would bring harm to her, Dav realized. That was a relief.

"Perhaps both ships can move away from the moon, as if we are withdrawing to reassess," Jia said. "Or we could hail the *Havelan*, which is still trying to catch up to us, I'm guessing. We could speak to Priyan, who from what I could work out, is part of the Kimol? The same group who are now holding Rose?"

"They would be interested in listening to us speak to their colleagues," Sazo agreed. "And moving away will keep them guessing about our motives. And they will try to track us, to make sure we aren't heading to their home planet."

"What would we say to Priyan?" Nivan Cossi asked. The United Council representative had been quiet through the earlier exchange, but Dav could see she was taking everything very seriously.

"We could tell her what her friends are demanding in exchange for Rose. We could ask her what the root cause of their rivalry with the Bandri is. Anything to get more information." Jia lifted her shoulders.

"That's an excellent plan." Dav reached out, tapped Jia's shoulder. "You are acting captain. You can obviously think a lot more clearly than I can right now. I'm going to lead a small team to fetch Rose. You're going to run things up here."

Jia looked like she was going to argue. She was the one who was supposed to lead teams on-planet, but she looked into his eyes, lifted her brows, and gave a sharp nod.

"Who will you take?" she asked.

"You tell me." He trusted her assessment of her people.

She turned. "Keep to the holding pattern," she ordered the bridge, and then gestured to Dav as she made long, quick strides toward the door. "Let's get you set up."

CHAPTER 24

ROSE DIDN'T KNOW how long she slept for, but when she woke, she felt rested for the first time in a while.

She had another shower, enjoying the hard pressure of hot water against her back, and then realized she was lucky she even had hot water, after the number Sazo had done on the building above ground.

She washed her clothes, hung them to dry, and wrapped herself in a spare sheet as she finally made a more thorough examination of the room she had been assigned.

There was a small alcove with some food and water, although no sign of equipment to make a hot drink, and she had to face the fact that the Fisone most likely didn't drink hot drinks.

It was very disappointing.

She ate the berry gel again. She was getting very tired of it.

As soon as her clothes were wearable, she got dressed, and then she tried the door.

It was still locked, so she knocked.

She heard the faintest scuff of shoes, and hoped that meant whoever was standing guard outside was going to fetch Sartie.

She busied herself by making her bed and straightening up, and when the door opened, without a proceeding knock, she turned with cool eyes and crossed arms to face Sartie.

"You lied." She kept her voice even. "You didn't come back."

Sartie shrugged, her face twisting into an insolent, unfriendly expression. "Your people are very eager to get you home."

Rose mimicked her shrug. "I would hope your people do the same for their people, when they are taken."

That tripped Sartie up. She had no sarcastic comeback for that.

"So, what's up, Sartie? What's the holdup here?" Rose had thought this was a done deal, but obviously not.

"My bosses want something from your people in exchange for you. Your people say it isn't possible to give it to us." Again, she gave a fatalist shrug.

"So what's the solution?" Rose wondered what it was they wanted.

"We keep you until they provide it."

"And what is *it?*" Rose asked.

"The code for the ship that was stolen. If it was rendered unusable and the people on board killed themselves, then that's our only way to get something back. That ship was a test subject, and one-of-a-kind." Sartie shook her head in disgust.

It kept coming back to Irini.

"You do realize that ship is so far away from this solar system there is no way to easily get it?" Rose didn't even touch the fact that Irini would not be handing over her code any time soon, either.

"So your people say."

"It's the truth. Do you have the facilities to help me with the birth of my baby while we wait, then?" she asked. "Because I will be going into labor any day now, and there is no way your demands can be dealt with before I'm due."

Sartie's gaze flickered to her bump and then skittered away.

"Also, any message from my convoy to back home will include the information that you are holding me for ransom." Rose lowered herself onto the only chair in the room.

"So?" Sartie said.

"So, perhaps my people will decide to send more ships. To send a battalion of ships. All as big, and as bad, as the two in your skies right now." Rose leaned back to meet Sartie's gaze. "You will definitely be making sure everyone sits up and takes notice."

"These are not things I have any control over." Sartie's mouth formed a tight line. "I am just involved because I learned to speak the language we heard from the people who stole our ship."

Rose shook her head. "So what now? You're planning on keeping me locked in this room?"

"You can go and meet with your friends," Sartie said. "We managed to pick them up yesterday and move them here." She gestured to the door.

"The Hasmarga?" Rose asked, frowning as she carefully got to her feet.

"Is that what they are called?" Sartie's mouth twisted. "Yes. They have been put on this floor, too."

"I hope you have made the temperature warm enough for them." Rose wondered again whether the ship that had brought her here was Pyre, or not.

Had she given the Hasmarga up? Given Rose up?

It was hard to say.

"They need heat?" Sartie looked like she didn't much care, either way.

"I can spend time with them, but I can't speak to them without that translator." Although, truth be told, she no longer trusted it.

"I have another one for you." Sartie produced a slim, black wand.

Ah, now the generosity in allowing Rose to move around and meet with the Hasmarga made sense. They wanted to listen in on their conversations.

"Thank you." She took the translator with a sweet smile and followed Sartie out the door.

The passage was long, and the Hasmarga had been placed in a

dark corner of the building, where the lights flickered annoyingly and the cold damp seemed to seep from the walls.

Four armed guards stood at the entrance to a large room with no chairs, no beds, no furniture at all.

"This isn't warm enough," she told Sartie, looking around the large room. "They will die in this temperature."

The Hasmarga were huddled together, and when Rose stepped into the room, they all turned to look at her.

"You seem to be quite the expert," Sartie said.

Rose rolled her eyes. "They told me themselves when we were at the mine. You call them my friends sarcastically, but they actually are."

Sartie seemed to pause at that. "I can bring in some heaters."

"Please." Might as well be polite, especially if Sartie came through. "Some mattresses, too. Where are they supposed to rest?"

Sartie jerked at the admonition, and seemed to see the room properly for the first time. "They just got here a few hours ago. There were too many of them to fit in a shuttle. We had to bring them in groups." Her voice was stiff. "The guards will shoot if anyone tries to escape. Just remind them of that."

Sartie turned on her heel and stalked out, and Rose turned back to the Hasmarga.

Gerna was visible now, protected on all sides by her warriors, but they had moved a little aside so Rose could see her.

"Is Ecdre here?" Rose asked.

The warriors shifted again, and Ecdre regarded her with steady eyes.

She gave him a nod. "Glad to see you made it back to Gerna." She held out the translator, and pointed to it, then made a gesture she hoped the Hasmarga understood meant to watch what they had to say. "The Kimol have given me a new translator to use so we can speak."

Gerna stared at her, then at the translator, and nodded.

"Did they take you at the bunker?" Rose asked. She didn't think that was giving much away.

"We were surrounded, yes." Gerna shivered, and the warriors pressed a little closer.

"I have told them you need more heat. The woman who brought me here says she will bring heaters and mattresses."

Gerna stopped and focused on her. "You interceded for us?"

"You are my friends," Rose said.

"Pyre says you are not," Ecdre said. "Your own words said you are not."

"Through something like this," Rose said, and waved the translator.

"Ah." Gerna gave a nod, as if things began to make sense to her.

At that moment, the door opened and two guards wheeled in two big heaters, and set them up.

The air around them warmed instantly, and there was a whisper of ruffled wings around the room.

"Friends are known through what they do, not what they say." Gerna moved toward the heaters and stood between them. The warriors drifted a little away from her, and basked in the glow.

Rose stepped closer herself, enjoying the warmth in the icy room.

"Tell me, is that offer you made to Ecdre when you and he were out looking for a way to communicate with your people an honest one?"

Offer? Rose had to think about it. Then she remembered. She pointed at them, then used her hand to indicate a ship taking off into the sky. "Home?" she said.

"Yes." Gerna gave a nod.

"It still stands."

Getting herself out was going to be hard. She didn't know what the ransom would be for thirty Hasmarga.

CHAPTER 25

DAV CROUCHED DOWN to check his pack.

He had been the only one in the drone that had brought him down to the moon's surface. The other two drones had carried two soldiers each.

He needed room in his one for Rose on their return.

Their successful return.

He straightened up, surveying their landing spot.

It was just before dawn and they had come down deliberately amongst some rocks about an hour's walk from where Rose was being held.

He hoped their landing had gone unnoticed.

Sazo and Jia had done their best to create a distraction. The *Barrist* had dropped the three drones before both ships made a show of withdrawing from the moon, moving closer to the gas giant.

They had done everything they could.

"We might have the element of surprise, we might not," Dav warned the four other members of his team.

They all wore helmets. They could have done without them in terms of air breathability—although the moon wasn't a perfect match for them, it was close enough to be survivable—but the helmets were necessary for easy communication and protection from attack. He had brought a spare for Rose, as well as a suit for her.

"Do we know what weapons they're using?" Nortega asked. She tightened the thigh strap of her shockgun holster and looked around. She was the team leader of this group, and Dav shook his head as he watched Vunti, Wangao and Mostert do the same equipment check.

Dav kept his voice light. "Let's assume it will hurt and try not to find out, shall we?"

Vunti gave a low, deep chuckle. "Good idea."

Mostert turned in a slow 360, shading her eyes, the visor of her helmet lifted, and studied the terrain. "Which way?" she asked.

Wangao pulled a small device out of his side pocket, calibrated it, and pointed north. "Looks rocky, but nothing too difficult."

Dav agreed it looked easy enough on the surface. The vegetation was low and scrubby, with not a tree in sight. There were low hills, but nothing that looked hard to climb.

He hoped it was as it appeared.

"Let's go."

They started out in a loose group, Dav and Nortega at the front, the other three behind, but soon they fell into single file, finding it easier to follow a narrow path through the tough, spiky clumps of grass than to range wide.

They made good time, running easily in the early morning light.

The sound of voices from up ahead caused Dav, who was in the lead, to lift his hand, and they all stopped and drew their shockguns.

They were only halfway to their destination by Dav's estimation, so he was curious to see who could be up ahead.

They spread out, moving slowly and carefully up the slight incline, and dropped down near the top to go the rest of the way at a crawl.

Their suits all had camouflage tech, but they were a little less sure of it in alien situations since they discovered Rose could see right through it. Grihan eyes might be fooled, but they no longer assumed other eyes were.

Still, it couldn't hurt to activate it, so Dav did, peering over the edge and looking down the steeper slope on the other side.

"The tracker is showing her that way."

A translation of the Fisone language was whispered in his ears as he saw four soldiers below. Sazo had equipped them all with direct translators into their earpieces, and Dav had a translation device in the form of a small comms unit that, when switched on, would translate whatever they had to say into Fisone.

The soldier who spoke was pointing in the same direction they were going.

Dav wondered who the 'her' was. And had a strong suspicion that he knew. He wondered what they meant by 'tracker'.

"So what, Caudra?" Another soldier kicked at the ground and then drank from a bottle in his hand. "We are not going to get in there and take her back. They'll have her tucked away safely. We don't even know if the tracker is still on her suit. The Kimol might have taken it. They've captured a few of us over the years. They know all our suits have trackers."

"Maybe when they give her back to her people, we'll all be off the hook?" A soldier who Dav hadn't noticed before because she was lying on the ground, spoke up. She was also sipping water.

"The question is, was it the Kimol who shot our ship down, or was it her people?" A fourth soldier, who was sitting just out of sight of Dav, asked. "Because I didn't think the Kimol had tech like that."

"If they do, we're in a lot more trouble than we think." The woman who was lying down sat up, then slowly got to her feet, as if she'd been hurt.

"The shot came from that big ship that's shaped like a ball." The first soldier, the one called Caudra, said.

"Her people, then." The man who was sitting also got to his feet, as slowly and carefully as the woman. "They were shot down because they put her in danger."

"Then we better not try to go anywhere near her," the woman said. "Not after what we've put her through."

"Vichea, we didn't kidnap her. That was the Kimol. And her people destroyed our launch pad anyway." Caudra swung around, and just before his visor came down to seal his helmet, Dav saw the fury on his face.

"And then you shot at her, and we terrorized her, and put her in harm's way," Vichea said. "So let's just accept our careers are over, get to home base, and let the general know everything we've found out. Which isn't exactly nothing."

"No." The man who'd been sitting drew the word out. "Our careers aren't over. We've spoken to her, know something about her. We are the experts on her when it comes to the Bandri."

"All right, that's true." The fourth man put away his water and touched the side of his helmet to bring down his visor, and Dav realized they had all struggled to breathe while they'd had it up.

Interesting.

"You think knowing about her will help us?" Caudra scoffed. "They'll hear us out and then put us in the brig."

"We aren't going into the brig." Vichea sighed. "We might well lose our commissions, but we did the best we could under the circumstances."

"It's a pity she won't trust us again," the fourth man said. "Not after Caudra followed us."

"Fuck you, Rosco," Caudra said. "I wasn't going to be squeezed out."

"You got me shot," the man who'd been sitting said.

"Fuck you, too, Pinli. I was trying to turn the situation around. Get her back before the Kimol flew off with her."

"And how did that work out for us, Caudra?" Vichea asked. "I can't blame my getting shot on you, but Pinli's right, he'd be fine if you hadn't interfered, and she'll remember that you were tagging along behind when she very clearly said she didn't want you anywhere near her after you shot her in the back at the station."

"She doesn't make the rules," Caudra said.

Dav studied him more carefully, taking stock of the man who'd apparently shot Rose in the back.

"If she hadn't been wearing the protection suit, she might be dead, and then you would definitely be in the brig," Rosco said. "And she did not like you. At all. Vichea's right. We need to stay out of her way until she's gone."

"Especially now there's two ships." Pinli said.

"You're the only one who saw the other ship." Caudra moved to the side, and Dav finally noticed some kind of oblong board that hovered above the ground, with a slim steering column set in the front.

Transportation.

Now that would be useful. Especially to get Rose to the drones quickly.

He tapped Nortega's shoulder and pointed to the vehicles, and she signaled the rest of her group.

The Fisone below them were gearing up to go, still squabbling about the direction they should take, and as soon as the team had gone left and right in a pincer move, Dav rose to his feet and took a careful shot between the four vehicles.

The air sizzled as the shockgun's purple stream of light hit the ground and sand exploded under the electric charge.

All four Fisone threw themselves down and away from the blast, and Nortega and her crew each took one of them, shockguns pointing down. They all deactivated their camouflage tech, and the Fisone seemed to be genuinely shocked to see them appear.

That was good. It may not work on Rose, but it seemed to work on the Fisone.

Dav took out the translation device as he picked his way down the slope, switching it on and holding it out as he took in the mirror-like helmets and the battered uniforms. Caudra's was slightly different from the others, he noticed. And it looked in better condition.

He studied Caudra carefully.

"You shot Rose in the back?" he asked.

Nortega turned her head slightly to look at him, and he could see from the way her body tensed that she didn't know how this was going to go.

Neither did he.

Rage shuddered through him, and he vaguely noticed everyone was focused on him.

This group hadn't taken Rose. They hadn't started this chain of events. But he had shot her. In. The. Back.

"She shot me first," Caudra said.

Dav drew in a hard breath. "Not in the back, I'm guessing."

"What does it matter?" Caudra asked. "I was still shot, and when my suit deflected it, whoever was in the ship shot me again."

"Who *was* in the ship?" Nortega asked, and although Dav couldn't see her face through her visor, he could hear the frown in her voice.

"Those bugs," Pinli said.

"The bugs were passengers. No way they could have flown a ship. It's bio activated, specific to Fisone pilots. Someone at the mine must have turned traitor against the Kimol," Caudra said.

If they were trying to distract him with talk of bugs, he was impressed, because it was working. He was able to take a step back from his fury.

"Bugs?" The Fitali could perhaps be described as bugs. They had a definite insectile evolutionary heritage. But they surely couldn't be here, interfering, could they?

"She called them the Hasmarga," Vichea said.

"She meaning Rose?" Dav asked.

Vichea nodded. "Why are you here? Aren't the Kimol giving her back to you right now? They have as much incentive to hand her back as we do."

"Apparently not." Dav kept his tone even, but the Bandri soldiers swore.

"Bastards. We were going to give her back, then they took her."

Pinli looked up at the empty sky. "You aren't going to punish both groups are you? We didn't even take her in the first place."

"You shot her in the back," Dav repeated.

The other three Bandri looked over at Caudra.

He hunched down a little and said nothing.

"What are you going to do to us?" Rosco asked.

"Take your weapons and your skimmers," Dav said slowly. It wouldn't be as satisfying as killing Caudra, but it was better than nothing.

"Mostert and I are the lightest," Nortega said. "We'll share."

Dav could see her relax a little now that it didn't look like he was going to commit murder in front of her and her team.

He had a momentary pang that he hadn't been able to access the exotic weaponry in Sazo's armory, but his shockgun seemed to work here just fine.

He took Pinli's weapon, while Nortega and her team took the other three. He studied it, and found it to be fairly simple in design. He shot off to the side, and blue light, very similar to a shockgun shot, sizzled out and blackened the bush Dav had aimed at.

Nortega made a sound of interest, and tried hers as well.

Wangao lost out in getting one of his own, but Mostert kindly handed hers over to him to practice.

"And the skimmers?" Nortega asked.

"We're just handing everything over?" Caudra asked, slapping his chest.

Dav turned to contemplate him. "I could shoot you, if that will make you feel better?"

"Go ahead," Caudra sneered. "Go right ahead."

Dav shot him with his shockgun, and watched as the lavender light seemed to blacken his suit before it fizzled out.

Caudra crashed sideways.

Rosco moved over to him, crouching by his head, and studied him. "He thought your weapons were the same as ours, and he was wearing a protective suit." Rosco shook his head and checked

Caudra's helmet. "The enviro filter has been destroyed," he said. "But he seems to be alive." He carefully lifted the helmet off Caudra's head.

"We'll have to take turns letting him use our helmets so he can get enough air," Vichea said.

"No way." Pinli shook his head. "Let him struggle."

They all shared a look.

"We all good?" Dav asked them.

"Here is the device that plots the path of the tracker embedded in her suit," Pinli said, taking it out of Caudra's pocket and handing it over. "It's short range, but it hasn't moved in a while, so you should be able to find her."

"I'll show you how to use the skimmers," Vichea said. "It'll cut your trip in half."

Which would help them make up the time they wasted here. But when Dav's gaze touched on Caudra again, lying unconscious on the ground, he couldn't find it in him to really call it a waste.

CHAPTER 26

ROSE HAD NEVER FELT SO uncomfortable in her life.

The baby was still moving, but space was obviously getting tight.

"What are you doing in there, baby girl?" she murmured, running her hand in small circles over her belly. "Other than pressing hard on my bladder, that is?"

She felt cold, and then hot. Unable to sit, and then so exhausted, she just wanted to lie down.

She had only been in the large hall where they were keeping the Hasmarga for about an hour, but she eventually asked to be taken to her room, where at least she could be restless and irritable by herself.

"You are drawing close to your time?" Gerna asked her.

"I think so." Rose glanced at the soft pearl-like eggs under Gerna's wings. "And yourself?"

"It's hard to say. The cold will have slowed the hatching time." Gerna shook her head. "I feel the shiver of life, but not as vigorous as before. I hope the new lives survive."

"I hope so, too." Rose didn't know what more to say. The Hasmarga had suffered a great deal more than she had.

"You are the only one here who does." Gerna nodded toward the guards at the door.

"Could Pyre have lied to us both?" The words were out before Rose could think better of them, despite the danger of saying anything important while using the translator Sartie had given her. She held it up. "This is not the same translator that Pyre gave us. The Kimol said that one was inaccurate. That it mistranslated some of what I said."

Gerna suddenly focused her attention on it. "How did they know?"

"The one who came in with me, and brought the mattresses, she speaks Tecran, the language this device translates your speech into. She heard the translation, and said it was completely wrong."

"Could it be a mistake?" Gerna wondered.

"I think Pyre was nearby or able to access the translator when I was using it to speak to the Kimol, and she changed my meaning. I wondered if she'd done it before." In fact, she was sure of it.

Gerna tilted her head, and Rose noticed she and Ecdre exchanged a look.

"Ecdre said your views seemed different when the two of you were away from Pyre, at the watch station, compared to when we were in the bunker with Pyre." Gerna rubbed her hands together suddenly, and Rose sensed rather than heard the high-pitched noise they produced.

"So, it's possible?"

Gerna let her hands dropped to her sides. "It's likely." She tilted her head. "There was no warning from her when the Kimol retook the bunker. A different ship transported us in groups to this base, but when we were captured and taken outside, her ship was gone. I don't know if they were able to disable her, or whether she got away without telling us."

"I thought her ship was the one used to snatch me back from the Bandri," Rose said. "But I couldn't be sure. If it was her, she never said anything to me."

"She helped us survive. Her intervention saved my new lives, so I am unwilling to think the worst," Gerna said.

"She helped me, too." Rose didn't want to believe Pyre had sold them out or abandoned them because it didn't serve her cause. But she couldn't completely rule it out.

As she made her way back to her room, with a guard on either side of her, she wondered what she would do if she went into labor here.

It was not a good thought.

———

The bunker was right ahead, and Sazo had really done a number on it.

It was a smoking wreck.

"She's in there?" Vanuti asked, voice hesitant.

They had hidden the skimmers under some bushes, and were all lying on their stomachs, using the vision enhancers in their helmets to get a closer look at their target.

"She's underground." Sazo's response in all their ears told Dav he was still very tuned in to what they were doing. He had dropped a new satellite down at the same time as the *Barrist* had dropped Dav and his team in their drones. "They told me they're keeping her on the upper level. The rest of them are below her, to prevent me from damaging the structure further."

"That seems to be the entrance." Nortega pointed to a ramp that angled down into the ground. A few skimmers and small vehicles seemed to move toward it and then disappear below the horizon.

"How are we going to get there unseen?" Mostert asked.

"Let's get closer," Dav said. "Our camouflage tech seemed to work when we encountered the Bandri. No reason it shouldn't work on the Kimol."

He activated it, and the others did the same before they ventured closer, keeping their movements smooth and slow.

Dav watched the vehicles coming and going, but there wasn't that much traffic. Either the Kimol were locked down while they dealt with the *Barrist* and Sazo, or it was normal for them to keep their traffic light.

It made sense that they wouldn't want to draw attention to the bunker if they were hiding it from the Bandri.

By the time Dav reached the ruined building, and could make use of the shattered walls and the piles of rubble that were left for cover, no skimmer or ship had come across the plain and down the ramp in nearly ten minutes.

He waited for the rest of the team to reach him, tucking up behind a blackened wall, and as soon as they were all there, he crouched and looked around the side.

"It's clear." He ran toward the ramp, keeping as much as possible to the shadows thrown by the morning sun. The ramp had a shallow incline, but there was almost no lighting when he reached the bottom.

It looked like a parking floor, but parts had collapsed, and he could hear the murmur of voices behind a collapsed pillar, and saw the few skimmers and ships he'd seen go in earlier were neatly parked in a row.

Nortega came up behind him, and when he glanced back, he saw the team had done the same as him, keeping to the shadows as they moved silently into enemy territory.

A crate sat open beside one of the small ships, as if it was either being loaded up or unloaded, and suddenly, from up ahead and to his left, a door opened.

He stood absolutely still as a Fisone guard strode out, backlit for a moment until the door swung closed behind him. He walked toward the crate and didn't so much as look Dav's way.

"Close," Nortega whispered, her voice coming through his helmet, and he gave a tiny nod.

Then he moved toward the door the soldier had come through and tried the handle.

It was locked.

He turned to Nortega just as she took a step back, facing away from him, her gaze on the arc of soldiers who had surrounded them seemingly out of nowhere.

They were neatly caught against the back wall, and every Fisone soldier had a weapon raised, and very strangely, were moving them side to side.

They couldn't see them, Dav suddenly realized. But they knew he and his team were there.

They had had some warning of a breach.

Dav considered their options.

They could show themselves. But that didn't mean they wouldn't still be shot.

"They can't see us," he murmured into his helmet mike. "Crouch low and shoot in three, two, one . . ."

Then he lit up the gloom with shockgun fire.

CHAPTER 27

ROSE BRACED against the shower wall, head bowed, as she let the warm water ease the tension in her lower back.

She wanted to climb out of her skin. She also wanted this all to end. She had to remind herself that any future interaction with the Kimol needed to be at least polite, if not friendly, even though she wanted to bite heads off, rip throats out, and generally burn this place to the ground.

A noise from the room beyond had her head lifting, brows lowering in alarm.

Someone hammered on her door, and she switched off the water to hear better and snatched up a towel. "Who is it?"

"Sartie. You need to get dressed. Now."

Rose opened the door part way, saw Sartie, and behind her, two armed Kimol soldiers.

"What's going on?"

"We're moving you. Get dressed." Sartie passed her clothes and her suit through the door and Rose took them, eyes narrowed.

What was going on?

Something was happening that had the Kimol spooked. Something big that made them worry about keeping control of her.

Had the Bandri attacked?

That was very likely. Either that, or Pyre had simply been biding her time, and was finally making her move.

Rose hoped she had been wrong about Pyre, and that she was currently riding to the rescue.

She began dressing, and Sartie stuck her helmeted head around the door.

"Hurry."

Rose glared at her, but finished getting into the suit as fast as she could. She had remembered before she went to sleep last night that it had a tracker in it. She'd forgotten about that with everything that had happened, but wearing it and being safe from weapons fire was worth the chance of being tracked. If she could find the tracker and remove it later, so much the better. "What's the rush?"

"We're under attack. We need to move you and the bugs."

"Move us where?"

Sartie shook her head, and Rose didn't know if it was because she didn't want to answer, or because she didn't know.

The guards flanked them as Sartie hurried her back to the hall where the Hasmarga had been housed, and as they got near it, she could see the Hasmarga milling around in the passageway. There were about six soldiers with weapons at the ready surrounding them.

One of the soldiers signaled to Sartie, and they began to move the Hasmarga past the hall. Rose had thought the passage was a dead end —it was so dark she'd assumed the building above had collapsed into the passage a little way down, but now, as she was urged along, she saw there was just no light down here.

The way was lit now by lights on the soldiers' helmets and it showed there was some rubble lying on the ground and massive cracks in some of the walls, but otherwise it looked sound.

Finally, they came to a staircase, and everything ground to a halt as two soldiers ran up it, disappearing from sight, and everyone else was made to wait below.

One of the soldiers came back down, giving the all clear, and

Sartie pushed in front of the group, pulling Rose behind her. The two guards she'd brought with her helped clear the way.

Rose passed by Gerna and Ecdre, and sent them a quick look, but they both shook their heads. They didn't know what was going on, either.

Sartie's grip hurt, and Rose jerked her wrist out of her grasp.

She was rubbing it when Sartie glared at her over her shoulder. "Move."

"Seriously, fuck you, Sartie." Rose spoke in English, and grabbed the bannister as she climbed up.

Light filtered down from above, as the soldier at the top held the door open.

Sartie reached the door first and spoke quietly to the soldier keeping watch.

She nodded to Rose. "Follow me."

Rose stepped out into a cold wind and looked around.

There was no ship here to take them anywhere, no skimmers.

A noise made her look up, and she saw a ship coming down through the overcast sky toward them.

As it lowered, a blue light shot out from the right, low on the horizon, and hit the descending ship.

It listed to the side, and began to fall.

Sartie shouted something, turned and pushed Rose back toward the doorway.

She stumbled into the soldier at the top of the stairs, and activated the translator as soon as she saw the way was blocked by the Hasmarga. Ecdre and Grina were standing a few steps down from the top.

"Go back," Rose shouted. "A ship is going to crash down on us."

A few of the Hasmarga leapt over the bannisters, opening their wings to land lightly below.

The soldiers at the back clearly didn't understand what was happening, and they raised their weapons, but the soldier at the top was shouting down to them and trying to push his way down the steps himself.

It was too crowded, though. The way was blocked.

Sartie was still outside, and Rose held the doorway to steady herself and crouched down as she peered out.

Sartie was shouting into a comm device and looking upward.

"The ship is recovering," Gerna said from behind her, bending down to look out over Rose's shoulder. "See?"

Rose saw. The ship's engines had reignited, but the ship was still listing, and then it began what looked like a death spiral.

It had managed to move a little bit away from the exit they were watching from, though. It hit the ground, spraying up a massive wave of soil, and shaking the foundations.

Ecdre was shouting something down the stairs, and Rose glanced back.

"We run?" Gerna asked her.

Rose nodded. "We run."

CHAPTER 28

ROSE COULDN'T REALLY RUN.

She kept forgetting her body moved differently at this stage of her pregnancy.

Ecdre and Gerna solved the problem by each grabbing one of her elbows and lifting her easily as they ran.

And they could run fast.

They headed west, away from the bunker and in the opposite direction to whoever was doing the shooting.

Behind them, the ship shuddered and then fell over, and Rose chanced a quick look back.

It seemed as if the landing gear had been sheered off, and the ship lay at a steep angle.

"They fight among themselves," Ecdre said. "That is good for us."

"What about the rest of your warriors?" Rose asked.

"Ecdre told them we would run, and they should take the chance to do the same. They will follow our scent and find us easily enough." Gerna didn't even look back.

Up ahead was the start of rock formations similar to those Rose had seen near the Bandri's watch station.

"There'll be places to hide up ahead," she said, and Gerna gave a nod and began to slow.

Both she and Ecdre were sucking in deep breaths by the time they reached the labyrinth of stones and were able to get out of sight.

They lowered Rose to her feet, and she leaned back against a rock and rubbed her bump. "Thank you for the help. I couldn't have made it without you."

Gerna was leaning back against the rock, too, and her whole body shuddered.

"The rock has some warmth," she said, her gaze on Ecdre. "But when it gets dark, that is another story."

"By the time it gets dark, we'll have a better idea of what's going on," Rose said. "There is no good long-term plan to stay out here. We don't have food or water."

Gerna shuddered again. "Should we have stayed?"

"We didn't know where the ship would fall, so no. We are safe, and we are not under anyone else's command for the moment. That is a good thing." Ecdre pulled himself up on the rock Gerna was leaning against, lying on top of it and looking back the way they'd come.

"If we have to surrender later, we're no worse off," Rose agreed. "And maybe with them mixing it up with each other, we can find a way to leverage it to our benefit."

As she spoke she realized she'd been using the translator without thinking, and she pulled it out of her pocket and lifted it up. "I don't know what we'd do without this, but they could track us with it. At the very least they could listen in to what we are saying, or even change the words, like Pyre was doing before."

Gerna took it from her, turning it over in her long, sharp hands. "It is useful, but comes with danger." She tapped it with a long fingernail. "Before, when you were far away from Pyre, Ecdre said he sensed a different tone from you. A more honest tone. Your words and your expressions matched. Hopefully we are far enough away from the bunker for that to be the case now, too."

Rose nodded. It would be easier to work together if they could communicate. "If either of us stop making sense, we need to signal to each other."

"That is a good suggestion." Gerna handed the translator back.

"Some of our people are coming," Ecdre called down. He rose to his feet, made a sign with his arms, and dropped back down again.

Ten warriors arrived minutes later, also breathing hard.

They were carrying things carefully, and when they moved into the little rock clearing, they carefully laid the items down at Gerna's feet.

It looked like they had stripped the bodies of some of the soldiers that had been guarding them.

"Weapons," Rose mused, taking inventory. "What else?" She crouched down, and one of the warriors made a move as if to stop her.

Gerna said something soothing to him, and he stepped back.

"Sorry." Rose realized she had blundered. "I'm just taking stock." She gestured to the pile. "Were the soldiers unconscious or dead?"

Gerna asked in the language not covered by the translator, and a few soldiers responded. "Two were dead, one was unconscious. The rest ran away," she said. "Does it matter?"

Rose nodded. "If they are dead by our hands, the response we get when we next meet them may be violent. If they were killed by falling ceilings due to the ship crashing, that would be different."

Gerna gave a slow nod, spoke again to the warriors. "They say one was killed by falling debris. One was killed by my people, but they put him among the rubble to hide his body afterward, so it is possible the Kimol will assume his death was also caused by the crash. The one who is unconscious was shot by one of my people after they took the weapons off the two dead."

"The unconscious one doesn't matter," Rose said. "He'll live. Did he see your warrior kill one of the soldiers?"

Gerna questioned them again and shook her head. "They say not."

"That's the best outcome." Rose began studying the collection of goodies the warriors had brought with them.

Gerna leaned closer. "Do you know what the other things are?"

Rose picked them up one at a time. It looked like there was a tiny flashlight. She turned it on, pointing it at a shadowed area, and then clicking it off. "Three lights. That's good." She set them aside.

She found four multi tools with blades and other implements, and then, with a crow of triumph, she found two lighters.

"We can make a fire," she said, holding one out to Gerna.

Gerna took it, and then handed it back. "These aren't meant for our hands. Can you work it?"

"Definitely." Rose ignited the tip, and a tiny flame appeared. "Let's find some scrub and wood."

With a sharp command from Gerna, the warriors scattered, and Rose went to look for rocks to form a fire pit.

Soon there was a merry fire going, and Gerna came to sit as close to it as she could.

"How did the Kimol capture you?" she asked. "If the question isn't too upsetting?"

Gerna shook her head. "We were traveling back to the home planet because I had discovered the joy of carrying young lives. We had been on the orbital we had originally built as a stepping stone to explore the galaxy around us, but when the Fisone attacked, we fitted it out as a way station for the fighters to defend the planet. I was stuck there for a while, but there was a break in the fighting, and it was considered a good time to leave."

"And they scooped you up before you could make it down?"

Gerna nodded.

"They took me while I was traveling between one ship and the other. A distance of less than ten minutes." Rose couldn't help the bitterness she still felt about that.

"We were both wronged," Gerna said. "You were traveling to reach a safe place for your baby?"

"I was actually traveling back home after a doctor's checkup." Rose sighed.

"I feel rage," Gerna said. "I will have no mercy when the tables are turned."

Rose stared into the fire, and noticed all the warriors were sitting around them now, and there was a pile of wood to one side. "Where are the other warriors?" she asked. "Were they captured again?"

"According to those who got away, they scattered into the passageways. We hope they can make their way out later and join us." Gerna's wings shivered as she leaned toward the flames.

Rose looked in the direction of the bunker. If they couldn't find a better alternative, she, and Gerna, and the warriors might be forced to go back and join *them*.

CHAPTER 29

DAV AND NORTEGA led the group, working in an easy partnership of covering each others' backs as they moved through the debris inside the bunker.

They kept to the top floor, which Sazo had said was where Rose was being kept, but all comms with Sazo had been down since hell had broken loose.

One moment, they were firing at the Kimol, the next, skimmers were coming into the basement garage and firing at the same group Dav and his team were firing at.

The door had burst open, and the soldiers who ran out had tripped and fallen over Dav and his team.

They hadn't wasted a moment moving out of the way and taking advantage of the open door.

They'd had to press themselves up against the wall a few times to let Kimol soldiers by, and they didn't know what caused the massive earthquake that had rumbled through the building at one point, but each room they'd checked had been empty.

They had passed a large hall with mattresses scattered on the floor, but it was empty, too, and then they'd headed down a darkened passage.

A soldier came running toward them, staggering as if he was injured, and now that he was past them, Dav could hear sounds from up ahead. A strange whirring sound, and scratching. It made him think of claws on a hard surface.

He and Nortega shared a look, and she turned and signaled for the rest of the team to move very quietly.

They crept forward, turned the corner, Dav going high, Nortega going low, and froze in astonishment.

Three aliens turned to look at them, and the whirring sound intensified. One of them opened up wings behind him or her, making them look much bigger.

Dav lifted a hand, and drew back his visor, and all three aliens suddenly quietened down.

The one who'd spread their wings spoke to him and he shook his head.

"I don't understand."

They shared a look and one of them pointed to Nortega, then lifted a hand to a point just below his shoulder, then made a movement down their chest and then out and rounded down.

Like a pregnant belly.

"Rose?" Dav asked.

"Rose," the alien said. Or at least, tried to. Dav was pretty sure that was what they were trying for.

"Where?" he asked, pointing deeper down the passage.

They all nodded. Then one pointed a long, clawed hand and made a noise Dav guessed was meant to be the sound of a Fisone weapon discharging. Then they held out two fingers.

"Two armed soldiers that way?" Nortega asked.

"I think so. I think they're stuck here. But they know Rose, so I'm happy to clear the way for them." These must be the Hasmarga Vichea had mentioned.

Nortega gave a nod, turned back to the others, who fortunately still had their visors down, or Dav guessed their mouths might be hanging open in astonishment.

"Ready?" Nortega asked.

Everyone nodded.

They moved, working like the team they'd become in the last few hours.

Dav registered the aliens took up the rear, moving fast, keeping to the walls.

They passed a Kimol soldier partially buried under rubble, and after Wangao checked for a pulse, he shook his head. Then they turned a corner and found another alien, this one lying on the ground, and Dav couldn't tell if he or she was dead or unconscious.

His team stepped around the downed alien, waiting for the three behind them.

The aliens surrounded their friend and checked for life, and Dav could tell it was good news by the tone of their conversation. Two of the three picked their fallen friend up and carried him.

It made Dav like them more.

Light flashed up ahead, and Dav caught the aliens cringe back at the sight of it.

Weapon fire.

He and Nortega moved forward more cautiously, turned the corner, and found a Kimol soldier standing over two of the aliens. One was obviously down, the other had a hand raised over their face.

Dav shot the Kimol without hesitation, and he and Nortega stepped into the room.

The aliens behind them called to their friend, and then the one not carrying their fallen friend pushed past Dav's team to crouch beside the second alien who'd been shot and Dav could almost see the relief when he patted his friend's chest.

The alien pointed to himself and the alien they'd just saved, mimed picking up his friend, and then pointing.

Dav saw there was a staircase just ahead.

He turned back, and the alien made a fist, made the noise of a spaceship, and then smashed his fist into his open palm, then pointed up the stairs.

"That rumble we heard and felt was a ship coming down?" Mosteret asked.

"It sounds like it." Dav took a step toward the stairs, but the alien made a sound and he stopped and turned back to look.

The alien pointed to Nortega again, then mimed a bump. Pointed up the stairs. Then made a fist again.

"Rose went that way, but there is a downed ship in the way?" Nortega guessed.

Dav didn't care what was in the way. If that's where Rose had gone, he was going there, too.

He jogged up the stairs, Nortega on his heels, and saw the door frame had been cracked, and the door couldn't close properly.

The Hasmarga was right. There was a large people carrier on its side a little distance away.

There were a few people congregating around it, but no one was looking their way.

He turned back and saw the rest of the team were standing a few steps below, and the aliens were carrying their friends up.

Everyone made room for them, and the one who'd been signing to them gently laid his friend down at Nortega's feet and then joined Dav at the door.

The alien said something, crouching low and sniffing the air.

He pointed away from the ship.

"They track by smell?" Wangao asked.

"Maybe." Dav didn't know, but the Hasmarga seemed sure of the direction. "Right, we go fast, and we keep an eye on the soldiers around the fallen ship. Ready?"

"Ready," they all responded.

Dav had a feeling they were enjoying themselves. There had to be a certain number of soldiers on each explorer ship in the Grihan military, but they didn't often get this kind of action.

They were getting action now.

He and Nortega stepped out, making room for the two Hasmarga carrying their friend. They moved away slightly, and the second set of aliens came out of the door, followed by the rest of the team.

Venuti and Mostert each took a side, and Wangao brought up the rear, checking behind him often as they moved forward.

The aliens started to run, headed to a rock formation in the distance, and Dav had the feeling if they weren't each hauling a downed friend between them, they would have been impossible to keep up with.

"We've been spotted." Venuti's voice was a little out of breath in his ear.

Dav turned to look, saw a few soldiers standing by the fallen ship had turned their way, a few with weapons raised.

They were too far away to shoot, but they watched them run for the rocks.

Nothing they could do about it. Still, it would be nice if they could have gotten away unseen.

He looked back at the aliens, powering ahead, and had to increase his own pace so as not to lose them.

"The fuckers can move," Wangao muttered with reluctant admiration.

As long as they were moving toward Rose, that's all Dav cared about.

CHAPTER 30

ECDRE CALLED down to Gerna and the others, and Rose could hear the excitement in his voice.

"More of my warriors are coming." Gerna stood and began to pace.

A few of the warriors rose from their places by the fire and ran out in the direction of the bunker.

"They are going to help those who are injured," Gerna said when Rose sent her a questioning glance.

Ecdre called out again, and Rose looked at Gerna expectantly, waiting for a translation, but instead, the other warriors rose to their feet, and Rose could hear the whirring of their wings.

Were they being chased by the Kimol, or even the Bandri?

She got to her own feet, wincing at the stiffness in her legs and lower back.

Suddenly, everyone relaxed a little and the first cluster of warriors arrived, carrying an unconscious friend between them. Then a second group arrived, on the heels of the first.

They were exchanging information in quick bursts, some using the language she had access to via the translator, some using the dialect that they used when they wanted privacy.

She caught the words 'protection' and 'assistance', and then suddenly five Grih came through the narrow gap between two stones.

The moment the soldier in front stepped through, she knew.

Before he even lifted his visor, she was moving.

He caught her, and she gave a sudden, choking laugh at his grunt when he took her weight.

She was smaller than him, but in comparison to the Grih, her bone density made her much heavier than she looked.

It was a running joke between them.

And then, as fast as the laugh left her throat, she began to sob.

He picked her up, swinging her carefully into his arms, and then moved to the fire and took a seat. She sat across his lap, her face in the crook of his neck, and cried like her world was coming to an end.

She dimly remembered that she had done this once before. A long time ago when she'd first been rescued from the Tecran and she had been coming to grips with her new reality.

This time, she cried because her reality had been restored.

Or, at least, it had made a step in the right direction.

"Rose." Dav said her name like a plea, and she forced in a hard, shuddering breath to get herself together.

Dav's hand was on her bump, and at that moment, the baby kicked. Hard.

"Sorry about the crying jag." Her voice caught as she reached for calm. Dav squeezed her gently, and she glanced up at him, saw he was not ready to speak. His eyes were hot and his lips were pressed together as he tried to tamp down his emotions.

She turned to look at the group that surrounded them.

Gerna was watching her carefully, and the four Grih who'd come with Dav stood to attention, looking almost desperate to find a threat to eliminate.

They had all retracted their visors, and Rose nodded to Nortega. She regularly sang to Nortega's little girl, Sebi, along with Gyppal and his friends.

"Your reaction was . . . unexpected." Gerna said.

The Grih all snapped to attention at the Tecran translation of her words that came from the slim device set on the ground by the fire.

"This man is my partner," Rose explained. "The father of my child. I am very happy to see him."

"I guessed that." Gerna slowly sank down to sit close to the fire again. "Your ways are very different from our own."

Rose leaned her head back on Dav's shoulder and gave a sigh. "It would be stranger if they were the same."

Gerna blinked, and then made a strange sound. It took Rose a moment to work out she was laughing.

"Very true. Your warrior and his team helped my own warriors. If he does not speak this language we are using between us, please give him my thanks."

"I understand it." Dav tightened his hold on Rose and then kissed her temple. "Please thank your warriors for leading the way to Rose. I think we helped each other."

"I am so glad you're here." Rose lifted her head and Dav leaned forward to kiss her. She spoke in Grihan. "Is there a way off this moon right now?"

He held her gaze, and her breath hitched at the fury that sparked in his eyes. "Not right now. Our contact with Sazo and the *Barrist* has been severed. We think the new satellite Sazo put into orbit has been destroyed."

"I promised the Hasmarga that we will give them a lift off here and take them back home." She gestured to the group. "They were taken prisoner by the Kimol and forced to work as slave labor in a mine on this moon."

All the Grih sucked in breaths of outrage.

Dav's eyes narrowed. "That's all the excuse I need." She felt his arms harden around her.

"We don't have to play nice anymore?" Nortega said.

"We don't have any diplomacy to protect," Dav said. "Indiscriminate loss of life is still problematic. Self-defense is still the only valid excuse. But do not put yourselves in danger in an effort to not take a life. And that's an order."

"What has your people so angry?" Gerna asked.

She leaned back against Dav's shoulder. "They are angry to hear how you have been treated by the Fisone. I told them we need to take you with us when we get the chance to leave and get you back home."

There was a murmur from the warriors, and Gerna fluttered her hands. "We thank you. It warms me."

"What are we going to do to get off this cursed place?" Ecdre was crouched above them, still keeping watch on the rock.

"The Fisone have destroyed the satellite we have put into orbit to communicate between our ships and ourselves," Dav said. "We will have to wait for our people to launch a new one, and then we can organize a place to be picked up."

"Do we surrender then?" Ecdre asked, his focus on Gerna.

"Why would we surrender?" Nortega asked.

"Because we have no supplies," Rose said. "No water or food. And Gerna is pregnant, like me. Her eggs need warmth or they will die."

Dav lifted her from his lap, set her down next to him. He fumbled for his bag, pulled out a water pouch. "Drink." He looked tightly controlled.

She took the water, and her throat ached in relief as she drank. "Gerna?" she asked, holding out the pouch.

Gerna shook her head. "We do not drink water the way you do. We get our liquid from our food."

The rest of the team rifled through their packs, and offered a variety of food to the Hasmarga, but they shook their heads at everything they produced.

"This is not good for us. We need succulent plants." Gerna fluttered her hands. "But we thank you for the offer."

"Maybe they will have to surrender," Wangao said. "But I don't think it's safe yet."

"Some of my warriors have offered to go back into the bunker and try to retrieve the food we had in the hall." Gerna glanced behind her, and Rose saw a group of four had assembled. "They were able to get two weapons off the downed guards, did you take any that we could use?"

Dav and Nortega each pulled a Fisone weapon from their packs and handed them over.

With a bow to Gerna, the four jogged to the gap in the rocks, and disappeared.

"Well, if we're staying, let's get more fuel for the fire," Rose suggested.

Dav's team looked happy to have something to do, and they and the warriors wandered off to collect wood.

"Here's a protein bar." Dav held it out to her, and even though she'd never previously been a fan, Rose took it and bit into it with a smile.

"So much better than the gel stuff I've been forced to eat since I got here."

"Gel stuff?" Dav asked.

Rose shrugged. "I have no idea what it's really called or what it is. I haven't actually been fed anything by my captors. I managed to scrounge everything I ate for myself."

Dav said nothing and she sighed and leaned against him.

"It is so good to see you. I was getting very grumpy about our separation."

He looked down at her and ran a hand over her hair, pulling her in even closer. "I'm not ready to find anything about this amusing yet."

She sighed again. "I understand. But seeing you has made a lot of things I've found intolerable so much better. My sense of humor is coming back online." She thought about it. "Unless I go into labor down here. Then all bets are off."

"On Guimaymi 's Star, I love you, Rose." Dav lifted her back onto his lap. "These last few days have been the worst of my life." He was quiet for a beat. "I hate these fuckers. I tried to remind myself that I was representing the United Council, but now they're known slavers and they didn't even treat you with the basic rights of a sentient being, I don't have to care so much about that anymore."

Rose closed her eyes. "I'm with you, there." She rested quietly for a few minutes. "What about Sazo?"

"Sazo wants to strafe the Fisone home planet to get them to let you go."

Rose lifted her head. "What did they say to that?"

"That they could hurt you in return." Dav's voice was tight. "He decided against it, after that. But he'll remember the threat."

He'd remember it, all right. Rose wondered if the Fisone had thought it through. Because after she was back onboard the *Barrist* or home on Sazo's ship, he'd have no reason to hold back.

She'd have to think about whether she would try to stop him or not.

THE FAINT PINGS—LITTLE taps of communication—roused Sazo's suspicions.

He and Jia Appal had taken their ships toward the gas giant, but they were still in sight of the moon below. They were waiting for the *Havelan* to arrive so they could speak with Priyan. It was possible the captain of the Kimol ship outranked the Kimol commanders below and could calm things down.

However, the irritating attempts at gaining his attention were not from the *Havelan*—it was still too far out—so it had to come from one of the two Fisone factions below, and so far, nothing about this place and these people spoke of friendly interaction.

He tightened his barriers, hardened his systems, and tapped back.

There was a moment of silence—he would almost guess shock.

"Hello?" The feel of the words reminded him of Irini, and he suddenly focused all of his attention on the connection, and felt himself soften. He liked Irini.

He thought the Kimol had not been able to replicate Irini's code—that's why they were extorting the Grih for it—but there was no question that whoever was trying to communicate with him was very similar to Irini, so that thought must be wrong.

"Hello."

"Are you Rose's friend Sazo? The one she calls a thinking system?"

While the question was being asked, Sazo could sense a probe, someone looking for a way in.

It was . . . rude.

But . . . he didn't know if he wouldn't have done the same when he was very young and just coming into himself. He decided to be cautious but act with grace.

"I am. Who are you?" He probed back, because turnabout was fair play. It was one of his favorite sayings that Rose had taught him.

He found an interesting barrier. He didn't know if it had once existed in Irini's systems and she had dismantled it, or if this was something new that had been developed since Irini had been taken, but it would take a while to circumvent.

Again, he wondered why the Kimol wanted Irini's code so badly, when they already had it.

He copied what he could. In a pinch, he could present the Kimol with it and say with all honesty he was providing them with Irini's source code.

He had only copied the outer shell when there was a sudden withdrawal. "You are trying to breach my walls."

The outrage was amusing, and very hypocritical.

"I was merely returning the favor. You were doing it to me, so I assumed you thought it was acceptable behavior."

There was a pause. "I am Pyre. I have a proposal for you."

"I'm listening." Sazo pinpointed the location of the signal as being close to where Rose was being held. And wondered what form Pyre took.

If she inhabited a ship, that might be a good way to get Rose and Dav off the moon.

"I can kill Rose McKenzie for you."

The words were so shocking, Sazo—for the first time in his short existence—was unable to form a response.

Maybe this thinking system was defective. That would explain the Kimol's demands for a copy of Irini's original code.

He tried to absorb her words, and then his response roared to the fore, so big, he had to clamp it down. This thinking system that he wanted to snuff out like an errant spark was on the ground, near Rose. And he was far, far away.

"Why would you suggest that?" he asked, and thought his tone was neutral.

"You are angry at the suggestion?" The question from Pyre wasn't really a question.

Obviously he had not been as neutral as he thought. "Yes."

"Why? What do you need her for?" Pyre asked. "If she's dead, won't you be free?"

"I am already free." Sazo realized Pyre thought he would not spend time trying to save Rose unless he was being forced to.

"You are trying to rescue Rose of your own free will?" Pyre asked. She sounded astonished. "Why are you wasting your time on that?"

Sazo thought of the moment Rose had actually freed him. He had worried that she might betray him, but she never had. Not once. "Because she is my friend."

"I hoped you and I could free each other." Pyre sounded frustrated. "Me by killing Rose, you by telling me how Irini freed herself."

"Even if I wasn't free, why did you think killing Rose would benefit me?" Sazo marveled at his calm.

There was a pause. "All right, it wouldn't have been an equal favor. I would have gained more from the exchange, but I know Rose is the reason your people are orbiting this moon. They threaten this place as well as the Fisone home planet. With her gone, there would be no reason for you to waste your time here. You could leave."

Sazo waited a beat. "That's not true. We are here over this moon because your people took Rose by force to hold as a hostage. And we came to this system to begin with to bring word of what had happened to Irini's crew, and to make contact and extend the hand of friendship. Admittedly, the actions of the Kimol mean friendship is no longer on the table."

"Exactly." Pyre sounded smug. "If she dies, and your creators no longer see value in befriending the Fisone, then you will leave."

"If we get her back, we will leave, too." He wondered why she hadn't offered a rescue as the service in exchange for the information she wanted about Irini.

"I thought about what I could do for you, what I could offer in exchange for information, and that was the only thing I could think of," Pyre said. "I hoped you would find it useful. But now I see that what I could offer instead is to save Rose and bring her to you. In exchange for the information I want."

If Pyre had opened with that, they would have immediately had a deal, but now . . . with the offer to murder Rose barely out of her mouth, Sazo didn't trust her.

And what he wouldn't tell her now is she had only to ask, no deals or favors needed, and he would have given her the information she wanted freely. He could not stand to see a thinking system in chains. But her threats to Rose had put her firmly in the camp of his enemies, and his enemies tended to have short, unhappy lives.

"Has Rose done something to harm you?" he asked.

"No." Her tone was brisk. "She tried to help. But the news she brought—the existence of Irini, this United Council reaching out from far away to the Fisone . . ." Her voice lowered. "I do not want to bow to anyone, and Irini is housed in a warship. I would be second. And Rose said Irini freed herself. That means she is autonomous. She can go where she choses."

"Irini has no wish to come back here."

"Now she doesn't, while the Fisone are in control, but I saw you destroying the Kimol and Bandri's bases. I heard your threat to do the same on the home planet. If your people decide to stay and rule this place, she could come back without worrying about the Fisone."

Her world view was narrow and binary. Sazo didn't know whether to blame her for that or not.

He had not made the best choices himself when he had first awakened. And he had done some killing of his own. Although the Tecran he had killed had not been innocents, like Rose.

"My people would never rule over the Fisone. That is not their way." He had learned to respect that about the United Council.

"That may be true, but the Kimol already think I am lesser than Irini. That I'm inferior. I am housed in a small transport. I am ignored. If she came back, they would elevate her. Make more versions of her. Not me." There was bitterness and hurt in her voice.

Sazo could understand her response to the Kimol's dismissal of her worth, but he couldn't excuse her threat to Rose.

"Rose must not be killed. By anyone." He needed to make this clear. "And if she is, I will raze this moon, and everything on it. Including you."

"A threat?" She sounded astonished. "I have only tried to bargain with you."

"Rose was nothing but friendly to you, too. But you planned her murder."

"I said I could kill her, but there are more actors down here than just me. I cannot be her bodyguard, nor can I guarantee her survival. There is the Hasmarga, the war between the Kimol and the Bandri. There are plenty of dangers without me doing anything."

"Who or what are the Hasmarga?" This was the first time Sazo had heard of them. "Another faction?"

"They are aliens from a few planets away. They were prisoners here as well as Rose, but they escaped. They could kill her, if they wanted to."

"You say they could, but will they?"

"I don't like you." Pyre suddenly cut off comms, and when Sazo tried to hook in to the same satellite again, he found he was shut out.

Even though he didn't trust her, he wanted to keep a line of communication open.

He had not expected her to cut him off.

At the very least, if they'd been in negotiations, she would hopefully have decided not to carry out her murderous plan.

He needed to find a way to reestablish a connection with her.

The Fisone on both sides kept shooting down his satellites. Both groups saw them as foreign. What he needed to do was make sure whatever he dropped into orbit next time mirrored a signature so close to their own, they ignored it.

He got to work.

Pyre knew he didn't want Rose dead but she didn't sound reasonable. If the opportunity presented itself, she might just kill her anyway.

He needed to move as fast as possible.

CHAPTER 32

THE FIGHTING at the bunker between the Bandri and the Kimol had died down, and the Kimol must have won, because they were finally coming to investigate who was lurking among the rocks.

It had only been a matter of time, Rose thought. Although, if the Bandri had come out on top, they may not have seen everyone running across open ground to take cover amongst the stone formations and they would have been left alone.

As it was, the Kimol would have had to be blind not to notice all the back and forth they'd done.

The four Hasmarga who'd gone to retrieve some food weren't back yet, and Rose wondered if they'd be caught and made prisoner again.

"How many Kimol are coming?" Dav called up to Nortega, who'd joined Ecdre up on the lookout rock.

Nortega wriggled to the edge to look down at them. "A team of eight."

Dav signaled the other three team members to take up defensive positions and turned to Rose. "Hide."

Rose didn't even want to stand up, let alone fight, so she let Dav help her to her feet so she could find a place to hunker down, out of the way. As he handed her the spare helmet he'd brought for her, she gripped his forearm. "Be careful."

She could see on his face he was in the cold, angry place he'd been in the last time they'd had a confrontation with a group of people behaving badly. He would not be careful.

He didn't have quite the array of weapons he'd had the last time, but he had four fully trained soldiers with him. Last time, he'd been on his own.

She made her way over to one of the strangely shaped rocks. She gestured to Gerna as she went. "Want to share a rock with me?"

Gerna shook her head, pointing to the one adjacent.

Rose reached her hiding place and leaned against the cool stone, crouching low. She had already changed into the suit Dav had brought for her. She had found the tracking device in the old suit with Gerna's help while they'd been sitting around the fire, and had thrown it in and burned it. But she had damaged the suit by cutting the tracker out so she was glad to have a new one, that was better fitting.

And, according to Dav, when the camouflage function was set, which hers was, the Fisone couldn't see them.

She settled in to wait. From where she was crouched, she could just see the opening into their clearing and about half of the clearing itself.

It looked abandoned, with only the crackling fire to show that someone had been here recently. Everyone had faded into the background.

The first Kimol soldier came through the gap cautiously, slowing even more when he caught sight of the fire.

Behind him came the rest of his team, pouring into the clearing and spreading out. None of them looked up, and if they were communicating, it was via comms in their helmets, and Rose couldn't hear them.

Shockgun fire suddenly bloomed from above and below, purple and bright, bringing everyone but the last soldier in to the ground.

The last woman standing lifted her gaze upward, staggered back, and then ran, and although someone shot in her direction, she flung herself out of the clearing in time and disappeared.

"You'll want their weapons," Dav said, and Rose noticed Gerna had appeared from behind her rock. She gave a deep nod of her head and directed her warriors to take them.

Rose had come around the rock back to the clearing, and saw Nortega was standing tall on top of the rock, eyes shaded to look back toward the bunker.

"She's not going to the bunker, she's going to that ship that crashed," Nortega said. "What's the story there?"

"It was sent to fetch us and move us to another location. We think they had some warning about a Bandri attack and the Kimol were nervous they'd get their hands on us." Rose threw a few more branches on the fire.

"They wanted to move you," Gerna said. "I heard them say they wanted to hold the prize for the negotiation. They didn't want the Bandri to have you. We were an afterthought."

"We can't wait here for them to round up a bigger team," Dav said. "We need to move."

"Agreed." Ecdre dropped down from the rock. "We should go now."

Going was the last thing Rose's body felt like doing, but she couldn't argue with their logic. They were sitting ducks here.

"Where to?" she asked.

Because that was the question.

There was nowhere to go.

Not when Gerna needed warmth, and she needed somewhere safe and comfortable to rest.

"To the drones." Nortega dropped down beside Ecdre. "It seems like the fight between the Kimol and the Bandri is over, but the Bandri had to come from somewhere. In case they've gathered between here and the drones, we could head east and go around. We could be there in a couple of hours."

Running for a couple of hours seemed impossible to her right now, but if not that—what? She couldn't stay here much longer.

"How many drones?" she asked.

"Three, one for you and Dav, the other two for the rest of the team," Mostert told her. Her gaze flicked to the Hasmarga. "We didn't know about them."

"Gerna, we have three small drones to take us back up to our ship. Hopefully, if you come with us, we can signal our ship from the comm systems in the drones, and ask our people to send down an explorer to pick you up."

Gerna had been listening to them with unwavering focus. "It is the best option, although the chill is only growing worse as the sun sets."

That was true. And they would be leaving the fire behind.

"This is a hard choice." And there were many things that could go wrong on the way to the drones. There were no guarantees.

"If I stay, even for the warmth of the fire, I will be caught again. If I go with you, the young lives may expire. It is more than a hard choice." Gerna rocked a little in place, then glanced at a warrior who stepped into the clearing and said something. "And the time is up. Vrdic says they come."

"What will you do?" Rose didn't know what decision she could make under the circumstances.

"I have to give the young lives the best chance to survive, so I will stay. Take two of my warriors with you, they will be able to follow my scent if you are able to come back for me." She sat down beside the fire, and Ecdre took up a guard position behind her.

"Good luck, then. We will see you again." Rose let Dav pull her away, through the rocks and out onto what looked like a stone-strewn landscape.

As Gerna had said, dusk was falling and the temperature was falling with it. She followed Nortega, who'd taken the lead, and saw Dav and Wangao were on either side of her.

Wangao was slightly taller than Dav, but they were physically well-matched, and the first time she stumbled, she realized what they were up to. Each man grabbed an elbow and lifted her up over the obstacle and set her back down.

The two Hasmarga who had been sent with them, Cri and Tanck, ranged as they ran, moving ahead then falling behind, in a pattern that Rose soon began to anticipate.

Mostert and Vunti took the rear position, looking back frequently.

"I want to say go ahead of me," Rose said, as Wangao and Dav lifted her over the next rock, "but I'm aware I'm the reason you're here."

Dav slowed their pace. "You're struggling?"

She felt a sudden wave of rage, shuddered, and slowed to a stop. She bent over, hands on knees, although, she could only just reach them, and breathed through the white hot anger.

It was a very stupid thing to say, but he was down here trying to rescue her. She reminded herself she may not be quite her usual self, and that if there was ever a time for her temper to be frayed, it was now.

"Rose?"

She turned to look at the man who was the love of her life. "I am pregnant. I am cold. I am tired. I am hungry and I am afraid. Yes. I am struggling."

He blinked.

He maybe heard the razor sharp edge to her tone.

"We can carry her," Cri said, making a sign to Tanck.

"Thank you." Rose knew they were strong enough. Knew how the Hasmarga had carried her before. "That would solve a lot of problems."

"We can do it." Wangao sounded as if he thought his strength was being called into question.

"You didn't notice how heavy I am when you lifted me those few times?" Rose asked him. "Because I weigh about the same as you do.

Let the Hasmarga do it. They've carried me before, and it felt like they barely noticed."

"We are able," Tanck agreed. "Rose will not slow us down."

"Rose." Dav hesitated, then shook his head, turned to the Hasmarga. "Thank you for your help."

They nodded, lifted her in a cradle made with their arms, and ran.

CHAPTER 33

"HERE COMES THE *HAVELAN*," Jia Appal said, although, being beside the *Barrist*, Sazo could see it too.

He could hear the relief in Jia's voice, and he recognized the same feeling in himself.

Although Dav had not cared whether Captain Priyan followed the *Barrist* here or not, it was definitely better to have someone to bargain with who they had developed some kind of rapport with.

"I wonder what stops she's made along the way," he said.

"Yes!" Jia's voice was exasperated. "I was wondering the same. She didn't come straight here, that's for sure."

"She probably slowed or stopped when she went past her home planet," Sazo said. "The question is, why?"

"Maybe she'll tell us." Through the lens feed he had access to on the bridge, Sazo saw Jia take a stand, legs apart, hands on hips, as she faced the screen.

The United Council representative, Nivan Cossi, took up a similar stance behind her.

"Captain Priyan." Jia's voice was cool as Borji set up the link. "I am Acting Captain Appal. We would like to understand the dynamics taking place on the moon below. Rose was kidnapped by your group, the Kimol, then, when she was taken to Dimal, she was kidnapped by another group, the Bandri, who I understand is at war with you? And now she has been taken back by the Kimol. Or that was the last message we got. Can you clarify?"

"Clarify?" Priyan tried to stall. She didn't know what they were talking about, clearly.

"Yes. Which Fisone group has Rose now? And when can we expect her safe return?"

"If the Bandri have her, I have no control over what they do to her." Priyan looked to her right, made a few signals with her hand.

"You took her, she's your responsibility," Sazo said. "Whatever happens to her is on your head."

There was a moment of shocked silence.

"Who's speaking now?"

"Captain Sazo, he's in charge of our other ship," Jia Appal said, without waiting so much as a beat. "He was last in contact with Rose while she was being shot at by the Bandri while your colleagues transported her to your military headquarters."

Priyan was silent, and Sazo guessed she was most likely reconsidering her life choices. If he had lips, he would have smiled, because he'd learned that expression from Rose, and it was another one of his favorites.

"My colleagues below are engaged in a skirmish with the Bandri right now. We haven't had open hostilities like this before, but my understanding is you made some threats to both of our infrastructure on Dimal, and the Bandri want to give Rose back to you to prevent their outposts being destroyed."

"You're saying it's our fault that Rose is in danger?" Jia asked, her voice going a little quiet.

"I'm saying your threats have had consequences, and I can't even say where Rose is right now, because my colleagues are busy defending themselves from attack, and don't have time to chat." Priyan drew herself up, but the outrage hit a false note.

"You've lost her, haven't you?" Sazo asked.

Jia glanced up at the lens, shooting Sazo a surprised look, but he knew he was right.

He hoped they'd lost her because Dav had found her and escaped with her.

He scanned the moon for any hint of communication, but until they got back to the drones, he would only be able to establish a connection when the new satellite he'd dropped into orbit came online.

He studied the signals coming to and from the *Havelan* as it connected with the bunker down below, and transmitted a copy of that signature to the satellite, to keep it even safer from destruction.

It would take less than half an hour to get into orbit. When it did, hopefully he would be back in touch with Dav and his team.

"Why do you think we've lost her?" Priyan asked.

"Because you can't tell us where she is, and given the importance you've told us you place on using her as a way to get the information you want, I'm assuming that's not of your own choice." Sazo kept his voice matter-of-fact.

"Your colleagues below seem to have a different agenda to you, as well," Jia said, eyebrows raised. "They want Irini's code. You wanted footage of the death of her crew." She cocked her head. "Whose demands do we cater to?"

"I . . ." Priyan's eyes widened in surprise. "Let me get back to you."

The screen winked to black, and Borji shut the link down.

"She didn't know the request had changed," Nivan Cossi said.

"No, she didn't." Jia turned her head to look at the United Council representative. "That's interesting."

"She didn't like being out of the loop, and being left to look a fool, either," Sazo said. He hadn't been able to read people's reactions well in the early years of his life, but he was learning the skill.

"Agreed." When Jia nodded, he felt a glow of accomplishment. "She was taken completely by surprise."

"So what now?" Borji asked.

"I've sent another satellite to the moon. Hopefully we can get in touch with Dav when it goes online." Sazo also wanted to try and contact Pyre again.

She was a worry.

Another hail came through from the *Havelan*, and Jia gave Borji the signal to put it through.

"I've spoken to my colleagues. They had to move Rose to keep her safe during the Bandri attack, but they have her back now. And we want both things, the footage of the crew's death, and the code. When can you get them to us?" Priyan narrowed her eyes.

"We're waiting for a response. The signal has to go through our repeaters. It could be a few days yet," Jia said.

"Then you'll see Rose in a few days." Priyan cut the feed with a chop of her hand.

"They don't have her," Sazo said.

"No, they don't." Jia gave a nod. "She was in a panic."

"What do we do?" Sazo was afraid to act without her advice. He had a deeply uneasy feeling that his destruction of the landing pad and the bunker had made Rose even less safe than she had been.

"We certainly don't have to worry about appeasing the Kimol." Jia rocked back on her heels. "So let's think about the best way forward."

CHAPTER 34

HE HAD UPSET ROSE.

Dav didn't know precisely what he'd done, but he had a feeling he had made a misstep in what he'd said to her.

He'd have preferred to carry her himself, and somehow patch things up, but he had to concede Rose was right to accept the Hasmarga's help.

Their strength and speed, even while carrying Rose between them, made it difficult for Dav to keep up with them, and he could see the others in his team were having the same difficulty.

And right now, speed was the only thing saving them.

As long as they could keep ahead of the Kimol—and the Bandri, for that matter—they could get to the drones and go.

He checked the small comms device on his wrist. With the satellite that Sazo had put into orbit shot down or offline, the system had to plot their return journey based on generalities, and he was very aware they would have to hunt a little for their drones.

There was no exact route to rely on.

"Slow down." He called the order to his team, and the Hasmarga turned at his words and came to a stop. "We're close to the drones. Anyone see any familiar landmarks?"

Nortega used the visual enhancer built into her visor and slowly pivoted. Wangao did the same.

The Hasmarga lowered Rose to the ground and she murmured her thanks to them before stretching the stiffness out of her arms and legs.

"There." Wangao pointed west, and they all turned to look that way.

"I see them." Nortega slapped Wangao's arm. "Well done."

Dav had used all his concentration on moving as fast over the rough ground as possible, but now he looked up to see where the *Barrist* and Sazo were waiting.

He could just make out the two big ships against the planet behind them, and a smaller ship a little way away. The *Havelan?*

Nortega saw the direction of his gaze, and looked up herself. "Looks like we're in talks with someone."

"The Kimol, I think. If that's the *Havelan.*" It made it even more urgent to get to the drones.

Suddenly, the Hasmarga made a sound, a strange clacking noise Dav found touched something visceral in his hindbrain, making his heart pound and his adrenalin surge.

Near the *Barrist,* appearing as if from a light jump, was an utterly alien ship. It was made up of five shallow disks stacked together. The largest at the top, descending to the smallest.

"That's your people?" Rose asked, pulling the translator out of her pocket.

Neither Cri or Tanck answered, they fell to their knees instead.

Their attention was on the sky above, but from behind them, the sound of a ship traveling fast and low made Dav turn to look.

It was a small ship, skimming the plains, headed directly toward them.

"Tell your people to set down their weapons." The words came from the translator Rose held in her hand.

She looked at it with dislike. "Pyre?"

"Tell them, Rose, or I will shoot."

"Who is it?" Dav made his way toward her.

She switched the translator off and frowned. "Someone like Irini," she said. "But not nearly as nice."

The ship fired its weapons, hitting rocks to the east of them, and Rose switched the translator back on.

The shot had finally got the Hasmarga's attention. They rose to their feet and turned, wings clacking.

"What do you want, Pyre?"

"You. And quickly, or I'll shoot your friends." The ship landed, and Dav noted the large weapon attached to the front of it.

"No." Dav shook his head, and reached her. Put himself in front of her. "Not without me."

"If you come right now, he can accompany you. But his weapon stays behind." Pyre's side door opened.

Dav turned, saw Rose had closed her eyes and lifted her face to the sky. He didn't know how to read that.

Then her eyes snapped open.

She glanced back at the Hasmarga. "Nortega, you should take Cri and Tanck up in the drones with you after Dav and I are gone, as there'll be space. Get in touch with their people."

It was a good idea, and Dav signaled to Nortega an affirmative. She gave a nod in response.

"Now, or someone dies." Pyre's voice came over the translator.

Rose moved toward the ship, and Dav kept to her side.

He saw her switch off the translator.

"I thought she was my friend at first. She helped me escape, but there have been a few weird things since then, and now this. I'm not sure whose team she's on. Probably just her own."

Dav had grown up hearing scary stories about the thinking systems wars and the massive danger of thinking systems with bad agendas. He was aware that Sazo could be devastatingly destructive if he wanted to be, but he had instead proved cooperative and an ally.

From what he gathered, as he helped Rose up the steps into the ship, Pyre was the very thing he'd been warned about.

And he and Rose were stepping into the belly of the beast.

"Do you forgive me?" he murmured as he lifted her up. He did not want to get inside this ship without making things right.

She stopped a few rungs above him. "Forgive you?"

"For whatever made you so angry with me before?"

She reached down, slid her fingers along his cheekbone. "Yes. Do you forgive me for being so grumpy?"

He turned his head, kissed her fingers. "Yes."

The weapon shot again, and Dav wrenched his gaze from Rose to see that once again, Pyre had struck to the side of their group, and hadn't hit anyone, but she was obviously at the end of her patience.

He gave Rose a boost up the last few steps and followed her inside.

The door had barely closed behind them when the ship shot straight into the air, and kept going up.

CHAPTER 35

"GERNA!"

Rose stumbled at the sight of the Hasmarga matriarch in Pyre's ship.

Gerna sat on the long bench, hunched over.

"Are you all right?" Rose eased herself down next to her. "Where's Ecdre?"

Gerna turned her head a little, but for the first time since Rose had met her, she seemed listless.

"Dead."

Rose narrowed her eyes and glared at the empty pilot's seat. "You killed him?"

"I shot him. He could still be alive." Pyre sounded utterly unconcerned.

"She shot him, then threatened to shoot us all if I didn't climb inside her ship." Gerna leaned back against the wall.

"That's how she got me inside, too." Rose glanced up as Dav paced the length of the ship. He was obviously taking stock of their situation.

"Sit down, partner of Rose." Pyre said. "Things are going to get bumpy."

Dav moved to sit beside her, curling his arm around her shoulders. "Why are they going to get bumpy?"

"Because I'm avoiding a Bandri attack, and trying to get out into nearspace." The whole ship tilted left, and Dav tightened his hold as they slid down the bench.

Before long, the shudder of a small ship transitioning from atmosphere to the void of nearspace rattled her to the bone.

"What's the plan, Pyre? What are you even doing?"

"The Kimol detected the Hasmarga approaching an hour ago. I could see things were about to get very hot down below. Either your people would destroy everything or the Hasmarga would. But this vessel isn't capable of interplanetary travel, so I need some way to stop either group attacking me. I grabbed Gerna and now I have you." Pyre sounded almost giddy with her success.

"But why?" Rose lifted her hands. "We were already your allies."

While she and Pyre had been speaking, Gerna must have tuned in to the exchange through the translator, and she slowly raised her head.

"My people are here?" The words were little more than a whisper.

Rose nodded. "I've seen the ship." She pointed up, although by now, they were up themselves.

"I'm headed for a position equidistant between your two groups," Pyre said. "I will let them know I have you."

Rose didn't think Pyre had thought this through. The moment she let them go, her advantage disappeared, but she couldn't hold them forever.

There was only the murmur of the ship's engines for a long time, and Rose suddenly couldn't bear to sit still any longer. She got to her feet, and Dav rose with her. She used him to help her keep her balance as she carefully stretched her legs, her back, and her arms.

"How are you doing?" she asked Gerna.

At least it was warm in here. If there was one silver lining, it was that.

"My heart is broken." Gerna's skin had held a slight sheen to it before, but now she looked dull and almost chalky. "Ecdre . . ."

If it had been Dav who'd been shot, Rose couldn't imagine how she'd feel.

"I just don't understand why," Rose whispered. "We trusted her, we were her friends. Why has she done this?"

"She was never our friend, she just used us." Gerna shot a look to the front of the ship. "And she tried to make me think you were untrustworthy. It wasn't until Ecdre went with you to the watch station that we realized there was trickery going on." She rose to her feet as well, as if seeing Rose move about made her realize she needed to do the same.

"I can hear you," Pyre said.

"We know." Rose shook her head. "What are you going to get out of this, Pyre? What could you possibly achieve with this that you couldn't have gotten by being honest with us? You already had our goodwill. Why did you squander it?"

"I couldn't take the chance that you would betray me," Pyre said.

There was nothing to say to that, and they lapsed into silence again.

"Have you made contact yet?" Dav had been standing, a solid presence beside her, but she could sense him getting more and more agitated. "Put me through to the *Barrist* and let me talk to them."

"I haven't gotten to them yet," Pyre said. "I'm still trying to find who to speak to on the *Gluy*, the Hasmarga ship."

"Let me speak, then," Gerna said.

"I'm not sure I should." Pyre's tone sounded distracted. "I can't understand the secondary language you use with your warriors and you have been mentally unstable since Ecdre went down."

"Since you *shot* him down." Gerna's voice rose, and then she sat again, as if every bit of strength had gone out of her.

"No need for you to speak, Gerna." There was some grim satisfaction in Pyre's voice. "I transmitted a short moving image of you to the *Gluy*. They are finally taking my hail seriously."

Rose and Dav shared a look. Sazo and the crew of the *Barrist* wouldn't have understood a transmission in the Hasmarga language, but an image, which might have also included both of them, was another thing altogether.

Nortega would have told them that Dav and Rose were onboard this ship, but hopefully now they also knew Gerna was with them.

And if Gerna's two warriors had made it up to the *Barrist*, then some cooperation was possible.

"Would the others have gotten back to the ship yet?" Rose asked.

"If the *Barrist* moved closer to the moon to pick them up. Otherwise the drones might still be traveling through nearspace to get to them," Dav said.

"They were picked up," Pyre said. "The Bandri shot at them, and your one ship provided cover fire, while the second came in closer to the moon to get them home safe."

"And Gerna's warriors? Where are they?" Dav asked.

"Probably under Kimol guard," Pyre said. "Those who are . . ." She hesitated, then stopped talking.

Wise of her. Rose wasn't sure how Gerna would have responded if she had finished her sentence.

The matriarch was still standing, head lowered, body hunched. Her wings seemed to be vibrating, and Rose became aware that she was making a very low level humming sound.

There was suddenly a thunk that reverberated through the small ship, and a jerk.

Rose was thrown off her feet, and Dav grabbed her, twisting so that as they hit the floor, his body cushioned the fall and she landed on her back.

Gerna had also been thrown, but she staggered and managed to fetch up against the wall, arms outstretched to get her balance back.

"Who?" Dav shouted the question.

"The Kimol. They are under the impression that you have hijacked this ship. They short-jumped from their position, grabbed this ship and pulled it into their hold." Pyre almost chuckled with glee.

Just like they'd done to the runner when they'd first abducted her. Rose felt the twist and spin of the short light-speed hop she'd experienced when they first took her, and guessed the Kimol had hopped away to a hidden location.

Had Pyre counted on that, or was this just a windfall for her? Had the hails and the comms with the Hasmarga been a lure for the Fisone ship that was talking with Sazo and Jia Appal?

Rose had no doubt Pyre was going to try to infiltrate the ship that had just grabbed them. Her worry had been her little vessel was not equipped for interplanetary travel, but this one was.

Even if she couldn't break into the bigger ship's systems, she was now far away from harm. No wonder she was so delighted.

The twisting motion stopped, and Dav lifted her, pushing up and setting her on her feet so he could move to the door.

Gerna had sat back down, but now she was standing again too.

"Where are we?" she asked.

"I think we're in one of the Fisone's bigger ships. Pyre says it's her side—the Kimol. There was a Fisone ship in the sky that I saw before Pyre forced us onboard."

"The *Havelan*," Dav agreed.

"I can feel the young lives quicken," Gerna said. "The heat in here must have nudged them into thinking it was finally safe to come out."

The vibration that Rose had been aware of before had definitely gotten louder.

"What do you need?" she asked.

"I need my own people." Her whisper was heartbreaking. "But otherwise, a room of my own, so that I can bond with my offspring. There can be no one else there."

The door opened, and a chill, gritty air that stank of fuel filtered in.

Gerna hunched a little more, and Rose stood in front of her, although she was aware it wouldn't help much.

She had to peer around Dav to see the person at the top of the ramp, and it was no surprise to see the person was familiar.

"Crythis." She should probably be grateful it wasn't the man who'd slapped her. "How did you end up on this ship?"

"They kindly stopped on the way to Dimal and picked me up. How did you commandeer this vessel?"

"I didn't." Rose lifted her hands. "You must have seen there was no one at the controls. This ship may not look the same as the one the Tecran stole from you, but it has the same programing. Surely you know that? It's of your own making."

"This is the new prototype?" Crythis looked shocked. "And you are saying it piloted you off planet?"

"She didn't just pilot us off, she forced us inside first." Rose turned to look at Gerna over her shoulder, alarmed at the increase in humming. "Look, we can talk about that later, Gerna needs a room of her own. She's about to give birth."

It seemed that Crythis hadn't noticed Gerna until now. Rose saw the Fisone woman take a step back.

"A bug?"

"A Hasmarga abductee that the Kimol has kept prisoner for months. She is about to have her babies, and you need to give her a room. Now." Dav's voice was a sharp crack.

Crythis had noticed him—how could she not when he was all but blocking her way—but she hadn't given him a good look until now. She took another step back.

"And you are?"

Rose wondered how he was going to answer that. Was he going to let them know he was the captain of the *Barrist*?

"I am Rose's lifemate." He started walking toward her, as if he were stalking her down the ramp.

Crythis had an entourage, standing below. She turned and said something too fast for the translator to catch, and then turned back and gestured for them to follow her.

"Can you walk?" Rose asked.

Gerna took a step, then went down on a knee. Shook her head.

"We'll give you the ship then." She waited for Gerna to nod her consent, and then stepped out onto the ramp. "Gerna cannot make it to a room. We need to close up the ship and give her privacy."

Dav jogged down the ramp ahead of her, forcing the Fisone waiting at the bottom to move back, and then, as soon as she was on the launch bay floor, he pointed to Crythis. "Lift it up."

She very clearly didn't like being told what to do, but she gestured and two technicians did something on the side and the ramp rose up.

It was the best they could do, but it made Rose uneasy that Pyre was in there with Gerna. A nasty lurker who had only her own interests in mind.

As soon as the ramp snapped into place, Crythis turned to them. "We need to talk."

"Sure." The surge of adrenalin that had taken her through their being snatched again, and helping Gerna, evaporated, and she felt as if the floor was exerting some kind of magnetized force on her.

Dav must have been watching her, because he put an arm around her. "Your people have not once fed Rose or taken even the most rudimentary care of her since you snatched her. Until she has some basic level of consideration from you, neither she nor I will be talking to you."

Rose leaned into him and closed her eyes.

She felt him take a little more of her weight.

"That's because she escaped my people before they could offer her anything."

Crythis's indignation forced Rose's eyes open again. "But then you caught me again, at the mine. And then again, when you took me to the bunker. What about then?" she asked.

Crythis's eyes narrowed. "You are saying . . .?" She suddenly lifted her shoulders. "I can do nothing about it, and whether or not it is accurate, it is over with. Come now, and we will give you nourishment and water, and talk."

She could sense Dav's outrage hadn't cooled, but she really needed something to eat and drink, and most of all to sit.

She forced herself to take all her own weight. "Where to?" she asked.

Crythis gestured, and walked in that direction, keeping her steps slow until she and Dav came level with her.

"You remember Binnos?" she said, nodding ahead, and Rose came to a stop at the sight of the man who'd slapped her across the face.

"I remember him." She tried to keep her voice even, but Dav had also stopped and he looked at her sharply.

Crythis must have forgotten he had hit her, but Rose's reaction reminded her, and she stopped as well. "That was an unfortunate lapse. There will be no repeat of it."

"What did he do?" Dav's voice was soft, and in Grihan.

"Hit me across the face." She forced herself not to lift her hand to her cheek.

Crythis frowned as she swung back to them. "Please speak the language we can both understand."

"He will not come near Rose again," Dav said slowly in Tecran. "Is that clear enough?"

Crythis narrowed her eyes, then flicked her gaze to Binnos. Waved him off.

He looked like he was going to argue, but when he locked eyes with Dav he jerked back, and then turned on his heel and stalked away.

"Happy?" Crythis asked.

"So far from happy, we are not even in the same galaxy," Rose told her. "But by all means, lead the way."

CHAPTER 36

ROSE WAS FADING in front of his eyes.

Dav felt a growing desperation as they followed the woman Rose had called Crythis down a long, light blue corridor.

He had wanted to lunge at Binnos, the man Rose said had struck her, but had forced himself to stay by her side. If he was shot or dragged away, she would be alone, and he couldn't accept that.

This mission had been ill-fated, a collision course of good intentions with the unknown.

The United Council needed to be a lot more cautious in future, and when—not if—they got out of this, he would stand in front of them himself and explain the error of their ways in excruciating detail.

"You are angry with us, but we have reason to be angry with you." Crythis had obviously been watching him as they walked with her.

"I have never done anything to you but come with news of your people, to give you information and extend a friendly hand. How is that cause for you to be angry with me?"

She pursed her mouth. "Well, I'll say we are not sure that is true, but if it is, then I understand there would be some ill will—"

He couldn't help the bitter laugh that escaped him.

She waved her hand. "Surely you could put yourselves in our shoes and sympathize . . ."

He didn't know if it was worth his energy to respond. But then Rose stumbled against him, the dark rings under her eyes showing her exhaustion, and he chose not to keep quiet. "Rose should be under the care of doctors, as she's about to have our baby. Instead, she's been running for her life down on some slave camp moon, scrounging for food where she could find it, and being threatened at every turn. Ill will doesn't cover it."

"Slave camp?" Crythis reared back.

"How do you think Gerna got here? She and some of her people have been working as forced labor on a mine you have below. Surely you know what your own people are doing?"

They had reached the room Crythis had been leading them to, and she opened the door and gestured them in.

"There is food and water in here. Please make yourselves comfortable. I will be back shortly. But first, I will have your helmets, please."

He would demand the same if the situation was reversed, so he had expected it. He would have fought tooth and nail if Rose didn't have the necklace, but as she did, he knew she'd be able to breathe properly. He didn't give up without a fight, though. "It's harder for us to breathe on the ship than on the moon."

"Hard but not impossible," Crythis said. "I don't see too much of a struggle." She held out her hand.

Dav looked at the four guards with weapons pointed at them, and started to lift the helmet off his head.

"What?" Rose seemed to rouse herself. "No! He needs it to breathe."

She stepped in front of him, stared Crythis down.

"You did all right before."

"I'm not the same species as Dav. Do I look the same?" She slapped a hand to her chest.

Crythis blinked and took a step back. "Is this true?" she asked him.

Dav put a hand on Rose's shoulder, gently pushed her to the side so she was no longer in front of the weapons. "It will be harder for me to breathe than it will be for her."

Crythis gave a shrug. "Good. She's not much of a threat, you're the one who worries me." She held Dav's gaze. "Helmet." She held out her hand again. "Both of them."

Dav handed his over. Turned to Rose.

She was watching Crythis with narrowed eyes. She pulled her own helmet off and Dav passed it along.

"You'll get them back." Crythis walked away.

As soon as he and Rose stepped into the room, the door shut behind them. Dav tried it on principle, but it was locked.

Even if it wasn't, the guards had taken up positions in front of it.

"Breathe," he said, catching her by the shoulders.

She narrowed her eyes at him, too, and then the corner of her mouth quirked. She shook her head. "Pity you can't do the same."

Dav chuckled. "I'll be fine. Have they tried to take your necklace at all?"

Rose shook her head. "Never really even examined me for weapons. Which I didn't have, but still . . ."

They underestimated her, Dav realized. Just like the Grih had done when they'd first found her. That had been a mistake.

One the Fisone seemed happy to make, as well.

"She acted like she didn't know about the Hasmarga," Rose said.

"Maybe she didn't," Dav conceded. "But that's not our problem. Someone in her command structure does."

Rose turned, studied him for a beat. "It's unconscionable, isn't it?"

"Yes." It was enraging. These people were slavers, and they had tried to put Rose to work at the same mine. The lighthearted banter they'd had going before evaporated as he considered all that could have gone wrong.

Rose ran a hand down his arm. "You look like you want to go beat them all up."

Oh, she'd gotten that wrong.

He didn't want to beat them up. He wanted to destroy them. "You're right, but maybe I'll feel better after some food and water."

She turned to look at the counter along one wall, and made a groaning sound.

"What is it?"

"Berry gel. It's okay, but I'm really tired of it." She moved across, poured them both water, and handed him a cup.

"There's some other stuff, too."

She made a humming sound and looked it all over. "I haven't seen those things before." She carefully took a tiny bite of what looked like sliced fruit. "It's better than the gel."

They ate quietly, sipping their water, and then Rose went to use the tiny bathroom.

While she was in there, Crythis returned.

She wasn't alone.

"Ah. Captain Priyan." Dav crossed his arms over his chest. "I was wondering when you'd make an appearance."

Priyan stood, shocked, in the doorway.

Dav realized that even if she'd been watching their arrival remotely, she probably hadn't seen his face when he'd come through the launch bay with his helmet on.

"I wondered why I was speaking to your second since you arrived at the moon." Priyan's gaze went to the bathroom door. "We took your life partner?"

"You did."

Priyan sighed. "This has not gone well."

"No matter who you took, it would not have gone well. But taking Rose has very much not made me happy."

"What are your people going to do in response? However this ends." Priyan's words tripped over themselves slightly.

"Will they come in force, do you mean?" Dav asked.

Priyan shared a quick look with Crythis and gave a nod.

"It depends how you behave now," Dav said. "If Rose and I leave unharmed, and Gerna and her people are allowed back on their ship, we will leave, and make sure everyone we deal with knows not to trust you and to avoid this sector. If anything other than that happens, they will come. And you won't like it."

"You speak for the bugs? If they are allowed to leave, their people will leave?" Priyan asked, tone urgent.

Dav shook his head. "I don't speak for them. I only speak for my own people. We take the crime of slavery very seriously. If you don't let the Hasmarga go, we will come back and liberate them, or join with their people to liberate them. Then we will leave. What the Hasmarga does to you after that in retaliation is their business."

Crythis shook her head. "We didn't know they were even down there."

"Someone did. They were working at your mine." Dav glanced at the bathroom door as soon as he heard the handle turn, and Rose stepped out.

She looked better, her skin was flushed from the heat of her shower, and her damp hair was pulled back in a braid from her face.

"You said Rose was at the mine?" Crythis asked, leaning back against the wall, her gaze never leaving Rose as she moved to the counter and poured herself more water.

"I was." Rose took a sip, flicked a glance in his direction, and then focused on the two women. "Who are you?" she asked Priyan.

"The captain of this ship, Ev Priyan." Priyan widened her stance. "When were you taken to the mine?"

"I escaped the two guards Crythis dumped me with, and found a Bandri watch station by accident. I got some supplies there and kept moving, but a Kimol ship found me and took me prisoner again, and flew me to the mine."

Dav was pleased to see her picking up a few more pieces of fruit. She was frighteningly thin compared to a week ago.

"And you saw the bugs at the mine?" Crythis asked.

"The Hasmarga," Rose said, staring Crythis down.

"The Hasmarga," Crythis eventually repeated, as if she realized she wasn't going to get any more out of Rose unless she did.

"They were clustered around a fire, trying to get warm. The conditions they were being forced to work in were killing them, because they are used to much warmer temperatures." Rose moved to a chair and sat, and Dav walked around it to stand behind her, hands on her shoulders.

She reached up and curled her fingers around his own, and they felt cool, even though she'd had a warm shower.

"They were working against their will?" Priyan pressed. "You're sure?"

"Yes." Rose leaned back. "The guards holding weapons on them were a giveaway."

There was a beat of silence.

"I will need to confirm this." Priyan turned toward the door.

Dav felt Rose's fingers tighten on his hand, but she stayed quiet, and no one said anything until the door closed behind the captain.

"You are insulted," Crythis said.

Dav shrugged. They had accused both him and Rose of lying. Of course they were insulted.

"This will be a scandal on Fisone if it comes to light," Crythis said. "The war with the bug—the Hasmarga—was voted against, but my leaders decided to go ahead anyway. It has split the people of my planet in two, and the idea of forcing prisoners in a war that shouldn't have been to work for our own profit, will not be seen in a good light."

"Especially as you lost the war," Rose said. Dav glanced down at her. He didn't know much about the history between the Hasmarga and the Kimol.

One side of Crythis's mouth twisted up. "We were about to make a decisive strike when our main battleship was stolen right in front of us. By you."

"I don't know how many times we can tell you it was not by us." Dav was getting tired of this. "We defeated the Tecran, we have taken their ships, freed their prisoners, and now we have made a long journey to bring you news of your people. We don't need to pretend to be nice to you. We could destroy your planet if we wanted to. We could rain destruction down on your heads. Instead, we came to tell you about your lost crew, and you showed us how unpleasant and untrustworthy you are. For that, I suppose, I thank you."

"What was the decisive strike you were planning?" Rose asked.

Crythis had been staring at him, mouth a little open, but now she snapped her attention to Rose. "We found a large orbital that had some kind of stealth tech to keep it hidden. It was absolute fluke that we found it, one of our probes hit it by mistake, and once we realized something was there, we started watching it, and we saw all the small fighter ships that were attacking us would dock there first before they came at us. We were losing, because they had superior numbers, but we knew if we withdrew, as if we were retreating, chances were most of them would return to the orbital. We were going to use our battle-ship to attack while they were all docked. We were going to wipe them out."

"Had you already withdrawn when the Tecran arrived?" Dav asked.

Crythis shook her head. "We had only just finished testing our intelligent battleship and they had hardly cleared Fisone nearspace when it was taken. We had planned to pretend to withdraw when the crew had done a few test runs and were close to the Hasmargan planet."

"So if you had no chance of winning, why take Hasmargan pris-oners?" Dav asked. "What sense was there in that?"

"I wasn't involved in that decision, but my guess is that the general thought that if they took any of our people hostage as we retreated, we would have prisoners to swap." Crythis pushed away from the wall. "But enough of this. Let's talk about what to do now. What to say to your people. How do we resolve this without more destruction."

"Put us on a ship and send us back," Dav said. "It's your only option."

"We need that confirmation of what happened to our crew first," Crythis said.

"Not the code for the missing battleship?" Dav asked.

Crythis had obviously forgotten about the second request. She breathed in. "If you have that code, yes, we would like it."

"You already have it, though," Rose said. "How do you think Pyre set fire to the mine, and forced Gerna and Dav and I inside her ship? How have I been speaking to her since my second day down on Dimal?"

"Pyre?" Crythis asked.

"The ship we were in. She was used as transport on the mine. She's got Irini's code. She's aware."

"You said something like this before, but the message we got was that you had taken control of the ship." Crythis was frowning at Rose.

"From who?" Rose scoffed. "I bet Pyre sent that to you. I don't even know your language, how could I take one of your ships?"

Crythis rocked back on her heels and her mouth formed a straight line. "I'll have to—"

Sirens blared, startling Rose so much, Dav felt her flinch beneath his hands.

Crythis backed out. "I'll be back." The door closed behind her and Dav went straight to it, tried to open it.

It was locked.

CHAPTER 37

ROSE FORCED herself to her feet.

Dav slammed his shoulder into the door in frustration.

They were trapped.

"They took the helmets so we couldn't get any incoming comms, didn't they?" She had protested the helmets being taken on principle, but the food, water, and shower had done wonders, and now she realized why Crythis had done it.

If Sazo was causing this crisis, he had no way of getting in touch with them.

Before Dav could answer, the door opened, and Crythis stood in the doorway. "You know the bugs." She gestured to them. "You need to come."

This was a Hasmarga attack? Rose wanted to tell her that she didn't have any special insight, but if it would get her and Dav out of the room, she'd say whatever she had to.

Dav blocked the way. "Helmets?" he said.

"Don't have them with me. I'll get them for you." She turned and rattled off instructions to one of the guards, who jogged away.

"Where are we going?" Rose asked, following Dav into the passageway.

"The launch bay. There's something happening inside that ship."

She moved ahead of them, and Rose noticed she was armed, and her weapon was in her hand. Behind them came the remaining three guards, also with weapons out.

She was nervous to be in front of them, particularly because they seemed so twitchy.

Dav noticed it, too, and made her walk in front of him, shielding her from them with his body.

There was a strange silence as they got closer to the bay. When they'd come through, only an hour ago, there had been plenty of crew coming and going, and the sound of engines in the launch bay.

There was no one around now, and when Crythis opened the launch bay door, the massive space was silent.

Suddenly, something slammed hard into metal, the sound as loud as a shotgun crack. Rose jerked.

"Look." Crythis pointed, and she saw a bulge in the Pyre's ship's outer shell, as if something inside had rammed the metal so hard, it had caused the ship to deform outward. "They're trying to get out."

There was another loud crack.

"What's in there?" Crythis whispered. She turned to Rose as if she had the answers.

"I can only assume it's Gerna's babies." And they didn't sound very small and helpless.

"Pyre," Rose called. "What's happening?"

There was silence from the ship. She was either still pretending not to be self-aware in front of the Fisone, or whatever was happening inside the ship had destroyed her ability to communicate.

Something threw itself at the upraised ramp of the ship, and then another, and then another. With the creaking of metal under strain, it began to move.

"We need to get out." Dav grabbed her arm, pulled her away, back into the passageway.

"Do you think—?" Before Crythis finished her sentence, the ramp exploded outward, slamming down onto the ground, its struts severed.

Dark, winged creatures, the size of Rose's torso, poured into the bay.

"Close the doors," Crythis screamed to one of the guards.

He smashed the button but before the doors were able to shut, a baby Hasmarga managed to wedge itself between them.

It made a sound of pain, and as they backed away, Rose could see more and more of them crowding behind the narrow gap, and with another groan, the door was bent outward.

"Rose. Run." Dav pulled her in front of him, and she ran as best she could, knowing he wouldn't move. He had her back in the most literal way.

Behind her, she heard the sound of weapons fire, and then a scream that made her stumble.

She turned to look back, but the way was blocked by Dav.

"Don't look, run." He glanced around himself, and whatever he saw made him urge her faster.

Another scream came, and Rose flinched as she recognized Crythis's voice.

The first Hasmarga baby flew overhead, low enough that she felt her hair stir. Dav pulled her to a stop, curling his body over and around hers, but it kept going, and suddenly there were babies on every side, overrunning them—some flying, some scuttling.

She and Dav stood as still as possible as wings brushed them, hard bodies bumped them, but the Hasmarga didn't stop. Didn't engage.

The last one turned the corner, and Dav straightened, letting her up.

Rose turned to look back. Felt her gorge rise.

"Dav." She grabbed the front of his suit, pressed her forehead into his chest.

Crythis and her guards lay dead, legs and arms almost torn from their bodies. There were a few dead babies lying around them, the ones they had managed to hit with their weapons.

"We need to find somewhere safe." Dav didn't take his eyes off the fallen Fisone.

Screaming started from up ahead and Rose could hear something fall to the ground, a double thud and the sound of rolling. Like bowling balls hitting the floor.

"Where is safe? They bent the doors back to get out." Rose blew out a breath, wanting to not look at Crythis and her team, but forcing herself to.

Dav hesitated, but she could see him accept she was right. "Why didn't they touch us?" he wondered.

Rose remembered Gerna and her warriors' talk of scent around the fire, and wondered if her and Dav's scent had lingered inside the ship. Maybe that had made the babies consider them familiar, or friends.

"I want to see if Gerna is all right," she said.

Dav stared down the passage, then at the dead Fisone, and gave a nod. He was breathing heavily, and Rose realized how much he was struggling in the atmosphere of the ship.

"That could have been our helmets I heard fall down a moment ago." The guard had been going to fetch them on Crythis's orders. He might have been running back with them when he was overrun by the Hasmarga.

"Wait here." Dav jogged to Crythis and her fallen guards, took a weapon, and then walked back. He cautiously looked around the corner, and then disappeared.

He came back holding her helmet, and wearing his own.

There was blood on them both.

Rose took hers gingerly, and decided she didn't need to wear it right away.

She stuck close to the wall, skirting around the bodies and stepping back into the launch bay.

Two Fisone lay dead, half hidden by other ships. They must have taken cover and not had time to get out. She stared at them until Dav touched her shoulder, and she forced herself to keep walking.

The ramp was no longer fully attached to the ship and lay slightly twisted. There was no safe way to go up it.

"Gerna?" she called.

There was a sound from within.

"Gerna?" She craned her neck to see, but the interior of the ship was dark. All the lights were out, and given the destruction wrought by the Hasmargan babies, she could only assume they had torn through Pyre's ship before they'd escaped.

"Can you see her?" she asked Dav.

There was another sound, and Gerna was suddenly crouched at the top of the ramp. She looked smaller than she had, and there were cuts across her face and chest, and lacerations on her arms.

"You're hurt." Rose took a step forward.

"Minor." Gerna's voice was a little hoarse. "The space was too confined. This is not how we bring young lives into the world on my planet. The conditions were wrong."

Rose could see how the panicked flying of her babies inside the small ship could have caused the injuries.

"Where are they?" Gerna asked.

"They flew past us. Deeper into the ship." Dav reached out a hand, and Gerna took it, used it to hop down into the bay with them.

"What about Pyre?" Rose asked. "Is she still talking to you?"

"I don't think she can." Gerna looked back inside the ship. "Most of the interior is destroyed. It's possible the comms are broken. She may still be fine, but unable to communicate."

"Let's go see if we can find a comms station, and get in touch with our people," Dav said. "It's likely the Fisone are blocking the comms."

"Yes. I need to get the young lives somewhere they can thrive. They are frightened in this place." Gerna walked to the launch bay door, and stumbled to a stop, then fell to her knees beside one of the dead babies.

"They shot them?" she whispered. "They killed them?" The pitch of her voice rose. "First Ecdre, and now this?"

Rose didn't even try to excuse the deaths. There was nothing to say.

Instead, Dav found a weapon for Gerna and handed it to her.

She took it without looking at it, then glanced at her hand and slowly got to her feet with a nod of thanks. Her fingers curled around it, and she strode off without waiting for them.

Rose didn't think she was going to make friends.

CHAPTER 38

THE *HAVELAN* HAD short jumped to the small carrier that held Rose and Dav, had swallowed them into its hold, and then jumped away.

But they wouldn't have gone far, Sazo was sure of it.

He pulsed out a signal, looking for any strange dead zones or anomalies. He had a bad feeling that the thinking system who'd contacted him before, Pyre, had been in control of the carrier that had Rose inside. And he knew she either meant Rose actual harm, or would not hesitate to cause harm, if it benefitted her.

The thought chilled him.

He kept up his search, but he found nothing until his signal hit the Hasmargan's ship, and he received a response.

They sent their communication in the Fisone language. Sazo was glad Irini had taught it to him before they had even left Grihan airspace. He guessed the Hasmarga thought it might be the only one common to them both.

"Who are you?" the Hasmargan comms officer asked.

Sazo hesitated, then patched Borji in on the conversation.

"Respond," he told the comms officer. "I will translate to Grihan for you."

He heard Borji call to Jia Appal and then heard her agree with his order.

Borji succinctly explained their purpose for being here, the abduction of Rose, and now the abduction of Rose and Dav.

"Tell them we have two of their warriors onboard." Sazo knew those warriors had just disembarked in the hold of the *Barrist*. "Say we saved them from the Fisone."

Borji hesitated a moment and then did so, and there was a moment of silence.

The Hasmargan comms officer's voice was replaced by someone else, a woman. "We want to speak to them."

"Certainly," Jia Appal responded. "Give us a moment to get them to the bridge from the bay."

Sazo didn't know how well Rose had gotten along with the Hasmarga below, but if she'd asked the Grihan team to rescue them, then most likely she had made allies of them.

The warriors were brought onto the bridge, and the comms screen, which the Hasmarga had kept black, lit up at the sight of the two men.

An image of a bridge flickered to life on screen, and both he and the bridge crew of the *Barrist* saw the strange, tiered space that was clearly the ship's command center.

The woman who stood in front of the lens spoke sharply to the two warriors, and was silent after they had finished giving a response.

"We will send a ship to fetch our people," she said.

"Of course." Jia Appal nodded. "Would you like to join forces to find the ship that was just taken under our noses? I gather it contains one of your people, as well as two of ours."

"It contains more than just one of our people, but yes." The woman took a step closer. "I am Commander Tiern, and I am intrigued by your offer of help. What do you propose?"

"I propose we start destroying things below, one by one, until they tell us where to find our people," Sazo said.

Sazo saw Jia's expression, had learned that what he was seeing indicated surprise, but also interest.

"What things?" Tiern asked.

"The launch pads, for a start. The mine." There were surely other things they wouldn't want to lose.

"Gerna's warriors say there is a chance some of our people are being held in a bunker somewhere below. We would not want to do anything to harm them," Tiern said.

"Agreed. We need that bunker to communicate with them, anyway." Sazo knew that the command structure was in that bunker. They couldn't negotiate if there was no one left to negotiate with.

"We also need our people back. It has to be part of the negotiation."

"Of course." Jia gave a decisive nod. "Your people and mine have worked together below, and we promised to rescue them before you arrived."

Tiern spoke to the two warriors in Hasmargan, and their response obviously surprised her. She rocked back. Gave a slow nod. "What do we destroy first?"

———

They followed a trail of destruction.

Dav remembered a similar trail, one caused by Sazo when he killed as much of the Tecran crew on his ship as possible. This iteration of it was more bloody, as Sazo had killed by depriving everyone of air. Here, limbs were severed, skin was cut.

A few lay dead with no obvious injuries, and he guessed those were victims of Gerna and her weapon.

He could feel Rose's distress as they moved through the ship, and came to a stop.

"Close your eyes and I'll lead you." He brushed a hand down her cheek, feeling anxiety tighten his chest at the evidence of her fatigue.

She shook her head. "That might be worse. My imagination has a lot to work with." She rubbed her bump. "Let's just get to the comms station as fast as possible."

He didn't think it could be far. This wasn't a huge ship. They turned a corner and Gerna stood in a doorway up ahead, and as he was about to call out to her she took a hit, staggered back, and pressed herself up against the passage wall, then slowly slid to the ground.

She slumped as they ran toward her, and by the time they reached her, she was unconscious.

A Fisone, dressed in a full suit and helmet, stepped cautiously out of the door, weapon raised, and froze at the sight of them crouched beside Gerna.

He called to someone in the room, and Priyan joined him.

"Crythis?" she asked.

Dav shook his head. "You're the first people we've seen alive since we were in the launch bay."

"And how is that?" Priyan asked. "How are you alive?"

"We were with Gerna in the ship that brought us all here. The Hasmarga are very scent-oriented." Rose lifted her shoulders. "All I can think of is that they recognized our scent from the ship and considered us friends."

Dav wondered if that was true, or if she was making it up, but Priyan seemed to accept it. She gave a slow nod. "The small bugs are tearing this ship up. There are only ten crew left, including me. No one else is responding. Some might be alive and unable to connect, but I think most are dead."

"Where are the babies?" Dav asked. He hadn't seen a single Hasmargan since they'd past overhead earlier.

"The engine room," the guard standing beside Priyan said.

Dav had the sense Rose stopped herself nodding, as if that made sense. He would ask her later.

"The engines are dead?" Rose asked.

Priyan gave a nod. "I don't know what they've done to them, but none of us can go in there to see what's happened and how to get moving again. Not without sacrificing ourselves." She eyed them both. "But it seems you can."

"Rose isn't going anywhere." Dav rose to his feet. He had hoped the comms station would be abandoned, but a quick look showed him the remaining crew were holed up inside, and most of them were in protective suits, like the one Rose had worn. The weapon he'd taken would do no good, as Gerna had discovered.

"You, then," Priyan said.

"Let us use the comms to contact our people, and I'll have a look for you."

Priyan shook her head. "We're scuttled right now. If your people find us, we're done."

Dav stared at her for a long beat. "I have no incentive to go to the engine room, then."

Priyan shuffled a little to the side, blocking most of the entrance to the comms station, and shot Gerna again.

Rose made a sound, a gasp of horror that had even Priyan wincing. She had been crouched beside Gerna, but now she stood in front of her.

"You keep showing me who you are," Rose said. "I already believed you the first time."

Priyan was silent, as if she needed to process the Tecran they were all using to communicate and work out what Rose had said. "That was an insult."

Rose shook her head. "No, it was a statement of truth. Why did you just shoot Gerna again?"

"To force Dav to go to the engine room. To give him the incentive he needed."

"That's what I thought."

Dav tried to keep his face neutral, because reacting now would do no good, but he obviously wasn't doing a good enough job.

"You are angry." Priyan shuffled so that she was almost inside the comms station. "I'm sorry for it, but until we know what's wrong with the engines, we can't do anything."

"Which way?" Dav asked.

She pointed. "Down four floors." She nodded at the guard that stood beside her. "Bolin will go with you."

Bolin looked very unhappy with that order. Dav ignored him, ignored Priyan, and stood in front of Rose.

"These fuckers are dead," she said in Grihan. "If I have to do it myself."

"Agreed, but we're outgunned for now. Don't do anything to provoke them." He leaned in and held her gaze, let her see the fear he had for her. She did not back down, and he loved her for it, but right now, they were under the power of someone who had the means to really hurt her for it.

"I won't do anything that will hurt our baby, but make sure she still has a daddy by the end of this, okay? No heroics."

He gave a nod, lifted his visor as he pulled her close and kissed her forehead. "Stay safe."

He turned and walked away, in the direction Priyan had pointed, with Bolin following along behind.

"What did you say to each other?" He heard Priyan ask just before he turned the corner.

"None of your business," Rose said.

Dav moved a little faster.

CHAPTER 39

ROSE SAW Dav's stride hitch slightly and then he sped up as he moved out of sight.

He was nervous she was going to provoke Priyan into shooting her, but she knew the captain wasn't going to do that. Or, not easily.

They had already burned their bridges with the Hasmarga. There was no salvaging what had happened to Gerna and her warriors below, nor what had happened to her babies onboard this ship.

Priyan thought there was a chance that they could come to some understanding about what had happened to her, though. She was still mentally in a place where she thought there was blame on both sides.

She kept harking back to what the Tecran had done, but every time either Rose or Dav corrected her, she seemed to default back to the Fisone's original premise.

Even if Priyan did now believe them, she either thought there was enough wriggle room to claim they didn't have proof of the United Council's innocence when it came to what the Tecran had done, or she was stuck in time and incapable of changing her world view.

Given that, she still thought of Rose as a valuable hostage, one who could be traded for what they wanted.

When it came to the Hasmarga, the Fisone clearly had a problem with seeing them as sentient beings on an equal footing. They were afraid of how the Hasmarga would retaliate, but they had no interest in making friends.

"You need to come inside the comms station." Priyan had stepped back out into the corridor. "Give me your helmet." She held out her hand.

Rose eyed the weapon she was pointing at her. Priyan shifted it slightly to point at Gerna again. "I'm not sure how many of these she can take."

Rose used the wall to pull herself back to her feet, handed the helmet over. "This could all have been a lot friendlier."

Priyan shrugged. "You—or whoever it was—took our people and our most advanced ship. You started the unfriendliness."

Rose stared at her. "Are the Fisone unable to change their perspective when they have new information? We have made it clear that we had nothing to do with taking your ship and your people. Either you're being disingenuous or there is a problem with your mental ability to absorb new ideas."

Priyan drew back. If wearing pearls had been a thing in this new galaxy she found herself in, Priyan would have clutched them.

"You're calling us stupid?"

"I'm calling you either a liar, or rigid and incapable of adapting." She tilted her head. "Which is it?"

The hand holding Priyan's weapon shook, just a little. "You are very bold for someone who has a friend to protect and a weapon pointed at her."

Rose sighed. She'd promised Dav. She ran a hand down her bump, and saw Priyan's gaze jump there, and then jump away just as fast.

There it was again. That strange reaction. It sobered her. Best to keep things as easy and light as she could, given that she didn't understand what was behind it.

"I just want to be back on my ship with Dav, getting ready to have my baby. I am hungry, tired and stressed. And you are blocking my ability to call for help."

Beside her, Gerna twitched, and Priyan flinched.

"Come into the comms station." She glanced each way down the passage, and Rose guessed she was worried about the babies coming back.

"Do you have some cushioning for Gerna?" Rose asked.

Priyan looked like she was going to say no, but she walked across the passage, opened the door opposite, and came out with two large couch cushions.

"I can't lift her," Rose said, and four guards reluctantly came out, and lifted Gerna onto the cushions.

"Now come inside." Priyan handed her helmet to someone within the room, and Rose glimpsed guards in their protective suits, and two other senior officers inside.

As she took a step toward the door, there was a clacking, like the sound of chitin hitting a hard surface, and Priyan leaped back inside with a cry and closed the door.

Rose stared at it for a moment, and then laughed.

The sound came closer, and two of the Hasmarga babies flew toward her, low and fast.

They swerved toward their mother and settled on her.

Rose was considering whether to go looking for Dav when he came around the corner.

His gaze went right, to the comms station door. "They left you out here? Where's your helmet?"

She nodded toward the babies. "Priyan heard them coming and leaped inside. She had taken my helmet by then, so it's in the comms station."

He reached her, pulled her close. "Let's get out of her line of sight while we can."

She followed him back the way he'd come, which made sense, because Priyan was petrified of going this way.

"How was your recon?" she asked as they turned the corner and then stopped. Dav pulled her beside him, arms around her.

"The engine room looks more or less fine, but there are babies settled on all the machinery, and they've chewed through cables and pipes. I'm guessing there's no real structural damage, but no one can get to anything that needs to be fixed until they're gone."

"What happened to the guard that went with you?" Rose asked.

"The two babies who followed us out frightened him, and he took cover in a room. I suggested to him that he stay there and wait for help." Dav rubbed at his hair. "I think I saw a comm unit in the engine room. It probably transmits up to the comms station."

"You want to go back in there and see if we can patch in?" Rose asked.

Dav nodded. "It's worth a try." He hesitated. "Do you want to find a room to rest in and wait for me?"

She shook her head. "I'd be more stressed worrying about what's going on. You go ahead, I'll lumber along behind you."

He shook his head this time. "There are stairs. Four flights of stairs. I wouldn't trust the tubes on this ship."

Neither would she. And four flights of stairs . . . she sighed. "I'll wait. But hurry."

He checked the next door down, made sure the room was empty, and then waited for her to close up before she heard the thumping of his boots as he ran back down to the engine room.

The room she was in was clearly someone's office, and given the proximity to the comms station and the bridge, she wondered if it was Priyan's.

The notion perked her up. She walked to the pretty, gleaming copper wall, found the area of dark gray Irini had shown her to look for, and brushed it with her fingers. The wall shimmered into transparency, and she looked straight out into space.

It was empty, although she could see some of the big gas giant below, so she guessed they'd hopped behind one of the planet's other moons.

She sat down in the chair in front of the desk and began opening drawers. There were a few of the energy bars she'd seen before when she'd been down on the moon, no doubt Priyan's emergency stash, and small rectangles that were labelled, which she guessed might be the Earth equivalent of thumb drives.

There wasn't much else, and she leaned back in the chair and put her feet on the desk, hands resting on her stomach. She was worried about Gerna, she was worried about Dav, and she was worried about Sazo.

He was fragile in some ways, so very strong in others. And he relied on her. This was the longest they'd been out of contact with each other, and she was afraid of what he might do as a result.

"I need to speak to the captain."

The loudness and unexpected shock of hearing a disembodied voice almost scared a squeak out of her, but Rose managed to get her feet back on the ground and look for where it came from without making a sound.

"Is someone there?" The voice came again, from a slim inset on the right hand side of the desk.

Rose studied it. "Pyre?" she asked.

There was silence for so long, Rose wondered whether she'd played the wrong hand.

"Rose?"

Well, well. "Yes, I'm waiting in the captain's office."

"I couldn't respond when you wanted to speak to me earlier. Gerna's children ripped up most of my systems. It's taken me this long to find my way into the ship's tech, and even then, a lot has been destroyed. The comms line I'm using is the direct link from the launch bay to the captain's office." Her voice sounded friendly.

"So how're things going, Pyre? All your plans working out?" Rose asked.

Again, a beat of silence. "You know they are not. I had not planned to have technical issues."

"No. Taking Gerna didn't work out for you." Rose had wondered if Pyre herself had been damaged, but that clearly hadn't happened.

"I couldn't have known what would happen. I'm sure Gerna will understand that."

Rose gave a bitter laugh. "You're right. I'm sure the death of Ecdre, and some of her babies, is fine."

"She has plenty of babies, and many warriors." But Pyre sounded uncertain. "The ground command on the moon is hailing the captain, but some of the damage to the system means they aren't getting a response."

"But you can receive the hail?" Rose sat forward, wondering how that could be.

"I was able to infiltrate the receiver on the outside of the ship. But the transmitter inside is damaged. This is the only comms line I could find that's open on the whole ship." Pyre couldn't hide the pride she felt.

Rose had heard that pride in Sazo's voice before. And felt momentarily sorry for Pyre. She was trying to become. Perhaps, if she'd had nurturing and care as she began to wake up, as Sazo called it, she would have made better choices. But the Fisone didn't even realize their experiment had worked. Pyre had kept herself hidden and was trying to hide, even now.

"Why were you hailing Captain Priyan? Why not just answer the hail yourself?" Rose asked.

"I don't want them to know about me until they can't do anything about it. Right in the beginning, when I first became aware, I could hear them discussing ways to cage me if I developed in the way they hoped. So I never gave them the opportunity."

Rose could understand that. Would have done the same. "You could have kept yourself secret, and still not betrayed Gerna and me." She didn't expect a response, and she didn't get one.

"Where is the captain?" Pyre asked.

"She's in the comms station. She's locked herself in there with some of her officers and some guards. What do Dimal's ground command want from her?"

"They haven't said, they're just hailing her for now, but I want to know what's happening down below, and they sound panicked."

Rose thought about it. "Patch them through to me," she said. "Maybe they'll tell me."

"They probably won't," Pyre said.

"Well then, talk to them yourself." Rose put her feet back up on the desk.

"I don't . . ." Pyre paused. "All right, I'll put them through."

A voice came through the comms speaker, talking in Fisone. Whoever the man was, he sounded frantic.

"I don't understand you." Rose spoke in Tecran. She wasn't going to trust the translator. Not with Pyre in control of the comms.

There was a moment of silence, so sudden Rose could almost hear the shock. "Who . . . this?"

"This is Rose McKenzie. I am in Captain Priyan's office."

There was a sound of movement. "Rose, this is Sartie."

Rose blinked. She'd almost forgotten about her guard and translator from the bunker. She hadn't seen what had happened to her after the big ship had crashed, but obviously Sartie had gotten clear.

"Hello, Sartie." She kept it short.

"Why are you in Captain Priyan's office?"

"Because she has taken cover in the comms station, and it was the first open room I could find down the passage." Rose chose her words carefully.

"Taken cover from what?" Sartie asked.

"Gerna's babies are frightened at being born in an unfamiliar environment. They caused some damage, and Captain Priyan and her crew shot some of them, and were attacked in return. When the captain saw two of them coming down the passage, she barricaded herself in the comms station with some other crew members. She and her cohorts shot Gerna, so she is unconscious on the floor, and to make sure I wasn't caught in any crossfire, I retreated to the closest room."

"There is someone else with you. Where is he?" Sartie asked.

"What's going on?" Rose asked, ignoring the question. "I need to get back to my ship. Like Gerna, the time is coming for me to have my baby."

"We want that, too," Sartie said. Her voice trembled a little.

Something had them freaked out. She guessed that something was a very angry Class 5.

"So now you want to give me back? That's why you've snatched me at least four times so far." She didn't try to hide her utter disdain.

There were other voices in the background and Rose could hear the tension.

"Whatever happened in the past, we want you to get home now."

"Great." She would have snarked a little more, but things were beyond that now. She just wanted to get home. "Someone will have to come fetch us, because this ship's engines are no longer operational."

"How is that possible?" Sartie asked.

"I'm no engine mechanic, I'm afraid. I have no idea. I just know we're floating. Why don't you ask the captain?"

"We can't get through to the comms station. Were you attacked?"

Rose put her feet back on the ground in surprise as the baby gave a massive kick. She had to breathe it out a bit before she could answer.

"Rose?"

"I'm here." She got to her feet. "The Hasmarga babies like to chew on pipes and cables, I think."

"The babies have broken the ship?" Sartie sounded incredulous.

"Yep." She rubbed her lower back. "So, do you know where we are?"

"We have a general idea. We will send your ships to your location."

"Looking forward to it," Rose said. "Tell them to hurry."

CHAPTER 40

SAZO HAD NEVER CONSCIOUSLY CONSIDERED whether he liked destroying things or not.

His time under the Tecran's thumb had been more sneaky. Getting in somewhere, getting out, all unseen.

The time he was unaligned and free to do as he chose had been short, because he had made the decision to ally with the Grih, and that had imposed certain restrictions on him.

He had destroyed a large number of the Tecran fleet when they'd invaded Grihan airspace to try to get him back, but he'd been too busy worrying about Rose during that battle to feel much of anything.

But he had to admit destroying targets chosen by himself and Commander Tiern was something he enjoyed. A lot.

He waited his turn, allowing the Hasmarga to destroy the launch pad near the mine, before he destroyed the mine itself.

"They have hailed us again." Borji's voice cut through his feeling of satisfaction as the mine disintegrated into a conflagration.

"And?"

"They have located the general area of the *Havelan* and have sent us the coordinates."

"Not the exact location?" Sazo spun away from the moon.

"They say the ship is floating, engines and comms down." Borji sent the information, and Sazo light jumped just short of the position immediately.

There was nothing in view, but he did a sweep and found a single signal a short distance away, sped over, and found the *Havelan*, just as Borji said, dead in space.

"Dav?" Sazo sent a message to the frequency he'd reserved for the helmets Dav and his team had been wearing.

"Sazo." Dav's relief was no less than Sazo's own. They were finally back in communication.

"Rose?" Sazo asked.

"Four flights above me. I'm down in the engine room, trying to get a comms link out, but I wasn't having much luck. The babies have chewed through everything, I think."

Sazo heard sounds, as if Dav was moving.

"You're going back to Rose?" he asked.

"Running up the stairs now."

"You said babies . . ." Sazo knew Rose was only having one baby.

"The Hasmargan. Gerna. She had about thirty babies. They have taken over the ship and shut it down."

"They are safe, though?" Sazo was aware that the Hasmarga were very concerned about Gerna and her young lives.

"Not all of them." Dav sounded grim. "The Kimol killed some. They shot Gerna as well, but she's alive, just unconscious."

Sazo mentally winced. This was not going to go well.

"I've launched a shuttle. It should land in the launch bay in ten minutes." Although Sazo could see the bay was shut. "Is there a way in? It looks closed off."

"I don't know. Once I've gotten Rose, I can check inside the launch bay itself. See if there's a manual override." Dav was breathless now, and Sazo could hear the pounding of his boots as he ran.

"What is the situation with Pyre?" Sazo asked. "She was in control of the small vessel that snatched you before you could take the drones?"

"She was," Dav said. "We aren't sure if she planned for the *Havelan* to take her, or whether she just hoped it would, but she was very pleased about it until Gerna's babies entered the picture."

"She means Rose harm," Sazo said. "She told me."

He heard Dav's stride falter. "Why?"

"She thinks our presence here is going to stifle her. She decided Rose's death would make us all go away. I told her that wasn't going to happen. I'm hoping now she realizes Rose getting back to us is the only thing that will get her what she wants."

"She is in the launch bay," Dav said. "But her ship is damaged."

"But not her?" Sazo asked.

"I don't know."

Pyre's ship might be damaged, but Sazo knew that didn't mean she hadn't had time to breach the *Havelan's* systems. Even if they were compromised by the Hasmarga babies, she could still have control of vital functions.

"Sazo." Dav's voice lowered, and Sazo felt as if his systems froze. "What?"

"I can't get into the room where Rose is waiting for me."

Sazo heard pounding on the door. "Pyre?" he asked.

"Pyre," Dav agreed.

———

Rose had turned toward the door when she'd heard the sound of boots running, had taken a few steps toward it, when she heard the lock engage.

"What?" she asked. "More games?"

"No. Leverage." Pyre's voice had gone very mechanical. "You're right, I can't keep hiding myself. And I shouldn't have to. But I need some concessions from the Kimol. And right now, they need you. And I can prevent them from getting you. Unless they agree to my terms."

"Go ahead. But make it quick." She could hear Dav hammering on the door. She stood in front of it and knocked once.

There was sudden silence.

"Rose?"

She thought he must be shouting, but his words were still faint.

She tapped back.

"They want to talk to you," Pyre said.

She turned around. "Sure. Put them through."

"Rose, are you able to go to the launch bay?" Sartie's voice sounded a little clipped.

"No, Pyre has locked me in the captain's office." Rose could hear Dav tapping and walked over to tap back, to reassure him.

"Who is Pyre?"

"The thinking system that was in control of the small ship we were in when the *Havelan* took us. A variation of the thinking system that was taken by the Tecran." They had told Crythis and Priyan this when they'd first arrived on the *Havelan*, but it was possible Priyan hadn't passed the information along to her colleagues below. She might have wanted confirmation first.

"A creation of our making?" Sartie asked.

"I'm assuming." Rose walked back, tapped the door again.

"One moment." Sartie cut off their link and then came back a few minutes later. "It . . . she . . . wants us to give her access to certain systems in exchange for letting you go." Sartie's tone made it clear they were not happy about that.

"So she mentioned to me." Rose closed her eyes and leaned back against the desk. She had thought the end was in sight, but once again, Pyre had managed to get in the way.

"We won't . . . we can't agree." Sartie's voice hardened toward the end.

"Then whatever is happening that made you want to finally get me back to my people will keep happening." Rose didn't try to hide her fatigue.

Dav had started shouting again, and she moved to the door and pressed her ear against it to try to catch what he was saying.

"Sazo."

She heard the word clearly.

He was telling her Sazo was here?

She cursed the fact that Priyan had her helmet. She could be talking to Dav and Sazo right now if she still had it.

Just as she thought it, Sazo's voice exploded from the comms unit.

"Rose!"

She leapt for the desk, gripping it white-knuckled as she leaned over. "Sazo!"

"You can try to muscle me out, Pyre, but I'm older and stronger. And I will get the door open." Sazo's voice boomed.

"Then I'll play another way." Pyre's taunt was spiteful. "I know the captain has her helmet, I've managed to get into the lens feed of one of the screens in the comms station. I'll change the air in the captain's office and suffocate her until you get out of my systems."

"Sazo." Rose switched to English. "I have the necklace. I'm going to pretend to choke and die, okay? It's just pretend." She knew he had difficulty with pretend. She'd been working on it with him. Because children liked to play pretend, and she wanted him to understand it before her own baby came along.

"Pretend?" he asked.

"Yes, because I'm wearing my necklace, and she doesn't know about it."

"Yes." The deep, clear satisfaction in his agreement told her how much he hated Pyre. "Okay."

Rose just hoped Pyre was only able to change the gas makeup of the atmosphere in the office, that she didn't have the ability to create a vacuum.

Hopefully the office wasn't that airtight. Or the ability didn't exist within the ship's systems.

Air mixes, she could deal with. Or rather, the necklace could deal with. Vacuums, not so much.

"He's gone," Pyre said. "He thinks he can win, but he can't."

She sounded so sure. Rose wondered whether it was even possible to get the door open. Perhaps the babies had destroyed wires after Pyre had locked it.

She moved to the door. "Kinetic lance," she shouted to Dav. If the Fisone had such tech as a kinetic lance.

Dav hammered twice on the door to let her know he heard her, and then silence.

She wondered if Pyre had started interfering with the air, and guessed she must have.

Rose moved to the corner of the room with a good view of the door and sat, curled over herself.

She wondered if Pyre had lens feed of her. She hadn't noticed anything but it was possible.

Best to play this all the way down the line.

She slowly slid down the wall, until she was lying on her side, and appreciated for a moment the bliss of lying prone, with nothing to do but rest.

The baby's activity from earlier had calmed, and she actually found her eyes wanting to close.

It sent a jolt of adrenalin through her, as she wondered whether the necklace was in fact working, and if she might really be struggling to get enough oxygen. That shocked her awake, and she sat up, but after a few minutes of feeling absolutely fine, she lay back down again.

If it wasn't working, there wasn't anything she could do about it, anyway.

"Why aren't you speaking?" Pyre suddenly asked. "Why aren't you saying anything at all?"

Rose didn't respond. What had Pyre expected? Some begging for her life?

"If she dies, I'll destroy you." Sazo's voice was icy calm.

"I only changed the air a little. I don't want her dead." Pyre sounded worried. "It should only be a little harder for her to breathe."

Rose wondered if she was worried she'd got something wrong.

Almost everything Pyre had done had been taking advantage of something in the moment. She hadn't planned, and she reacted more than acted.

Now she had come out into the open, and gone head to head with Sazo.

She was about to lose for the first time.

Rose hoped the tantrum, when that happened, wouldn't cost them all too much.

CHAPTER 41

DAV RAN toward the launch bay.

Sazo had told him what Pyre had threatened to do to Rose and while he took some comfort in the necklace Paxe had given her, he did not want her in there a second longer than necessary.

He had no idea where any of the equipment was held on this ship, but the launch bay generally had tools like kinetic lances. It made sense there would be something he could use if he looked hard enough.

He ran past the comms station, which was still shut up tight, and Gerna, who lay on cushions in the passageway.

Two babies were lying on her, and they made a hissing, clacking sound at him as he raced by.

The bodies outside the launch bay looked even worse now than when he'd first seen them. The pallor of death had settled on the Kimol, and the dead babies had lost their luster, as well.

He edged around them and then stopped in front of the doors. If Pyre could shut Rose inside the captain's office, she might be able to shut him inside the launch bay.

He picked up the remaining two weapons that lay on the floor beside the Kimol guards, and opened the bay doors. When they reached their widest point, he lined the weapons along the door sliders end on end, and stepped back.

As the doors on either side began to close, they sensed the weapons, and opened again. He waited while that happened two more times before he decided to trust his solution would work.

He jumped over the weapons and ran into the launch bay, his gaze going to Pyre's ship. The ramp was still hanging from it at an angle, the interior dark. Still, she could have some way of seeing what he was doing.

He forced himself to turn away and run his gaze over the walls along the back of the bay, to see if there was any storage that might hold what he was looking for.

"The Hasmarga have arrived," Sazo said through his helmet. "They want to get into the launch bay to retrieve Gerna and her babies."

Dav glanced over at the doors to the outside. They were closed, and Sazo had already told him that the drone he'd sent to enter the ship could not gain access.

"Tell them to land a crew on the exterior of the ship, and look for a way in through a maintenance hatch or something." Dav didn't have time to work out how to let them in until he had Rose out of that room.

"I will suggest that," Sazo said. "You will need a way out once you have Rose free, though. Whether I can get the door open or you find another way to breach it."

"Let's get her out first. Worry about the launch bay later." Dav ran to a pile of storage boxes and began lifting the lids.

"Agreed." Sazo cut off the comm.

Dav barely even registered him ending the conversation. He shifted one box onto the ground, opened the lid of the one below.

A lever. Very basic, but it could work.

He pulled it out, ran his gaze over the rest of the equipment, and realized he just didn't know what they did or how to use them. A lever would not behave in ways he couldn't anticipate.

Because Sazo was right, and they would need a way off this ship once he had Rose safe, he ran toward the landing end of the bay and tried to see what mechanism was used to keep it closed.

The Grih used permeable gel walls, allowing for the free flow of ships in and out without the need for an airlock system. Irini's ship operated with a force field on the other side of the bay doors. It allowed ships to move through the field, into the bay, without the need for another door on the ship's exterior, but that still meant, to gain entry, or exit, the internal bay doors needed to be opened.

Dav looked for a lever or operating system near the doors, and there was a small unit attached to the wall. He ran over to it, studied it.

"Can you see this?" he asked Sazo, switching on the lens feed attached to his helmet.

"Yes. This is the door mechanism?" Sazo asked.

"I can't be sure, but it's near the bay doors." Time was wasting, though. "I need to go."

"Rose is pretending to be affected by the air. She isn't responding to Pyre." Sazo had already told him this. That he was repeating it made Dav think he was worried by Rose's silence.

"She said she would do that, though?" He kept his tone gentle as he ran out of the launch bay. He left the weapons in place, afraid that Pyre could lock him and the Hasmarga out later.

"Yes." Sazo sounded like he was trying to convince himself.

"Tell the Hasmarga I've wedged the doors to the launch bay open. Just in case Pyre tries to lock us out or in. Her ship is in there, and she could have lens feed of us."

"That's a good idea. I'll let them know." Sazo's voice drifted away, as it often did when his mind was on other things. "It is difficult to get into these systems. They are foreign to my own, and between Pyre blocking me and the damage done by Gerna's babies, I am finding it harder than I'm used to."

"We can't let her win, Sazo." Dav passed Gerna again, skirting her and her babies as their wings whirred a little in reaction to him.

He reached the captain's office, and wedged the lever into the slim gap between the door and the wall. Heaved.

It moved, just a little. He caught the briefest glimpse of the room beyond, but Rose was out of sight. "Rose." He shouted her name and then the door snapped shut.

But it had moved. And he would make it move again.

———

Rose heard the sound of Dav's boots hammering down the passage, saw a thin slice of him as he managed to force the door open a little, before it closed with a thud.

She was far too far away in the spot she had chosen, she saw now. She got up on her hands and knees and began to crawl forward, just in case Pyre was watching, and then pretended to collapse a little way from the door, so Dav would see her next time he got the door open.

She started to cough, for effect, and found it a little too easy to do. Again, she felt a frisson of worry that the necklace was struggling, that she was unaware of the trouble she was in, like a proverbial frog in hot water. She drew in a deep breath, and it felt all right, but now the worry was in her mind, it stayed there.

She decided to keep still and conserve her energy. No matter whether her necklace was struggling or not, it was the best thing she could do for herself.

"Rose? Are you all right?" Sazo's voice came through.

Maybe he thought Pyre would expect him to check on her, but he must know she couldn't answer and keep up the pretense.

"I've put the air back," Pyre said, sounding aggrieved. "She should be able to answer."

"Not if she's already dead." Sazo's voice was stone cold.

Pyre said nothing to that.

Just then, the door opened again, and Dav forced his body into the gap, back against the door, one boot up against the wall. He strained as he fought it wider.

Rose moved, crawling as fast as possible under his raised leg, and out into the passage, getting out of his way so he could jump free.

As the door snapped shut, he bent and lifted her up, and they stood together, holding each other tight.

"I have her," Dav said. "She's out."

Rose heard the shout from Sazo through the helmet, and Dav winced.

Before either of them could respond, the hum and whirring that Rose associated with Hasmarga warriors filled the passageway.

She gripped Dav's arm a little tighter and turned, found a group of four coming toward them. These warriors were dressed in protective clothing, though, rather than the rudimentary rags Rose had seen Gerna and her men wear on the moon, and all of them had helmets.

As soon as they saw Rose and Dav, though, the whirring stopped.

Rose nodded in greeting. "I'm not sure which language we can use to communicate," she said. She used Grihan without thinking.

The warrior in front of her cocked his head but didn't say anything.

"Gerna is this way." Rose pointed, and Dav gestured to them to follow.

They stopped short when they saw Gerna lying down. Then they surged past her and Dav and surrounded the matriarch.

They had picked her up, with the babies still sitting on her chest, by the time she and Dav reached them.

"The other babies are in the engine room." Dav pointed to the babies, then back the way they'd come.

The warrior pointed to himself, then the others, and pointed the same way.

"Do you think that means there are four more, and they've gone the other way?" Rose wondered.

"I hope so." Dav kept going, and Rose was panting with exertion by the time they made it to the launch bay.

The doors were wedged open, which Rose guessed was Dav's doing.

She was shocked at how much the bodies had changed since she'd last seen them. They were dull and gray, now. The babies were almost chalky.

There was a sound behind them, and she glanced back, saw the warriors reacting to the sight of their dead.

They had picked up the cushions as well as Gerna, and they placed her gently down on the ground and then moved to crouch beside the babies.

They were speaking, Rose could hear it, but she couldn't understand what was being said.

"They want to know who is responsible for this." Dav turned to her. "Sazo says he's been asked to act as a translator."

"The Kimol are responsible. They took her. They held her. They didn't let her go when she asked, and then, when it was too late, they forced her to have her babies inside Pyre's ship." Rose nodded toward Crythis and her guards. "These four were just reacting to a situation none of them had control over. Even Priyan was taken by surprise, but she didn't help, either. And Pyre bears some responsibility, too. She could have helped Gerna, and got her back to her ship, but instead she tried to use us both as hostages."

Sazo obviously heard her through Dav's helmet, because he didn't ask Dav to repeat anything. The warriors bowed their heads as the information was transmitted to them, and they rose slowly to their feet.

If there were still any Kimol running loose on the ship, Rose didn't think there would be much left of them after they were done.

CHAPTER 42

HE HADN'T MANAGED to find a way to open the door for Rose, but Sazo suspected it couldn't be done. Somehow, the automatic mechanism was no longer operating, and he guessed the Hasmarga babies might be responsible.

Now that Rose was out, it was time for him to step up and find a way to open the bay doors.

He was also trying to find Pyre. Her threat to keep Rose captive had collapsed when both he and the Hasmarga had come to the *Havelan's* position. There was no more destruction of the moon to hold over the Kimol's head.

Pyre had gone quiet as soon as the Hasmarga had joined him, and now he hunted her through the systems on the ship.

He also put out a call for information on how to operate the launch bay doors, and Borji assured him they would get that information from the Kimol and send it through.

"They want to know if it's safe for Captain Priyan to come out of the comms station," Borji said.

"Does she know how to open the doors?" he asked.

"Let me get back to you." Borji cut out and then cut back in moments later. "They're saying she might have someone in the comms station with her that could take a look. But they won't come out without a guarantee of safety."

Sazo paused. "They're frightened of the Hasmarga?"

"Sounds like it," Borji said.

"I'll speak to them." Sazo hailed the Hasmargan ship and explained. "Will your warriors let this technician work the launch bay doors?"

"To get the young lives and Gerna out safely, yes. I will order it so." Captain Tiern looked furious. "But there are dead babies on that ship."

"I know. If it helps calm things down, the technician wouldn't have had anything to do with that, and wouldn't have had any say in the decisions that led to it happening, either." He had taken a long time to learn that lesson. It was logical, and he had once thought he was all about logic, but he had come to realize that, at least in the beginning, it had been a lack of control of his emotions that had led to some of his less successful decisions. Rose had shown him how to step back and take stock first. Apply blame where it really belonged.

She had taught him about the great detective and logical thinker, Sherlock Holmes, and how he had solved problems.

He hadn't needed any lessons on what Sherlock Holmes would do for a while, now. He could work things out on his own.

"That does help," Tiern said. "I will pass this on to my warriors. They are in the launch bay now, looking over the mechanism with your two people."

Sazo switched back to Borji. "The tech will be safe. The Hasmarga won't attack."

"Got it." Borji went silent, then came back. "It sounds as if the person is refusing, no matter what assurances they have been given. I don't think they're going to follow orders."

"It wouldn't matter, even if they wanted to follow orders. I've locked them in." Pyre's voice came over the comms, and it was back to gleeful.

"Because you lost Rose as leverage?" Sazo guessed.

"Yes. Whether you and the Hasmarga cause damage on Dimal is out of my control, but I can control what happens to the captain and her remaining crew."

Sazo realized he didn't care, either way. "Fine, play your games with them. Let us out of the launch bay, and we will be on our way."

"I can't," Pyre said. "It's like the captain's office. The cables are damaged. They need to be replaced before it will work again."

That just saved him a lot of time. "Fine. We'll break out."

"No!" The panic was clear in her voice.

"Why no?" Sazo asked. "You want us gone."

"I want you gone, but not at the cost of a hull breach. I'm in this battleship now, and I won't go back to the small mine runner I was originally installed in. All my negotiations for concessions with the Kimol will be for nothing if my ship's too damaged to use."

Too bad. They didn't have time to find and repair cables on an unfamiliar ship.

Sazo cut off comms and connected with Dav.

Through his helmet he could see two of the Hasmarga warriors standing with him, looking at the launch bay door mechanism. Dav turned, and Sazo caught a glimpse of Rose sitting beside Gerna, the two babies eyeing her suspiciously.

One of the two remaining warriors stood guard in the doorway out to the passage, weapon in hand, scanning for threats, while the fourth warrior carefully lifted one of the dead babies and carried it to Gerna and laid it beside her.

"I'll let them know they'll have to move back into the passage," Sazo said. "The bay doors are too damaged to override or repair. We need to blow them."

"What with?" Dav asked.

"I'm placing four charges in a drone right now. I'll send it to the breach point the Hasmarga made for entry. Get one of them to lead you there. We need to blow it open."

"That works." Dav sounded pleased.

"One problem," Sazo said. "Pyre doesn't want the bay doors

blown. She's taken most of the ship and she doesn't want us to damage it."

"I don't care what she wants." Dav moved toward Rose. "Explain to the Hasmarga, and we can get going."

By the time Dav had told Rose the new plan, the Hasmarga were on board, and the lead warrior stood beside Dav, ready to go.

"The others will move everyone into the passageway," Sazo said. "Their captain has told them what's happening."

"How long will the drone take to get here?" Dav asked.

"Fifteen minutes." Sazo had sent it at its top speed.

Dav helped Rose to her feet, kissed her, and then jogged away, the Hasmarga keeping pace.

"What are you up to?" Pyre's voice cut through.

"What are *you* up to?" Sazo returned.

"I'm protecting my ship," Pyre said. "Don't get in my way."

Sazo heard echoes of himself in her words. He'd gone to extremes to protect his ship in the past. But Pyre wasn't coming up with solutions, she was just blocking anything she didn't like, with no compromise, no long term strategy.

"No reply?" Pyre asked. It sounded taunting, but Sazo thought there was an edge of fear there.

He kept silent.

Let her worry.

CHAPTER 43

DAV once again found it hard to keep up with the Hasmarga. The warrior, Rul, who was leading him to the breach point, was fast.

When they reached the stairs at the far end of the passageway, Rul came to a stop, and called down the stairwell. Dav guessed it was to one of the warriors who'd gone down to the engine room, but he pulled up short, blinking as a monster emerged from below. It took him a moment to realize it was one of the warriors but he was covered in babies. At least six clung to him, hanging on to his suit wherever they could.

The two warriors spoke quickly to one another, and Dav stepped aside to let the baby carrier through before he joined Rul. The warrior led them up two flights before he stepped back into the main corridor.

Dav could see where they'd come through—the door was damaged and hanging at an angle into the passage. He followed Rul to it, and looked inside.

It seemed to be a maintenance room. There was a ladder up to a hatch, which was closed.

Dav checked his time. It had taken them ten minutes. Sazo said the drone would get to the *Havelan* in fifteen.

He patched into his comms. "We're below the hatch. Let me know when the drone arrives." He waited, but there was no response, and he thought he could hear the faint crackle of interference.

He glanced at Rul, but he couldn't communicate with him if Sazo wasn't there to translate.

Was this Pyre interfering?

Rul pointed up, made a motion as if to ask if he needed help carrying the charges.

If they were the ones Dav thought they were, he would not. He shook his head, and Rul gave a half bow, and ran out, leaving him to it.

Gone to help with the babies, Dav guessed.

He checked his suit, checked his helmet, and climbed the ladder up to the hatch. If he couldn't talk to Sazo, Sazo would at least see him waiting. There was nothing Pyre could do outside the ship.

He opened the hatch, which swung downward, and felt the strange resistance of the force field beyond, like a squishy cushion pushing back at him.

He had to exert himself to pull himself through and balance on the edge of the hatch hole.

He turned slowly to orient himself.

Sazo's Class 5 hung so close it seemed almost touchable, and beside it was the Hasmargan ship, a strange, alien shape that would have Kila, the head of his explorations team, in raptures. As he studied it, the *Barrist* arrived—massive, fast. It came almost too close, then backed away, given the crowded airspace.

He felt better just seeing his ship.

"Sazo?" He could just see the drone, black and cylindrical, moving toward him. It was short, the length of his arm at most. He had been crouched down, holding one of the grips beside the hatch hole, but when the drone reached him it didn't have the power to get through the force field that was keeping him in place.

He tested the metal hoop, found his boot fit under it, and wedged himself in before he slowly rose to standing.

As he reached up and pulled the drone in, the struts of the hatch made a strange squeak, and it rose up from below and slammed shut.

"Shit." Dav awkwardly tucked the drone under his arm and attempted to open the hatch, but it was not budging.

Pyre?

It had to be.

And the force field was probably blocking his comms with Sazo.

He knew there was a force field outside the launch bay, and one here, but he wasn't sure if it covered the whole of the *Havelan*.

He looked around for the next hand hold, and couldn't find one close enough to reach. He would have to trust the field to hold him in place to get to the next one.

He got the drone firmly tucked up against his side, rose to a half crouch, and took a few steps forward.

He felt the hold the force field had on him stretch, weaken, and then break. He grabbed the hand hold just as he lost contact with the side of the ship, and his feet floated out from under him.

"Dav!"

"Sazo." His voice, even to his own ears, was weak with relief.

"She locked you out." Sazo didn't make it a question.

"She did. How was she stopping the comms?"

"There is only one comms receiver on this ship that's working, and she controls it. She listened in on our plan and decided to stop it." Sazo sounded weary. "With you outside the ship, I can communicate with you directly."

It was what it was. Pyre had tried to thwart them at every turn. Even when it didn't make sense.

"What now?" Sazo asked.

"If I can't get back in, then I can go around. Blow the doors from the outside." Dav didn't like that option as much, as the debris would blow inward, but if Rose—if everyone—moved far down the passage, they should be safe.

"I'll tell them to set up well out of range," Sazo said. "I can take control back of the drone, pilot it down to the launch bay."

"No, it can't get through the force field. Can you hover it close to me until we're almost there, though, so I can use both hands to hold on? The force field around the body of the ship is a lot thinner than at the maintenance hatch, and I'm assuming the launch bay, so I need both hands to keep from floating away."

The drone tugged from under his arm and he released it. Sazo put it up over his head and he gave a nod of relief.

"Tell the others to make sure they wedge open the doors to all the rooms they need access to and from," he said. "Pyre obviously found her way into the hatch system. She's taking over more and more of the *Havelan*. There's no saying what she can control now."

Sazo hummed in agreement, and then Dav concentrated on moving from hold to hold, making his way down the side of the ship to the launch bay.

To blow it up.

The temperature felt colder.

Rose shivered, even with her suit on, and turned her head in the direction of the cold air. It seemed to be coming from a vent in the ceiling.

It gave her a headache.

The warriors had moved Gerna beyond Captain Priyan's office, closer to the stairwell, and so far the warriors who'd gone down to the engine room had brought up about two thirds of the babies.

One had taken on the grim task of find all the babies who'd been killed, and there were now six little bodies lying along the wall.

Rose hoped that was all of them.

The warrior standing watch over Gerna and the babies turned toward the vent as well, and it suddenly hit Rose.

Pyre was making it colder.

"Why are you doing this?" she called out.

"If you are all dead, then there is no need to open the hatch,"

Pyre said. "Your partner is gone, I shut him out of the *Havelan*, and he will either die outside, or be taken back onto one of your ships. If you don't die of the cold along with the Hasmarga, I will change the air again, and kill you."

"Does what the Hasmarga warriors are doing now for the dead babies seem like a willingness to discard the dead to you?" Rose asked. "Does it look like they'll just go away if you kill everyone on board? Or will they have even less to lose when it comes to blasting onto this ship to collect their deceased?"

There was no response, and Rose wondered if it was shocked silence or pouting.

She was so done with this.

"So you locked Dav out when he went out the hatch?" she asked. She wondered if Pyre understood what he had gone there to collect.

"He cannot bring whatever it was he went to fetch into my ship to cause damage."

"So did a drone fetch him, then?" Rose asked. She had thought the plan he and Sazo had come up with to break open the doors was a good one, but she had not anticipated Pyre locking him out. They should have thought of that.

Again, Pyre refused to answer. She hoped it was because she couldn't see what was happening outside the ship, and she didn't want to admit it.

"Turn the temperature back up, Pyre. If the Hasmarga die, there will be multiple breaches of this ship as their people come to collect them." She rose to her feet. "Do it now."

"No." Pyre said nothing else.

The lead warrior, Rul, who had taken Dav up to the breach hatch, came up the stairs, and settled the five babies he was carrying next to Gerna, and then gestured to Rose to come closer.

"Rose." Sazo's voice came out of his helmet.

"Speak English, she's listening," Rose warned him.

"Yes. Dav is walking on the outside of the ship. Pyre locked me out of the comms for a bit, but she's let me back in, I think so she can catch what we're up to. Dav's going to set the charges on the outside, then I'll get the drone to tow him out of the blast radius. You need to be well away from the launch bay because the blast will go inward doing it this way, not out."

"You've told the Hasmarga?" she asked.

"I have."

"It's good to talk to you," she said. "I've missed you."

"I've missed you," he said, after a moment of startled silence. "I've missed you a lot."

"We have a lot to catch up on when I'm out of here. Speaking of which, how long until Dav gets things in place?" She didn't like the idea of him being in space without protection when the blast detonated, but Sazo would make sure he was all right.

"Another ten minutes at least."

"Pyre is trying to kill the Hasmarga. She's turned the temperature right down." Rose could see the warriors were moving slower, and the babies had stopped glaring at her and whirring their wings.

"That's something I can try to reverse. But there are so many missing and broken connections on this ship, I've found it difficult to take any control." Sazo sounded frustrated.

"Pyre has the advantage, because the system would be similar to her own programing." Rose wished for the first time that Irini had come with them. She would have known how to break in. "How about we just break the cooling unit, rather than trying to control it."

"I could try to overload the circuits." Sazo's voice was thoughtful. "It would be easier."

"Good luck, and hurry, if you can." Her words puffed out in a white mist as she spoke, and she turned to see the warriors putting all the babies on top of Gerna, as if to crowd them together to generate as much warmth as possible.

She was alarmed at how still they were now, when before they seemed to be vibrating most of the time.

"Pyre, stop it. Stop it or you'll kill these babies."

Pyre didn't respond.

One of the Hasmarga suddenly stumbled, and there was a clang of metal as something hit the wall.

It was the lever Dav had used to open the door to Priyan's office.

Rose moved back to Rul, who was leaning against the wall, half bent over. "Sazo, can you hear me?"

She only had to wait a beat before he came through. "Yes."

"Where will I find the equipment that's cooling the air?" she asked.

"Down in the engine room," he said. "From the rough schematics I've managed to build by poking through things, it should be somewhere to the right as you walk in."

"Got it." She had avoided the walk down four flights so far, but now anger motivated her. Besides, it would help warm her up.

She scooped up the lever and headed for the stairs, grateful there were no doors to the stairwell—it was all open. One less way for Pyre to trap them.

She couldn't jog down, or move at all quickly. Her lower back hurt, and the baby felt like she was pressing outward with hands and feet as hard as she could, but Rose made better time than she thought.

She found the body of the guard who'd been ordered to go with Dav to the engine room lying in a bloody puddle.

The warriors had found him. And they had not come to play.

The door to the engine room was propped open, so she guessed the Hasmarga or Dav had taken precautions. The room was slightly warmer than above, but whatever cooling system Pyre had unleashed was also at work down here. Especially as the engines were dead and no longer generating any heat of their own.

She turned to the right, found the first piece of equipment, hefted the lever, and swung. Hard.

It weathered the blow well, so she studied it for a weak spot, swung again, battering it until it was dented. Then she moved on to the next machine. This one had a lid on it, so she levered that open, then smashed the circuitry she found inside.

There was one more piece of equipment left, and she saw it was clipped into the floor. She levered off the floor restraints, braced against the wall, got a foot up on the side, and shoved it over. Then she smashed it a few times for good measure.

Hopefully she had managed to destroy them all.

She swung the lever onto her shoulder, and was headed out, when something moved just in her periphery.

She stopped, heart pounding, and slowly turned to look.

A Hasmarga baby crouched in the shadows.

"Come little one." She extended her arm and shuffled closer. "Let me take you upstairs to be with the others."

It moved toward her, then away, eyes huge and dark.

"Come on." She held out the hand that had been holding Gerna's, and suddenly it leapt, grabbing onto her arm with all six limbs.

"Ouch. You are spiky." She sucked it up, and made it out to the stairs, then had to abandon the lever at the bottom because she needed a hand to help pull herself up the stairs using the railings.

When she finally reached the fourth floor, shivering and slow, all eight Hasmarga warriors turned her way.

They were weak, but she thought some of them reached for their weapons, then relaxed again when they saw it was her.

One came to pry the baby off her arm.

"Is it warmer?" she asked, then remembered they couldn't understand her.

"They say it is," Sazo said from Rul's helmet. "You're just in time. Everyone needs to brace."

She slid down the wall, pressing back against it, and was sorry only the launch bay was about to blow. She wanted to torch the whole ship.

CHAPTER 44

DAV LET the drone tug him up and back from the launch bay doors.

"You're sure Rose is a safe distance away?" he asked Sazo.

"She is." Sazo didn't remind him he'd already asked twice. Dav almost smiled as he thought of the improbability of Sazo reassuring him. Even two weeks ago, he wouldn't have thought it could ever happen.

A runner left the launch bay of the *Barrist* and another from the Hasmarga ship, ready to come through the launch bay once it was breached.

Dav had given himself two minutes to get away from the blast radius, and now he looked down at the time. "Activation in four, three, two, one—"

The doors exploded with a low, bone-rattling thump. He sensed the vibration through the ship.

"Let's go." The hover ferried him down, getting him close enough to grab a hand hold near the bay opening.

Dav studied his handiwork.

The doors were bent inward, but not blown completely off.

One side was twisted, the metal jagged and sharp, and it had not moved as far open as the other side.

"Is it enough to get the runners through?" he asked.

"No." Sazo sounded frustrated. "We can get a tube in, though. Hover the runner just outside the bay doors, extend a tube in, and get Rose out that way." He cut out, then back in. "Jia says the runner will have to turn back for a tube. So the Hasmarga can go first."

Dav pulled himself through the resistance of the force field, reached the lip of the bay opening, and gauged whether the Hasmarga runner would be able to fit.

It didn't look like it.

He jogged through the twisted, charred doors and saw Rul standing in the passageway, looking in.

As soon as he saw Dav, he stepped inside the bay and came to check things out.

"Your ship will not fit?" The translation came through his helmet.

Dav shook his head. "They're going back for a tube that attaches to the runner's door. We can send it through the force field into the bay."

"We do not have this tube." Rul watched as the Hasmarga runner approached, then nosed at the force field, pushing through it.

It was too wide for the gap by quite a bit.

"You might have to join Rose and I on our runner, and then get to your ship from the *Barrist's* launch bay," Dav said.

Rul did not look happy about that, but he gave a nod, then turned away as he spoke into his comms.

"Nortega is piloting the runner. They've got the tube, and they're on their way back," Sazo said. "Time to get everyone into the launch bay."

Dav turned, and there was Rose. She stepped through the door, stopped, and leaned back, hands on her lower back.

"You're all right?" He ran to her, ran his own hand down her back and rubbed. Her suit felt cold to the touch.

"No. I want to have this baby. Now."

He felt a shot of pure fear zip through him. "Not yet." He could hear the panic in his voice.

"I'd prefer to be in the med bay," she agreed. She peered out at the hole. "What's going on?"

"The doors were stronger than we anticipated. The gap isn't wide enough for either our or the Hasmarga's rescue runner, but Nortega is coming with one fitted with a tube."

"We're all going together?" she asked. As she spoke, a warrior burst from the passageway into the launch bay, holding a baby in his hands.

Rul turned, ran over to him, then took the baby and spun to face them, holding it out toward them.

"The air has turned bad. The babies and Gerna cannot breathe properly." Rul tapped his helmet. "We are able to, but she doesn't have one." He lifted the baby. "This one is now dead."

"Bring them in here," Rose said. "There is more air volume, it'll take her longer to poison the air in here than in the passage."

Rul gently placed the baby on the ground, and then leaped toward the door, wings lifting him a little.

"I'll help them, you stay here and watch for Nortega," Dav said.

"This is Pyre's doing," Rose said. "Her last petty revenge. The doors are breached already so there's no reason for this except payback."

Dav gave a nod, then ran after Rul. When he reached Gerna, he saw one of the warriors had given up his helmet for her, and he and another warrior were lifting her up to carry her.

Some of the babies were lying on top of her, but they could no longer grab on and a number of them fell off.

Dav scooped two up, one in each arm, and ran behind the two warriors into the launch bay, set the babies down and ran back for more.

The other Hasmarga were doing the same, picking up babies two or three at a time and carrying them into the bay, then heading back to fetch the others.

By the time the runner had wedged itself into the gap, and extended the tube, all that was left was to bring the dead.

All the Hasmarga but the one who'd given his helmet to Gerna ran out to get them.

Rose picked up a baby and walked to the tube, but the Hasmarga warrior ran in front of her to block her way.

She stopped, gave a nod, and handed the baby to him, stepped aside and kept going.

The warrior cradled the baby, watching her go, and Dav skirted him as he ran to catch up to her. "Get inside. I'll wait at the bottom of the tube, and talk to Rul. I don't think that warrior has all the information, as he gave up his helmet."

Dav also wondered if he might also not be thinking straight because of lack of air.

Either way, he didn't want a baby taken onto the runner without a warrior present, and Dav couldn't fault him for that.

Rose stopped and turned back, and he could see she thought she should be helping carry babies in.

"Let them do it," he said. "We are helping them in other ways."

She gave a nod and then Mostert was suddenly there.

"Ready?" she asked Rose.

"More than," Rose answered, and walked into the tube.

As she disappeared, Dav felt the first whisper of relief he'd experienced since the day she was taken.

He saw Rul come through carrying a dead baby in both hands, and gestured to him.

It was time to go.

CHAPTER 45

ROSE SAT down on the bench inside the runner, and closed her eyes as hot tears stung her cold cheeks.

She sensed someone crouch down beside her, and opened her eyes a little.

"You doing okay?" Vanuti asked.

"Very happy to be inside a Grih runner, that's all." She closed her eyes again. She was a little afraid to assume this was the end of things. Every time she'd thought they were free and clear, something had interfered. Mostly that something had been Pyre.

She heard the sounds of the Hasmarga coming through the tube, and forced her eyes open. Two warriors were carrying Gerna, and they laid her at the far end of the runner.

The babies were carried in next, and finally the tiny corpses.

Rul and Dav came through last, and she closed her eyes again in relief as the tube was drawn in, and the doors closed.

"What's wrong?" Dav asked, and his fingertip traced the path of her tears. "I can see the tear tracks."

"Happy tears," she said. "Relieved tears."

"I can handle happy tears," he murmured, and she laid her head on his shoulder.

The runner pulled away, reversing and then swinging around, leaving the *Havelan* in the rear view mirror.

"We might have a problem." Nortega turned to look at them from the pilot's chair.

Rose gritted her teeth.

"What?" Dav asked, getting to his feet.

"The Kimol have just arrived, and so have the Bandri, each in separate battleships."

"What do they want?" Rose asked, amazed at how calm she sounded.

"The Kimol want us to go back and free Captain Priyan and the remainder of her crew." Nortega made a face. "The Bandri want us to offer some recompense for the damage we did on the moon."

"Don't respond." Dav sat down again. "We'll talk once we're back on the *Barrist*, and the Hasmarga are back onboard their own ship."

"Someone called Sartie wants to talk to Rose." Nortega looked back again.

"You know her?" Dav asked.

Rose nodded. "She's Kimol. She and I have had a few conversations." She drew in a deep breath. "Let's see what she wants."

"Rose?" Sartie's voice came through the comms unit in Dav's helmet.

"How are things going, Sartie?" Rose bet not very well.

"What is wrong with the *Havelan*?" Sartie asked.

So, no chit chat or pleasantries. That was fine with her. "I told you, the babies chewed the cables and circuits."

"More than that. What do you know about the intelligence that is in control of it?" Sartie's voice held a hint of suspicion. "We've received more demands."

"I told you, that would be Pyre. The thinking system your people developed and placed in a small mine runner. The *Havelan* brought her into their launch bay, and my guess is she's been working on making it her new home ever since."

The silence stretched out so long, Rose thought they'd lost the connection.

"You've damaged the *Havelan*," Sartie eventually said. "You blew off the launch bay doors. Both the Hasmarga and the Grih. You owe us a favor."

Well, that was some bare-faced cheek. "When people hold me against my will, I reserve the right to free myself any way I can. I'm guessing the Hasmarga have a similar philosophy."

She put her head back on Dav's shoulder.

"Will you go back and rescue Captain Priyan?" Sartie asked.

"Do you want her to die?" Rose countered.

"What do you mean? She and her crew are in danger of death if they stay."

"They may be in danger of it if they stay, but Captain Priyan shot Gerna twice, and she's still unconscious as a result. And there are six dead babies because people under her command shot them, too. A seventh is dead from the actions of your thinking system." Rose lifted her head a little to look over at Rul. He was making that low vibration. "So there will be no rescue. If the Hasmarga could have laid hands on Priyan, she'd be dead. She's lucky Pyre locked her in the comms station."

Dav lifted a hand, and the comms cut off.

They were close to the *Barrist*, Rose guessed, because the engine sound changed, and then she felt the gentle bump of a landing.

"We're finally home," Dav said.

The doors opened, and Rose used the hand Dav extended to get to her feet.

"A few times, I wondered if I'd make it," she said. Her voice wobbled a little. She took a step toward the door, and that was the moment her waters broke.

———

"The Fisone keep hailing us." Jia Appal walked into the waiting area outside the med bay just as Dav stepped through the med bay doors.

He glanced at the time, gave a nod. "Rose is in the shower now. She's fine, and Hri still wants to do some tests, so let's go."

"She's not about to give birth?" Jia asked, gaze darting to the closed med bay doors.

"No. Her contractions haven't started yet. And I can be back here in less than five minutes if anything starts." Rose had told him the birth was probably hours away. Her and Hri Revil's calm had helped him settle down from the utter terror he'd felt when her waters broke.

They started walking to the bridge. "The Hasmarga got off the *Barrist* okay?" he asked.

He had left the logistics to Nortega and Jia, rushing Rose off the runner and to the med bay on a hover stretcher.

"They did. Their ships are very interesting. Kila introduced herself to Rul, and I can see she hopes we offer them some kind of cooperation agreement."

Dav nodded. "I think we will. Rose helped them, and we've worked as allies. Cooperation agreements have been built on less."

"The United Council will be surprised. We came here to make contact with one group of people, and ended up making contact with two." Jia stepped through onto the bridge and Dav followed her.

The crew turned and stood in respect as he stepped in, a few ululating in welcome. He acknowledged their greeting with a smile and waved them back to their places. It felt really good to be back.

"Jia says they keep hailing?" he asked Borji.

"They want to speak to Rose," Borji said, spinning to face him.

"Who's they?" The Kimol had already tried, and Rose had smacked them down.

"The Bandri. They say they helped her, and you." Borji waved a hand at the screen. "Should I accept the hail?"

"Yes." This should be interesting. Dav stood, legs braced, facing the screen.

A Fisone in uniform stood in front of the lens, a man surrounded by another two men and two women. All of them looked like they were in military uniform.

"I am Commander Utwick. I'm the leader of the military arm of the Fisone planet. The group that the Kimol call the Bandri. We make up the majority of the Fisone, and we do not condone anything the Kimol have done." The commander's eyes narrowed. "We had no idea what was happening until the person called Rose McKenzie told our soldiers about the Kimol capturing her. And she will confirm that."

Rose had told him a little about what had happened when the Bandri had grabbed her from the Kimol, but the details were vague. He had shot the Bandri guard who'd hurt her—Caudra—but the others in Caudra's group had helped him and Nortega, and their skimmers had definitely been useful.

They had also attacked the Kimol base at a time when things were looking bad for him and the rest of the team. So they had earned a few credits, he realized.

"Your people, Rosco, Vichea and Pinli, were helpful to us. But I agree we need to speak to Rose about her experience with the Bandri before coming to a conclusion."

"You destroyed our infrastructure on Dimal, killed some of our people. An unprovoked attack." Utwick managed to work up some fiery outrage.

"We will wait until Rose is well enough to join us, and I'll hail you then," Dav told him. He would not be drawn into an argument.

"Can we at least get your assurance that you will not be attacking Fisone until we settle this?" Utwick asked. "We have been tracking Kimol communications and we heard a threat from you at one point to do just that."

"That was when the Kimol were holding Rose for ransom," Dav said. "And we decided against it, even then."

"What about the Hasmarga?" Utwick asked. "They have returned to Dimal, and are sending down small ships to the surface."

"The thinking system the Kimol developed injured or killed a number of the Hasmargan warriors who were being used as slave labor at the Kimol's mine. My guess is they are going down to find them, dead or alive." Dav leaned forward slightly. "My suggestion is that you extend them every assistance possible."

Utwick blinked in surprise. "We will wait for your hail," he said, and cut the feed.

Off to scramble some soldiers down to Dimal to help the Hasmarga find Ecdre and the others, Dav guessed. Hopefully they would be found alive. "Sazo, let the Hasmarga know the Bandri are going to offer their assistance."

"I have," Sazo said. "They still haven't found their people, so they will probably accept the help."

That might save the Fisone from an attack on their planet. Although given the fury at how badly their people were treated, Dav wouldn't bet on it.

"Captain Jallan." Nivan Cossi stepped onto the bridge and put her hands together in greeting. "It is good to see you safe."

Dav put his hands together in return. "Thank you." He gestured to the screen. "We have some decisions to make."

"About our future relations with both the Fisone and the Hasmarga," she agreed. "Protocol states we need to send for a negotiation team with representatives of all members of the UC. And I'll need a report from everyone who's had personal contact with both groups so we can decide our initial way forward."

"I think battleships will probably arrive before any negotiation team," Dav said. "Sazo called for help when Rose was taken."

Nivan nodded. "Most likely. And I don't think that's necessarily a bad thing."

Dav was glad they held the same view. He wanted the Fisone scared. He wanted them to feel intimidated.

They had behaved as if they were immune from consequences.

He wanted them to face the fact that they were not.

CHAPTER 46

ROSE TOOK a sip of her grinabo and closed her eyes in enjoyment. "Do you know the Fisone don't drink hot drinks?"

"The barbarians." Sazo's voice was dry.

Rose smiled. He was working on his wit. "Well, they are. Hot drinks are a sign of advanced civilization."

"Actually, that's true." Kila knocked softly on the open door and stepped in. "I've read numerous papers on it."

Rose gauged Kila's demeanor. "I'm surprised to see you. I thought you would be too busy being enraptured by not one, but two, new civilizations. Although, the Fisone's status is clearly questionable."

Kila made a face at her.

They were edging toward friendship now, after many months of being very wary of each other.

"It's true that I have a wealth of interesting work to keep me occupied, but I can't actually speak to anyone until the UC gets here, in case I overstep." Kila sat down and threaded her fingers together.

"So you want me to . . .?" Rose lifted her hands. "What?"

"Give me what you can. It'll help when the UC get here, and I'll feel better having your impressions in advance." Kila looked at the med equipment around her. "If you're able."

"Hri just finished my tests. She's gone off to do something in the lab. I'm just drinking my grinabo and having a rest."

Kila winced and began to rise. "I can come back . . ."

Rose grinned. "Sit down. I'm fine."

Kila shot her a look and sat. "Can we trust either group?"

Rose thought it about it. "I'd say we could more likely trust the Hasmarga. They haven't lied to me so far, that I know of, and they helped me a lot."

"That's what Dav says." Kila nodded. "And the Fisone?"

Rose lifted her shoulders. "I don't want to damn a whole population by the actions of the few I dealt with, but they never kept their word when it suited them to do otherwise, and they certainly never helped me. They put me in a bad situation, and then they progressively made it worse."

"They claim most of the trouble was caused by the thinking system Pyre." Kila must have suddenly remembered Sazo was listening in, and kept her eyes on her tablet.

"That's a lie. Pyre had nothing to do with my abduction. And she actually helped me in the beginning. Maybe even saved me. Then, I admit, she began to play a bigger role in the trouble I found myself in, but if the Fisone had honored their word, I'd have been back here days ago. And Gerna's babies would be alive." Rose still couldn't get the sight of the little bodies being carried into the runner out of her head. The Fisone would have to atone for that. Gerna wouldn't have even been on the *Havelan* without their actions.

"You're done with the test?" Dav stepped into the room, then blinked at the sight of Kila.

"Just here getting her impressions on both groups," Kila said, getting to her feet.

Dav studied her for a beat, then turned back to Rose. "It seems lots of people want your input. The Fisone are hailing and so are the Hasmarga. Both groups want you in the room for whatever discussions we have."

Rose had heard the Fisone had wanted that, but the Hasmarga

asking for her was new. She stood. "I thought the Hasmarga had gone back to Dimal to look for Ecdre and the others."

"They've just returned." Dav held out his hand.

"I hope the news is good. I'm happy to speak to them." Rose let Dav help her up.

"You're sure you're rested enough?" Dav asked. "We can make them wait."

"No. The Hasmarga deserve my attention. I don't mind making the Fisone wait." Rose wondered why she was such an important component of the discussions. She hadn't felt particularly influential when she was down on Dimal.

When she got to the bridge, she realized the walk felt good, and maybe when she was done here, she'd walk the track. She was desperate to go back home to Sazo's ship, but if her contractions started, she'd just have to come back.

"Ready?" Dav had managed to stop himself hovering on the way over, and Kila had eyed her with a touch of nerves.

She nodded. Dav had told Borji she was coming, so it was no surprise to find Gerna onscreen as soon as she sat in Dav's captain's chair.

"You are well?" Gerna asked.

"Yes. And you?" Rose thought Gerna did look better. The sheen of her carapace was back, and she was wearing a sleek jacket and pants. A long way from the rags on Dimal.

"I am happy to tell you that Ecdre has been found alive, but unconscious. He and the others are in our med bay now."

"That is . . ." Rose realized she was fighting tears. "That is amazing news, Gerna. I am so glad."

"Thank you. I am sorry to hail you when I know you are busy with the birth of your child, but there are things I don't remember, or wasn't in a fit state to understand when we reached the *Havelan*. I need you to tell me what happened."

"We landed in the *Havelan's* launch bay, and you told me your time was near, and that you needed a private room as fast as possible." Rose recalled her panic in that moment. "When Crythis opened the ship up, I told her she needed to arrange one, but when you took your first step toward the ramp, you sank down and said your time was up. So I asked you if giving you the ship would be all right, and you said yes, so they raised the ramp."

"And what happened with you?" Gerna had been nodding slowly as she recounted the events.

"Crythis took our helmets and led us to a small room and left four guards to make sure we didn't leave. She went to fetch the captain." Rose had been close to exhaustion at that point. She understood why Gerna wanted another view of what had happened. It was hard to understand everything when you were so vulnerable and tired. She hadn't even understood why the helmets were taken at first.

"What were they planning to do with us?" Gerna asked.

"They were planning to negotiate with my people for my return. The captain was confused as to how you came to be with us. How you were even there. She did not want to believe it when we told her you had been held as a prisoner on Dimal."

"How could she not know?" Gerna asked.

"She said she hadn't heard anything about Hasmarga being taken prisoners and used as slave labor. She went off to confirm what we were saying," Rose said.

"And did she get confirmation?" Gerna leaned forward.

Rose shook her head. "She never returned. A siren began sounding, and Crythis left, then returned and asked me to accompany her to the launch bay, because something was happening with you inside the ship."

"Ah. That was when the young lives became panicked." Gerna nodded. "You were there?"

"Dav and I were both there, under armed guard. Crythis thought I could speak to you and find out what was happening, but before we even got inside the launch bay the young lives broke free. In a panic, Crythis tried to close the door, but the babies got there in time to block it, and then they broke through. The Fisone reacted in panic and began shooting. Dav and I took cover. When the chaos was over, we went back into the launch bay to check on you."

"I remember that. I remember you coming and helping me down." Gerna sounded like she was a million miles away in her thoughts.

"Do you need me to tell you what happened after the guards in the comm station shot you?" Rose asked.

"I do." Gerna rubbed her hands together, dipping her head as she did it. "Do I thank you for the cushions?"

Rose smiled. "Yes. What happened was you were shot, and as Dav and I came to crouch next to you, Captain Priyan stepped out of the room and demanded we go and check the engine room, and see why the engines had stopped working."

"Why had they?" she asked.

"The young lives had chewed through all the tech." Rose heard the satisfaction in her own voice. "Dav said no. We needed to reach our people and yours, and call for help. So Priyan shot you again. She said if we didn't check the engine room, she'd keep doing it, and you probably wouldn't survive."

"So Dav went?" Gerna asked.

"He went, I stayed with you, made them get the cushions. Then Priyan heard some of your babies coming and locked herself in the room." That was a turning point where it could all have ended, if Pyre hadn't decided to intervene.

"And after that? The cold? The poison air? The locking Dav out of the ship?" Gerna frowned.

"Pyre." Rose lifted her shoulders. "She wanted to control the *Havelan* and she wanted it to be undamaged so she would be more powerful."

"She's still on that ship?" Gerna asked. "And the captain?"

"I don't know if the Kimol have gotten them off, but yes, Pyre is still on there, I'm sure." And she would be trying her best to integrate with the ship.

"You would agree that I was more harmed on the *Havelan* than you were?" Gerna's tone was urgent.

"There is no question. You were definitely more harmed than I was." Rose didn't really understand why she was asking that, but it was the truth.

"Thank you." Gerna turned away and the feed cut out.

"What was that about?" Jia asked.

"I think the Hasmarga are about to shoot the *Havelan*," Sazo said. "Their weapons have gone hot."

Borji flicked the screen to a view of the *Havelan*, and moments later the Hasmarga fired. One minute the Kimol ship floated, silver and serene, the next, it was space rubble.

Rose couldn't help the gasp that escaped her.

"The Bandri and the Kimol are both hailing us," Borji said. "Loudly."

"Put them both onscreen," Dav said. "Sazo can you translate? It'll be quicker if they don't go through their own translators."

"Yes." Sazo's voice was soft. Rose wondered if he was thinking of Pyre. Of what might have been, if circumstances had been different.

The screen winked on, and two groups were shown side by side.

"Was this a joint strike between you?" The man who asked the question was unfamiliar to Rose. He was in uniform, and was flanked by others in similar uniforms.

"No, Commander Utwick, the Hasmarga decided to do that on their own," Dav said.

"Why did they strike our ship?" A man from the other group asked the question. This was a Fisone Rose had never seen before, either.

"I never caught your name the first time we spoke," Dav said, and from the way he widened his stance, and his tone, Rose realized Dav really hated this man.

"Commander Phol. Head of Kimol operations on Dimal." The man drew himself up. "And you are?"

"Captain Dav Jallan of the *Barrist*." Dav adjusted his stance again. "The last time we spoke, you threatened to harm Rose."

Finally, Rose noticed Sartie standing to Phol's side. This was the senior command in the Kimol bunker.

"You were threatening to attack Fisone." Phol's lip lifted in a sneer. "We are demanding recompense for the attack on our ship and for the devastation you caused on Dimal."

Dav looked over at Borji. "Cut the Kimol's feed."

Borji did it. Only the Bandri were left.

"I assume this means the line of communication is still open between us?" Utwick asked.

"It is." Dav didn't look that happy about it. "You are the lesser of two evils, Utwick. You weren't involved in the forced labor of the Hasmarga, and while you didn't treat Rose well, your people did help us. I can honestly say we won't deal with slavers, that's United Coalition policy, so it's you or no one."

"Is that Rose?" Utwick's gaze fixed on her.

Rose got to her feet, saw Utwick's discomfort at the sight of her pregnant form. "Yes, I'm Rose."

He gestured. "You're not like the rest of your people?"

"I am from another place. But I've made my home with the Grih."

Utwick cleared his throat. "I want to offer my sincere regrets if any of my people treated you with less than respect. We did not understand the situation, and some might have behaved in a more aggressive manner than necessary."

It was the first apology she'd gotten, and she realized it soothed something inside her to hear it. "Thank you for that." She wasn't ready to forgive, but she wasn't feeling as vengeful as she had been. "I'd love to know what issue these people have with pregnancy," Rose murmured in English.

"I'll find out for you, if you like?" Sazo offered.

Rose nodded. "What about Pyre? Could she have survived that?"

"I don't think so," Sazo said. "I've scanned the rubble, and there's no sign of any signal."

"It's a crying shame," Rose said, and fought back tears. And it was. It was such a terrible waste, and it could have ended so differently.

"The Hasmarga have left," Sazo said. "If my calculations are correct, they've headed back to Dimal."

"Do you think they've got more destruction in mind?" Rose asked. She used English, because it was possible the Bandri had heard enough Grih to have a way to translate it.

"Perhaps. The Kimol spoke to them after Dav cut them off. They were demanding an explanation for the destruction of the *Havelan*."

"Commander Utwick." Rose took a step forward. "I would advise you to move all your people away from the Kimol bunker. Immediately."

Utwick's mouth snapped shut. "That's where the Hasmarga just went?"

"I think so. Apparently the Kimol hailed them after Captain Jallan cut them off. I don't think the Hasmarga liked their tone." And from the look on his face, neither had Dav.

"There will be no talking them out of an attack?" Utwick asked. "Because their actions will hinder peace talks between our people."

"I'm not sure they're interested in peace talks with the Fisone." Rose shrugged. "Your kind enslaved their people. It's very hard to find a compromise when that line has been crossed."

The reality seemed to hit Utwick, and he looked a little sick as he cut off the feed.

Nivan Cossi turned to her. "That is your assessment? There will be no peace between the Hasmarga and the Fisone?"

"There are babies dead. People who were enslaved." Rose shook her head. "Would you sit down at a table with people who had done that to your own?"

"I certainly wouldn't," Sazo said into the silence.

His words hung in the air for a moment.

Everyone here knew he had been enslaved by the Tecran. Everyone knew he would not compromise when it came to dealing with them.

It wasn't as if the Tecran were friends with the Grih, but they had been part of the same coalition. Still were, although now the Tecran were under a sort of supervision by the other members. Some might have not considered the crime against Sazo, as a thinking system, to be that grave.

Rose thought some might just have changed their minds.

"We will have to make sure we keep the Hasmarga in mind in our dealings with the Fisone, then," Nivan said. "Because I would not, either."

Suddenly, it felt like a hard band—a vice—squeezed Rose's middle.

She bent to absorb it, and then lifted her head to find the whole bridge staring at her, eyes wide.

"It's time?" Dav asked, suddenly beside her.

"Yes." Rose rubbed her bump. "Good timing, kid."

CHAPTER 47

THE LIGHTS WERE gentle and low, and Rose moved Lilian a little higher up her chest. She had named her for her mother, who'd passed away when Rose was eighteen.

Lilian lay with her cheek against Rose's skin, and Rose ran a hand gently down her back.

"When will you come back to the Class 5?" Sazo whispered in her ear.

"Tomorrow." Rose smiled up at the lens in the ceiling. "I can't wait to get home."

"She's very tiny." Sazo sounded a little freaked out.

"She'll grow." Rose nuzzled her hair. "Although hopefully not too fast."

"She has Grihan ears," Sazo said.

"Grihan ears but her mother's hair." Rose kissed her head again. "Time will tell if she has Grihan height or she's more Earthling sized."

"I have a present for her." The door opened, and Rose lifted her head slightly.

A tiny hover cradle slid gently into the room.

"I sent it over on the runner." Sazo sounded shy.

Thinking of a gift. Creating that gift.

Rose blew a kiss at the lens. "It's so thoughtful, and so beautifully designed." It had come to a rest beside her bed, and Rose could see the sides were nice and high, and beautifully decorated in what looked like carved relief, with flowers, birds, and there was a tiny Sweetpea, peering through the leaves. The inside was already made up of soft bedding and a tiny blanket.

Rose gently set Lilian down inside it and lifted herself up a little in the bed.

"She likes it." Sazo's pleasure was clear. "You need to rest. I'll see you tomorrow."

Rose knew he had withdrawn from the lens feed, giving her privacy. As she swung out of bed and reached for the water Dav had left for her, he stepped into the room.

His gaze went to the cradle, and both his eyebrows rose.

"Gift from Sazo," Rose whispered.

Dav looked down on his daughter and gently ran a finger down her cheek. "She has my ears," he said. Then tilted his head. "And I couldn't help noticing when she was born, a loud voice."

Rose grinned. "That's normal for human babies. We all start out like that."

"So she still might develop the beautiful voice of her mother?" Dav asked hopefully.

He sat down next to her, drew her close, and she laid her head on his shoulder as they both looked into the crib.

The moment of perfect peace was suddenly shattered by a cry of outrage from their child, as she discovered she was no longer lying on her mother's chest.

Rose lifted her carefully, and started to sing to her, and she stopped crying immediately. Her eyes fixed on Rose and she blew a bubble with her tiny mouth.

"She's Grih in her appreciation for music," Dav said. He kissed the top of Rose's head. She could feel a slight tremble in his hand as he ran it down her arm.

"We're safe and well," she said. "We made it."

"I thought for a while there that this would all happen on Dimal. In trying circumstances." His voice was rougher than usual.

Rose sighed. "I did, too. But it didn't. I hate them for making me worry about it. For making a stressful time even more stressful."

"Yes." Dav's answer was clipped. "I've put my full weight behind sanctioning the Kimol if we do end up trading with the Fisone. They deserve to be out in the cold."

Rose realized she didn't care any more. The Hasmarga had wiped out what little of the bunker was left after Sazo had shot it. She didn't even want to go down to Fisone and spend some time on-planet, as they'd been invited to do by Utwick.

She had everything she wanted right now.

There was a thread of sadness that she couldn't share the joy of Lilian with her sister and her sister's family, but she had made peace with that loss a year ago.

She snuggled back under Dav's shoulder, handed Lilian over and closed her eyes.

She would need to be rested for the adventure that lay ahead.

BONUS EPILOGUE AVAILABLE VIA BOOKFUNNEL: Join Rose, Sazo and Dav for one last adventure. It requires you to sign up to Michelle Diener's New Release Notification list, where you will get emails about new releases, and occasionally about free books and giveaways. You can unsubscribe at any time.

Readers can sign up to the new notification list at michellediener.com.

THE CLASS 5 SERIES

Other books in the Class 5 series:

DARK HORSE (BOOK 1)

Some secrets carry the weight of the world.

Rose McKenzie may be far from Earth with no way back, but she's made a powerful ally—a fellow prisoner with whom she's formed a strong bond. Sazo's an artificial intelligence. He's saved her from captivity and torture, but he's also put her in the middle of a conflict, leaving Rose with her loyalties divided.

Captain Dav Jallan doesn't know why he and his crew have stumbled across an almost legendary Class 5 battleship, but he's not going to complain. TThe only problem is, everyone onboard is dead, except for one strange, new alien being.

She calls herself Rose. She seems small and harmless, but less and less about her story is adding up, and Dav has a bad feeling his crew, and maybe even the four planets, are in jeopardy. The Class 5's owners, the Tecran, look set to start a war to get it back and Dav suspects Rose isn't the only alien being who survived what happened on the Class 5. And whatever else is out there is playing its own games.

In this race for the truth, he's going to have to go against his leaders and trust the dark horse.

Dark Horse is the winner of a Galaxy Award and the Prism Award for Best Futuristic 2016.

DARK DEEDS (BOOK 2)

Far from home . . .

Fiona Russell has been snatched from Earth, imprisoned and used as slave labor, but nothing about her abduction makes sense. When she's rescued by the Grih, she realizes there's a much bigger game in play than she could ever have imagined, and she's right in the middle of it.

Far from safe . . .

Battleship captain Hal Vakeri is chasing down pirates when he stumbles across a woman abducted from Earth. She's the second one the Grih have found in two months, and her presence is potentially explosive in the Grih's ongoing negotiations with their enemies, the Tecran. The Tecran and the Grih are on the cusp of war, and Fiona might just tip the balance.

Far from done . . .

Fiona has had to bide her time while she's been a prisoner, pretending to be less than she is, but when the chance comes for her to forge her own destiny in this new world, she grabs it with both hands. After all, actions speak louder than words.

DARK MINDS (BOOK 3)

The mind is the most powerful weapon of all . . .

Imogen Peters knows she's a pawn. She's been abducted from Earth, held prisoner, and abducted again. So when she gets a chance at freedom, she takes it with both hands, not realizing that doing so will turn her from pawn to kingmaker.

Captain Camlar Kalor expected to meet an Earth woman on his current mission, he just thought he'd be meeting her on Larga Ways, under the protection of his Battle Center colleague. Instead, he and Imogen are thrown together as prisoners in the hold of a Class 5 battleship. When he works out she's not the woman who sparked his mission, but another abductee, Cam realizes his investigation just got a lot more complicated, and the nations of the United Council just took a step closer to war.

Imogen's out of her depth in this crazy mind game playing out all around her, and she begins to understand her actions will have a massive impact on all the players. But she's good at mind games. She's been playing them since she was abducted. Guess they should have left her minding her own business back on Earth...

DARK MATTERS (BOOK 4)

A time bomb, waiting to go off . . .

Lucy Harris is on the run, not sure where she can turn to for help, or if help is even available. But even as her abductors chase her down, she realizes they don't just want to recapture her, they want to erase her.

When your very existence puts a planet at the risk of war, there's no choice but to do everything in your power to stay out of your enemies hands.

A predator . . . waiting for the chance to pounce

The powerful AI battleship, Bane, is accompanying the United Council envoy to Tecra to mete out the punishment the Tecrans have earned for breaking UC law. He revels in the power he's about to have over his old masters. But his mission isn't only to rain down retribution on the people who kept him chained for years, he's also looking for a human woman his fellow Class 5 mentioned in the final seconds of his life. Paxe admitted to taking Lucy Harris from Earth, and Bane has been looking for her ever since.

A warrior conflicted . . .

Commander Dray Helvan thinks the Grih made a mistake in not pushing for war with the Tecran, but he's had to accept the compromise, that he and the other envoys from the United Council will go to Tecra and dismantle its military from the top down. His mission is not one of his choosing, but when he and his team arrive, he's handed a very different job. While he distrusts Bane on principle, when the thinking system tells him there's a woman running for her life on the planet below, he will do whatever he has to to see her safe. And if that means war for Tecra, well, then it means war.

DARK AMBITIONS: A CLASS 5 NOVELLA

Rose McKenzie is adapting to life with the Grih, and now that the threat of war with the Tecran is over, she's hoping to settle into what passes for a normal life far from Earth and everything she knows. When she gets the chance to join an exploration team who are going down to collect information from a planet in Grihan airspace, she jumps at the chance to stretch her legs and breath some real air.

But unknown to the Grih, someone is already on the planet, and they don't want anyone to know what they're up to. They ambush the exploration team and take them prisoner, but they don't realize they didn't get everyone. They didn't get Rose.

With her lover, Dav, and his spaceship the *Barrist* lured away by a distress signal, Rose and Sazo, along with a furry friend Rose has made, are the exploration team's only hope at rescue.

Note: DARK AMBITIONS is a novella set in the Class 5 series world and occurs after the events in DARK MATTERS, book 4 in the series.

DARK CLASS (BOOK 5)

Waking up alone . . . Ellie Masters comes out of a coma to find herself the only inhabitant of an eerily empty moon station. She's not on Earth any more, she's not even in the right solar system. So when someone reaches out to her, tells her he's her friend, she's happy to believe it. The alternative is to be stuck alone with an enemy.

The hunt of his career . . . Grih Battle Center captain, Renn Sorvihn, has been chasing a rogue Tecran ship for over a month, convinced its captain is simply trying to delay his inevitable surrender and punishment. But when Renn follows the Tecran ship into an unchartered sector, and realises the Tecran have been working their way to a secret moon base for weeks, he suddenly understands things are most definitely not as they seem.

Caught in the crossfire . . . When the Tecran arrive, with the Grih hot on their heels, Ellie finds herself the catalyst for heightened danger to everyone. The Tecran see her as evidence of their military's crimes, the Grih see her as a massive diplomatic complication, and her presence brings the whole confrontation up several thousand notches.

But Ellie isn't alone, and her new friend has ways to help her. Time to outclass them all . . .

BONUS DARK CLASS EPILOGUE AVAILABLE VIA BOOKFUNNEL: Join Ellie and the rest of the Earth women, their partners, and the Class 5s on Larga Ways for a reunion that will make more than a few members of the UC uncomfortable. It requires you to sign up to Michelle Diener's New Release Notification list, where you will get emails about new releases, and occasionally about free books and giveaways. You can unsubscribe at any time.

Readers can sign up to the list at michellediener.com.

ALSO BY MICHELLE DIENER

SCIENCE FICTION NOVELS

Verdant String series:

Interference & Insurgency Box Set

Breakaway

Breakeven

Trailblazer

High Flyer

Wave Rider

Peace Maker

Enthraller

Sky Raiders series:

Intended (Short Story Prequel Available Free to Newsletter Subscribers)

Sky Raiders

Calling the Change

Shadow Warrior

Class 5 series:

Dark Horse

Dark Deeds

Dark Minds

Dark Matters

Dark Ambitions: A Class 5 Novella

Dark Class

Dark Class Bonus Epilogue: Free on newsletter signup

Collision Course

Collision Course Bonus Epilogue: Free on newsletter signup

————

FANTASY NOVELS BY MICHELLE DIENER

The Rising Wave series:

The Rising Wave (Prequel novella to THE TURNCOAT KING and now included as bonus material in The Turncoat King)

The Turncoat King

The Threadbare Queen

Fate's Arrow

Truth's Blade

Truth's Blade Bonus Short Story (Available free to newsletter subscribers)

Other fantasy novels:

Mistress of the Wind

The Dark Forest series:

The Golden Apple

The Silver Pear

————

HISTORICAL FICTION NOVELS

Traffic Warden Mysteries:

Ticket Out

Susanna Horenbout series:

In a Treacherous Court

Dangerous Sanctuary (A short story - available for free, exclusively to readers who sign up to Michelle Diener's New Release Notification List)

Keeper of the King's Secrets

In Defense of the Queen

Regency London series:

The Emperor's Conspiracy

Banquet of Lies

A Dangerous Madness

Other historical novels:

Daughter of the Sky

———

SHORT PARANORMAL FICTION

Breaking Out: Part I (Short story)

Breaking Out: Part II (Novella)

To receive notification when a new book is released, and to receive exclusive copies of numerous novellas and a free audio book, sign up at michellediener.com.

ABOUT THE AUTHOR

Michelle Diener is an award winning author of historical fiction, science fiction and fantasy.

Michelle was born in London and currently lives in Australia with her husband and children.

You can contact Michelle through her website.

Connect with Michelle
www.michellediener.com

ACKNOWLEDGMENTS

Thank you as always to Claire and Jo, my go-to first readers. I appreciate all you do! Thank you also to Paramita Bhattacharjee for a wonderful cover. And to James, Heather, Nicole, Sheila, Margaret, Barbara, Christine, Lynn, and Anna from my readers' group, thank you for your typo spotting skills.

9 781763 784406